WORTH THE TROUBLE

JENNIFER J WILLIAMS

JJW PRODUCTIONS LLC

For all the women who are told they're "too much," "too dramatic," or "too sensitive." Fuck 'em. You are absolute perfection, exactly as you are.

Play List

Listen to the playlist on Spotify

I Knew You Were Trouble - Taylor Swift

Trouble - Josh Ross

Halley's Comet - Billie Eilish

Guys My Age - Hey Violet

Trouble with a Heartbreak - Jason Aldean

Always On My Mind - Elvis Presley

I Touch Myself - Divinyls

...Baby One More Time - Britney Spears

Don't Blame Me - Taylor Swift

Secret Love Song - Little Mix, Jason Derulo

Save Me The Trouble - Dan + Shay

Tennessee Whiskey - Chris Stapleton

I'm Yours - Isabel LaRosa

I Knew You Were Trouble (Taylor's Version) - Taylor Swift

*A*rianna

It's official.

I've hit rock bottom.

Sobbing in the middle of the gala I've spent months planning, because my jackass of a now ex-boyfriend decided to announce his engagement. Twenty minutes ago, I still had a boyfriend. Unbeknownst to me, he had a fiancée. Turns out, I was the side chick.

"Ari, what can I do?" My brother's girlfriend, Hannah, softly pats my back as she attempts to keep me calm. Easier said than done, obviously. I'm two seconds away from my sobs echoing across this grand ballroom in downtown Denver. "Should I get Bradley?"

"No!" I sob. "Didn't you hear what he did? Why would I want him near me?"

"What? No, I was with Luca. We stepped out for a moment," she murmurs. Of course she did. I open one eye a sliver and notice her swollen lips, and hair that is distinctly frizzier than it was only thirty minutes ago. I don't know why I'm surprised that Luca would grab a quickie at this event. And speak of the devil ...

"Where is that motherfucker?" Luca snarls.

"Honey, why are you shaking?" Hannah asks, grabbing on to

Luca's tuxedo jacket. He's taut with animosity, his eyes dangerously dark with venom.

"The jackass she's dating is fucking engaged to someone else," he seethes. Hannah gasps, her eyes whipping to mine, as a fresh wave of tears pour down my cheeks. Humiliation. Utter and complete humiliation. Shit. Now I see my mother approaching, my older brother Dominic stalking behind her, and I realize my rock bottom of moments ago just got worse.

I'm the youngest of seven kids. Yep, you read that right. Seven. Two older sisters and four brothers. Four guys who have attempted to reel me in, scare any man I've dated, and tell me I'm not allowed to have sex until I'm forty. Sorry, bros, that ship sailed quite a while ago. And generally I take their thoughts and advice on my love life pretty seriously. But watching Luca fall for Hannah made me incredibly jealous, and I said yes to Bradley around the same time. Dom hated him immediately. Luca was hesitant, his own lovesick heart making him second-guess his gut decision, I think. He wanted to trust me and my ability to pick out my own men. My remaining brothers, Alex and Leo, are both overseas on military assignments and haven't met Bradley yet. I'm sure I'll hear about how they felt, regardless of that fact.

Bradley and I weren't exclusive. I knew that. He insinuated he didn't want me dating anyone else, but I don't think I reciprocated the feeling. Maybe I knew he wasn't end-game. Or maybe I knew he was a conniving snake. I should have known, however, this week when I asked if he'd like to attend the gala with me, and he said he'd see me there.

Him showing up with another woman, then telling anyone who'd listen how he proposed *earlier in the month*, was not on my bingo card for the night.

"*Paperotta*," my mother soothes as she reaches me, "go. You don't need to be here for the remainder of the event. I'll handle everything."

"It's my event, Momma. I'm not leaving because of that asshole,"

I pout. Usually I find it calming when she calls me *paperotta*, which means little duck, and is a cute term Italians use for their kids. But right now, I'm barely hanging on. I try to catch my breath as a sob threatens to break through. I've been begging my family to let me take point on this specific event, our fundraiser for the Children's Hospital in Denver. I've wanted this for as long as I can remember, and considering we started this fundraiser because of me, it's about time they let me take the lead.

"You don't need to prove anything, Arianna. This is the best event we've ever hosted. Everyone is talking about it. You can leave with your head held high," my dad says quietly, alerting me to his presence. He's the voice of reason. The observant one who notices everything, but only speaks when it's truly important.

"I'll be fine," I murmur, my voice stuttering as I try to rein in my emotions.

"Go splash some water on your face. Take five or ten minutes. We're not sad to see him go, *cara*. None of us liked him," Dad says with a flip of his wrist, as if he's casting Bradley away for good. It'll be hard to do, considering we both work at the same hotel. My family's hotel.

"Okay, I'll be back," I whisper, turning on my heel and quickly walking out of the ballroom and into the closest bathroom. Two stalls are occupied by giggling women, and I scurry into the third stall to hide out until they leave. It gives me a few minutes to control my breathing and focus on calming thoughts.

I met Bradley at work. While I manage the hotel spa and hot springs, he is one of the chefs. He pursued me for months, flirting at every opportunity. I welcomed the attention, but evaded his advances. I worried about mixing business with pleasure. Bradley assured me it wouldn't be an issue. That should have been a major red flag. But I was going through a pretty long dry spell, and I let my hormones make the decision. Now I have no idea how I'm going to deal with seeing him every day at work.

I knew from an early age that I'd work for my family's hotel,

Everlasting Hotel and Spa. It's an institution in Eternity Springs, having been part of our family for three generations. First my grandfather, then my father, and now my brother Dominic. We all work here in some capacity, even our mom. But my heart was always pulled toward the spa.

People who don't know me, or those who assume things about me, would think it's because I'm a typical woman and enjoy anything that is labeled as self-care. But in reality, it's how the spa helps others feel. There's nothing better than seeing a frazzled mom come in, stressed about life, and watch as she relaxes and unwinds. When she's done with her treatments, she vows to make it a priority to take time for herself. Or teaching a teenage girl who suffers from cystic acne how to care for her skin, and watch as she grows confident when the acne begins to fade away. I won't take for granted the times I've gotten to witness a toddler experience the hot springs for the first time. I'm amazed by how satisfying it is to help a bride, and her bridal party, get ready for her wedding. The happiness and excitement are contagious.

I love my job, and I was born to have this role.

Don't get me wrong, it's exhausting. The spa is open long hours, and seasonal employees only help so much. It's left to me to cover any open times, and I couldn't even begin to guesstimate how many times I've fallen asleep in my car in the parking lot because it was too much to drive back to my apartment.

This year especially, I regretted my decision to live in western Denver. I wanted to be closer to my friends, and the nightlife of the city, and didn't take into account how tired I'd be most nights after work. I guess part of the reason Bradley wore me down was because I was too busy to actively look into dating. Obviously, that's a decision I regret more than the location of my apartment.

Once the coast is clear, I sneak out to the sinks and address my makeup. All in all, it's not looking too bad. My eyes are red-rimmed, but the crying jag left my cheeks with a natural blush that matches my sequined baby pink dress. The gown I chose for the gala has thousands of crystals and sequins, a small train that just grazes the ground as I walk, and a plunging neckline that showcases my boobs amazingly. My dad was not thrilled with the dress, but he didn't see it until I arrived at the gala, and he couldn't force me to go home and change. I'll probably get Hell from him about it tomorrow.

Stepping out of the bathroom, I look down as my favorite pair of Christian Louboutin ribbon ankle-wrap stiletto sandals catch on the hem of my dress, making me stumble forward. I close my eyes tightly as I fall, blindly reaching out to brace myself, until arms wrap around me and pull me into a hard body. I gasp as the scent of leather and cedarwood sweeps over me, and I lean into it reflexively. I know this scent. It's the same cologne he's been wearing since I was a teenager.

Stone Dixon.

My brother's best friend, and the one man who has never given me the benefit of the doubt. Why? I don't know. I honestly don't. He's been belligerent and standoffish toward me for well over a decade. My earliest memory of him revolves around one of Luca's hockey games, and me asking Stone if he liked the dress I was wearing that day. I don't remember exactly what he responded, just that he was horribly rude, and he made me cry. That's when he began calling me Princess, and he's never stopped.

I've never again asked him what he thought. It's clear he doesn't think highly of me, and I'd rather not learn the specifics as to why.

"Princess," he says grittily. I instinctively shiver as if his voice is speaking directly against my skin. Stone's voice is deep, so deep, the vibration makes me feel the words. I can only imagine what he sounds like when he's talking a woman through an orgasm. Demanding her compliance as he gets them both there. As I take a step back, I rake my eyes quickly down his body, admiring how well his tux fits him. Around the time I turned thirteen, I realized how attractive I found Stone. Just over six feet, with unruly brown locks that always look perfectly tousled, slate blue eyes that appear to see into my soul, and lips that I'd beg to experience just once against mine. "Powdering your nose for your perfect boyfriend?"

And then he speaks, and I'm reminded of what an ass he can be.

I mean, his ass fills out any pants exceptionally well, but still. Stone Dixon isn't a nice guy, and I don't know why my entire family loves him.

I can't even say that lie convincingly. He's an amazing guy. Just not to me. Everyone loves him, except for me. Well, and my dad. Dad doesn't like anyone really, though, so his opinion can't be trusted.

"Shows what you know," I retort. "I don't have a boyfriend."

I hate showing weakness, especially to him.

I hate that he can tell when I'm lying.

I hate how my voice threatens to quiver as emotion clogs my throat.

And I hate that I want him to comfort me, instead of what he'll inevitably do, which is to poke at me incessantly.

Stone's smug expression falls as his eyes sharpen on me. "What happened? What did that motherfucker do?"

"Why do you care, Stone? Go ask him. I'm sure he'll enjoy the two of you making fun of me all night. He started calling me princess because of you, you know."

"I didn't —" Stone stutters before clearing his throat, "I didn't know he was calling you that."

"Yeah, well, there's a lot of things you don't know about me, old man. Let go of me," I say clearly as I push away from him. He looks down, as if confused to find he's still holding on to my waist. When he lets go, I'm acutely aware of the stark coldness that replaces the warmth from his hands.

"Worried I'll contaminate this perfect dress, Princess?" he taunts. "How much did this set you back? Or rather, how much did Daddy pay for it?"

"Why are you so concerned with my clothes?" I ask. He doesn't need to know that my beautiful dress is a rental. I don't buy dresses for these events. It's a waste of money. The only money I spend on fashion is on my shoes.

"I'm not concerned with your clothes."

"But you obviously are. You comment on them almost every time we interact. How much did it cost, where did I get it, did my dad buy it. It's insulting, Stone," I tell him. "I don't comment on your clothes."

"I wear the same six things, Arianna. Pretty sure your mom got most of them for me," he says exasperatedly.

"So? Who cares? I don't. Why should you?"

"I doubt your mom spent as much on the sweater she got me for Christmas as you clearly spent on your fancy shoes," he mutters.

I roll my eyes. Knowing my mom, the sweater might have cost more than my Louboutins. My love of fashion is a genetic trait passed down from her. And while we're both pretty stingy in everyday life, my mom enjoys spoiling her kids. Stone has always been considered an adopted son of hers. Which is why no one, not even my mother, knows that I've had a crush on him for as long as I can remember.

"Excuse me, I need to go back into the ballroom," I say snootily, holding my head up and flouncing past Stone.

I hate that he still affects me.

I hate that I want to impress him.

I hate how I still want him, even though he despises me.

But mostly, I hate myself because I compare every guy I date to him. The man I can't have. The one I don't even know what it would be like to have.

As I walk back into the ballroom, I'm ambushed by Bradley.

"Princess," he sneers.

"Don't call me that. That was never okay," I respond. A tiny blonde approaches him, sliding her left arm into the crook of his elbow, her massive engagement ring proudly on display.

"Darling, who is this?" she whines. There's no other way to explain her voice. It's a whiny voice, that after only four words, already grates on my nerves.

"Sweetheart, this is Arianna," Bradley coos.

"Oh, the easy lay," she says nonchalantly. My mouth drops open in shock, making her break out in a fit of high-pitched giggles. I'm reminded of Janice from *Friends*. "Did you think I didn't know about you? Oh my God. That's just too adorable. Bradley told me all about you."

"You were okay with him dating someone else? While you're engaged?" I ask incredulously. She hyena laughs again.

"That's not dating, Adrienne. He fucked you. That's it," she snarls. I don't miss her mistaking my name. Now she's just being hurtful. Game fucking on.

"Ahh. Just sex. Got it. You should know, then, that he told me how he's never had it as good as he had it with me, and I rocked his world," I tell her. Her eyes narrow.

"Of course he would say that. We're waiting until our wedding night. That's the only reason why I was okay with this asinine situation," she retorts. "I told him to find some stupid whore and get his kicks before we get married. He found you, and the rest is history."

Before I can respond, my arm is grabbed, and I'm whirled around. I see Stone's eyes only a second before his lips are on mine.

I gasp into his mouth, and Stone takes the opportunity to slide his tongue against mine. I shudder as his arms tighten around me, and find I've slid my arms snugly around his trim waist. I feel his groan as my body connects with his. I'd always wondered what his lips would feel and taste like, and this is so much better than my imagination. This is perfection.

I wonder if Stone can feel my heart beating wildly in my chest. When his hand skirts up my spine to latch into my hair, I shudder as endorphins spread throughout my body. Goosebumps erupt along my skin in the wake of his touch.

As he breaks off the kiss, his hand slides along my neck and up to my cheek, cupping it reverently. I'm about to ask what the hell is going on, but he discreetly taps my lips before turning me back to face a stunned Bradley and his fiancée. "Hello. I'm Arianna's man. And you are?"

"Her man?" the fiancée asks, turning to Bradley, whose face is getting quite red.

"Your man? You two-timing bitch," he seethes.

"Considering you seem to be engaged to someone else, and half the people in attendance knew you were dating Arianna, I don't think you have any room to judge," Stone points out.

"Always knew you had a thing for her, Rock," Bradley spits out. Stone chuckles.

"You know my fucking name, asshat. Take your trailer trash and get the hell out of here. Oh, and I'd start looking for a new job if I were you."

"I'm very happy where I am, thank you very much," Bradley responds.

"You won't be," Stone says lightly.

"Is that a threat?"

"It's a promise, man. You know much about her other brothers?" Stone asks.

"The ones that don't live here? Not really, no," Bradley says warily. His fiancée, who I still don't know by name, watches with interest. I'm weirdly intrigued with Bradley saying he doesn't know much about Alex and Leo. He's been working at the hotel for eighteen months. Both of my brothers have been home in that time. Then again, I'm realizing how self-involved Bradley really is, so it's not that far off the mark for him to not pay attention at work.

"They're both in the military, man. One is special ops. And," Stone says, as he whips out his phone and begins to furiously type, "when they hear about this bullshit you pulled tonight, I can assure you they're going to have all kinds of thoughts."

"Well, they're not here, so ..." Bradley trails off.

"Baby girl," Stone says, turning to me, and damn it all to hell if my heart doesn't skip a beat at the pet name, "what's that lake where Lex used to take us fishing? The one he talked about being the deepest in the state."

"I don't remember," I murmur with a smile, captivated by this new side of Stone I've never seen.

"Damn. I can't remember either. I just know he said it would be really easy to drop a body there," he says pointedly, staring at Bradley. "Have I made myself clear?"

"Crystal," Bradley mutters, before taking his fiancée's hand and making a quick dash to the exit.

I turn to Stone, expecting some kind of explanation, but he just shrugs.

"What?"

"What the hell was that?" I shriek.

"You're welcome, Princess."

"I didn't thank you." I stare at him indignantly. He has the audacity to smirk at me, his eyebrows raised in sheer defiance.

I hate how suave he can look.

I hate that I can't read him.

And I hate that I want him to kiss me again.

Stone chuckles. "You should. You obviously needed help."

"I was handling that just fine," I growl, my hands fisted at my waist.

Stone smirks. "Go ahead and keep thinking that."

As he pats me on the ass — THE ASS — and walks away, I stare at his retreating form in complete shock.

I repeat: what the hell was that?

Arianna

Ring.
Ring.
Ring.
Is that my doorbell?
Buzz.
Buzz.
I groan.
It's too early for someone to be texting me.
Ring.
"ARIANNA!"

I scream, jumping out of bed, as someone beats loudly on my apartment door. I immediately grab my head as the pounding seems to reverberate inside my brain even louder than whoever is at my door. Who am I kidding? It's a brother. It's always a brother being this loud and obnoxious.

Grabbing my watch, I see that it's just after seven in the morning. Jesus. I was home before midnight, but then I may or may not have polished off a bottle of rosé all by myself, and I vaguely remember singing Christmas carols while taking a bath. Oh, God. Did I bathe in my rental gown?

"Arianna, I'm two seconds away from kicking this goddamn door down!"

Deep and growly. That's definitely Dominic.

My second oldest brother, the CEO of the family hotel, has always been a serious person. But when his marriage fell apart, and he took on sole custody of his three children, it was as if every little bit of joy he was able to find previously just evaporated. He gives one hundred percent to the hotel, and his kids, and has nothing left for anything, or anyone, else.

I struggle to the door, breathing a sigh of relief when I see my dry rental dress in an unladylike heap next to my couch, and open the door for Dominic.

"Alex is going to kill you," he comments as he bursts into my space.

"Huh? Why?" I ask, confusion evident in my tone. Alex is deployed. What could I have done to aggravate him?

Dom turns to me. "Seriously? You're hooking up with his best friend, didn't bother to tell him about it, and you're confused why he'd be upset?"

Suddenly, the entirety of the night comes back to me in a flash: Bradley and his fiancée, Stone, the kiss to end all kisses.

"Oh my God," I moan, flopping on my well-loved corduroy couch and covering my face with my hands. "How did he know about all of this already? Who got in touch with him?"

"Who do you think?" Dom says.

"Nonna," we both say simultaneously. Our meddling grandmother. The woman gets too much joy from gossiping about our love lives.

"You're the front page of the site, too."

Shit.

Of course.

The Eagle Has Landed is the unofficial town website. Technically, it's just gossip, but more people use that than the actual town website. My family is featured often. Way too often, if you ask me. We aren't that important. We don't even know who runs the damn thing. It's like a genuine version of *Gossip Girl*.

"Ari, there's a compelling picture of you and Stone," Dom says quietly. I gasp, turning to look for my phone. Finding it on the floor next to the discarded dress, I pull up the site and stare. Holy hotness. It's not just one picture. There are three.

The first picture is us within the throes of the kiss of the century. My arms are wrapped around Stone's waist, and he has one arm around me while his other holds my face against his. It is alluring and sexy, and I'm wet just looking at it.

The second picture must have been immediately after the kiss because we're staring into each other's eyes. The angle shows only Stone's profile, but my face is in full view, and I look utterly besotted with him. No one would question our relationship.

The third picture showcases Bradley and Stone, who almost look like they're having a spitting contest. Bradley has his chest puffed out, and his heels are slightly off the ground. Stone looks at him amusedly, clearly knowing he's the superior man in this particular rat race.

As I scroll past the third picture, a very small paragraph is written in accompaniment.

Resident barber Stone Dixon has never been one for PDAs or relation-ships, so we definitely couldn't have predicted this. Staking his claim at the Everlasting gala in support of Children's Hospital, the gala our very own Arianna Santo was responsible for organizing? These two have had spats over the years, but it's clear these enemies have turned into lovers. We have two questions: how long has this been going on, and has anyone told Arianna's brother Alex, Stone's best friend, about this yet?

When my phone rings with a number marked private, I groan.

It's Alex. When he's overseas, the phone calls are always marked as private. Fantastic.

"Hello."

"What the fuck do you think you're doing?" Alex growls.

"I'm not doing anything, Alex." Sighing, I sit down on my couch and rub my forehead. My brothers are not making my hangover headache any better. I look to find Dominic leaning against the wall, his arms crossed, and he nods at me as if he agrees silently with his older brother.

"I beg to differ," he scoffs.

"Look, I know you've always had a thing for Stone, but —"

"What?" I shriek. Dom rolls his eyes.

"You thought we didn't know?" Alex asks.

"Who is 'we,' Alex?" I ask.

"Everyone."

"Everyone — everyone including Stone?" I whisper.

"Jesus, Ari, yes. You would stare at him with stars in your eyes. Everyone knew."

"I was a kid!"

"You aren't a kid now. Break it the fuck off," Alex demands.

"Excuse me! I can't believe you're calling me from God knows where to tell me who I can, or can't, date. You have some fucking nerve! You don't get to tell me how to live my life, asshole!" I shout, ending the call. Dom stares at me in shock. I rarely lose my temper with my brothers. Possibly it's due to all the emotional trauma I've dealt with over the last twelve hours, then imbibing in way too much alcohol, but having to interact with both Dom and Alex this early is grating on my nerves.

When someone knocks on my door again, I growl. "I swear to God if that's Luca, one of you is getting punched in the nuts."

When I open the door and find Stone, I don't know which one of us is more surprised.

"What the fuck are you doing here?" Dominic snarls.

"Oh my God, you seriously need to go!" I shout.

"Oh, I'm sorry, I should have called first," Stone stammers.

"Shit. Not you. I meant him," I say, pointing to my brother. "Dominic, I love you and know your heart is in the right place, but I'm a big girl. I can make my own decisions. You need to go."

Dom studies me for a moment before reluctantly nodding. "Call me if you need anything."

He passes by Stone without acknowledging him, which makes Stone sardonically chuckle. "I see your family is already closing the ranks, huh."

"Evidently. I just hung up on Alex, so I'm sure more people will be here within the hour."

"Funny you mention it because I hung up on him too."

Laughter bursts out of me. "Really?"

Stone nods. "He was being an ass."

"I told him the same thing."

An awkward silence overtakes us as I stare at the floor.

Why is Stone here? A quick glance at him tells me he's still wearing his tux shirt, although it's unbuttoned to reveal an undershirt. Dark circles under his eyes make me assume he hasn't slept. Did our kiss rattle him as much as it did me?

"Can you get dressed, please?"

"Hmm?" I murmur.

"Princess," he snaps. "Look at me."

My eyes whip to his, and I find him glaring at me. "What?"

"You always greet guests almost naked?"

I look down at my body, noticing I'm wearing a tank top and bootie shorts. "No, I don't greet *guests* this way. But considering I certainly didn't invite you over here, this is what you get."

Stone rolls his eyes. "But you dress like that in front of your brother?"

"Jesus, Stone, I didn't invite him either! I'd still be asleep if it weren't for you two Neanderthals! I could have just answered Alex from bed, or ignored him completely!"

He looks momentarily chagrined before shuttering his expression. "You answered the fucking door like that, Arianna. It could have been anyone."

"It's the crack of dawn, Stone. I knew it was most likely family. Never in a million years thought it would be you," I snap. "How did you even know where I live?"

"I've always known," he shrugs.

"Why?"

"Alex."

"That doesn't make sense."

"I always keep tabs on you when he's gone," he explains.

"Excuse me?" I shout.

"Lower your voice, Princess. You're trouble. Someone has to keep track of you."

"Are you fucking kidding me?" I seethe. "Alex put you up to this?"

"Oh, uh, no. He never asked, per se. It was just a gentlemanly understanding."

I'm furious. So upset, in fact, that I'm shaking. How dare he. How fucking dare he. I begin pacing, so mad at all the men in my life who think they know better than me. "I am twenty-six, Stone. Twenty fucking six years old. I have been living on my own for years. I am perfectly capable of keeping track of myself. I have enough brothers, and I certainly don't need you playing some fucked up version of proxy."

Stone laughs sardonically. "Seriously, Princess? You're gonna sit here and claim you don't need looking after?"

"I don't!" I screech. I whirl around to find his eyes trained on my legs, and when he realizes I caught him, he goes on the defensive.

"Sure. What about when you flooded your bathroom six months ago and needed Dom to show you how to shut the water off?"

"So? Plumbing isn't my forté," I say, crossing my arms in defiance. I don't miss the quick glance Stone makes, tracking my arms as they push my breasts up.

"What about when you went to fill up your windshield wiper fluid and somehow poured it into the oil gasket?"

"That was an accident, and you know it!" I sputter.

"And the time you thought you hit Mason and made Alex search your entire car engine for the carcass?"

"Mason is a treasure, and I was devastated!" Mason is a marmot. Marmots typically live above tree line in the mountains, which is partially why Mason is revered in Eternity Springs. But he's also a troublemaker and constantly wreaks havoc on the area. So much so, in fact, that there are signs all over the town for tourists to watch out for him. He has an affinity for men's shoes, cotton candy, and Denver Wolves paraphernalia. No one can figure out why he's so taken with the Wolves merchandise. Still, if someone leaves something unattended, it will disappear. Within a week, a resident will find Mason on a doorbell camera posing with the missing item.

"What would have happened had I not shown up to help you last night, Arianna?" Stone asks, his voice decidedly deeper than it was just a moment ago. I have a quick vision of our kiss, and as I see Stone's eyes grow hooded, I know he's thinking about it, too.

"I would have been just fine. I'm perfectly capable of handling uncomfortable conversations, Stone."

"Yeah, well, your boyfriend left a lot faster after I arrived," Stone comments.

"He's not my boyfriend."

"Clearly."

"Okay, why are you even here? Did you really show up here just to argue with me?" I ask. Generally, I enjoy arguing with Stone. He's a worthy adversary. He doesn't take shit from me, and he has excellent zingers. But right now, I'm emotionally drained, slightly hungover, and I'm on the cusp of a breakdown. If he says another mean thing, I'm likely to start crying.

Stone sighs as he runs his hand through his hair. I wonder if it's as soft as it looks. I was so stunned when he kissed me that I didn't take full advantage. Since it'll never happen again, I wish I had explored his body more.

"I just wanted to make sure we were on the same page. About what happened."

"Okay …" I trail off. Where is Stone going with this?

"I mean, it's not — that's not happening again."

I don't speak. Did Stone really show up here this early to tell me he wouldn't kiss me again? As if I expected it?

"I know you've had a thing for me. I get it. But you're a kid. And Alex. And I'm me. And it's not — not gonna happen. So get that out of your head," he stammers.

Oh, he did not.

"Are you fucking kidding me right now?" I whisper. I step toward him, and he automatically takes a step back. "Did you hear yourself? Really. That's what you're going with? I really hope you didn't plan that amazing speech. If so, not your best work, Stone."

"I can't think right because you're in your fucking underwear, Arianna," he snaps.

"Why does it matter? I'm just a kid, remember? And you're just you." I take another step toward him, and he hits the wall. His eyes are stricken with fear, but I can see a little bit of lust as well. He can claim I'm just a kid, but he's as thrown off by our chemistry last night as I am.

"It's moot. We aren't happening."

"I never said we were."

"You're looking at me like you want to climb me like a tree, Princess."

"You're looking at me like you want me to, old man."

I don't know who moves first.

Suddenly I'm in his arms, and he turns so my back is against the wall, his very hard cock pressing against my core, and his lips against mine. We groan simultaneously as my legs wrap around his waist and his hands find my ass. He skirts his fingertips under my panties, kneading my ass as his tongue thrusts into my mouth. My hands finally grab onto his hair, as soft and silky as I imagined, before he breaks off the kiss and drags his tongue down my neck to nip on my collarbone. One hand moves my tank top to the side before Stone sucks my nipple harshly into his mouth, and I cry out as exquisite pleasure washes over me.

This.

This is what I dreamed it would be like with him. Somehow I knew he'd be better than every other boy out there. And that's what they are: boys. Stone is a man.

As I'm about to tell him where my bedroom is, someone knocks on the door next to us. Again.

"Arianna?" Luca calls out.

"Motherfucker," I swear. When I open my eyes to find Stone's stunned expression, I realize whatever spell we were under is broken. He untangles himself from me, and I regretfully remove my legs from his waist. Stone yanks my tank top to cover my breast, but the damage has been done. The headlights are on, and they are standing proud. Frankly, it's all Stone's fault.

I thought the kiss last night was spectacular — I'd never been kissed like that. But this one was better. It was *more*. It had heat, promise, and history. Stone has basically been in my life since I was born. I don't remember much until I was around ten, but I know he was there. He's always been there.

Now that I know what kissing Stone is like, and how it feels to have his tongue on my skin, I can only imagine what sex would be like. It would be earth-shattering. Time stopping. Life changing.

As if he can hear my thoughts, he shakes his head. "That was a mistake, Arianna."

"No. No, it wasn't," I respond, my steely gaze locked on him as he looks anywhere but my face.

"Yes, it was," he says quietly as he opens the door. "Luca."

"What the fuck? Did you sleep here last night?" Luca asks.

"No. I was just checking on her for Alex. And now I'm leaving." Stone walks out without a backward glance, leaving me with my brother. Luca raises an eyebrow at me.

"What?" I ask nonchalantly.

"What the hell was that, sis? I don't care what Dom and Alex think. I know you aren't dating him," Luca says with a crooked smile. Fuck. Out of all my siblings, Luca and I are the closest. We're both extroverted and jokesters. Even though he's four years older than me, he's one of my best friends.

I sigh loudly. "I need coffee if we're doing this."

Luca calls after me as I walk into my kitchen to start a pot. "Put some clothes on. I don't need the girls staring at me while I interrogate you."

"You don't have to be crass, Luca," I shout, but I grab shorts and a sweatshirt while the coffee brews. I giggle as I think back to teasing Hannah about the same thing only a few weeks ago while they stayed at the hotel after Hannah was assaulted by her ex-boyfriend. Honestly, I'm surprised Dominic didn't tell me to put on some clothes. Maybe his anger clouded his vision.

Once I make both of us a cup, Luca follows me back to the couch.

"Alright, start at the beginning. How did Stone end up kissing you last night?" Luca asks. I explain the conversation outside the bathroom and about how Bradley and his fiancée cornered me.

"Stone just turned me around and kissed me. I was as shocked as everyone else," I admit.

"And then he told Bradley he was your boyfriend?" Luca asks.

"Technically, he said he was my man, not my boyfriend."

"Same thing."

"I guess."

"And Bradley bought it?"

"Him, and everyone else. Alex already called to yell at me, and Dom showed up right before Stone this morning."

"Oh, shit. I bet that was awkward as fuck," Luca chuckles. His lip twitches with a smile, causing me to giggle. Awkward doesn't even begin to describe the events this morning. Luca has always been my best friend. While I won't go into explicit detail with him, he's the person I trust the most with my deep thoughts. I can share more with Hannah, who I honestly think is my person. She's the Meredith Grey to my Christina Yang.

"About as awkward as you showing up just now and interrupting us," I comment.

"Seriously? Gross. You didn't do it on this couch, did you?" he makes a face, jumping up and swiping dramatically at his pants.

"Ew, no. We just kissed. Then you knocked on the damn door, Stone freaked, and he hauled ass out of here."

"You know, there's something so extraordinary about knowing I cockblocked you, considering you did it with me and Hannah," he says with a grin.

"Oh shit, I forgot about that!" I laugh. I got into a car accident and broke my wrist. Since I was in Denver, I called Luca. He stayed with me all weekend to ensure I was okay. I, of course, took advantage and let him fawn over me until he realized I could take care of myself.

"So Dom and Alex both think you're really dating Stone?" Luca asks.

"I guess," I sigh.

"When are you going to tell them the truth?"

"I'm not saying a damn word right now. Those assholes need to stew. The fact that all three of you have either called, or shown up here, before eight in the morning is absurd. I'm an adult, and you guys treat me like a child that needs protecting."

"That is true, but you are the baby. And it was rough all those years when you were in and out of the hospital, sis."

My childhood wasn't as ideal as Stone paints it to be. I had a rare disease called Hemolytic Uremic Syndrome, and it wreaked havoc on my entire body and immune system. Way too many hospital visits to count over the first ten years of my life. An eternal optimist, I channeled my energy into what is now the Children's Hospital Gala. I had to give back somehow.

"I get that, but seriously, Isabella is two years older than me. You don't intercept her boyfriends. You don't show up at her house, or work, like you do me. It's bullshit, Luca."

"Well, you are very different people, Ari. I mean this with love. Okay? You and Isabella can't be treated with the same gloves. Isabella was basically an adult by the age of ten. She's an old soul, and she rarely trusts anyone. You, on the other hand, have rose-colored glasses on. You're full of life, and you inherently believe that there's good in everyone. We worry about you on a different level than her because we think people will take advantage of you. We worry about her because we don't think she lets anyone in."

He's not wrong about my sister. I love Isabella. She's incredibly smart and driven. But we are as different as night and day. I'm an open book, and she's closed off. I can talk to anyone, whereas she feigns politeness. After knowing her for five minutes, I told Hannah, Luca's girlfriend, that we were best friends. I don't think Isabella even has Hannah's number yet.

"Regardless, you guys need to back off. Let me make my own decisions. My own mistakes. Live and learn, right? You can't fight my battles for me, Luca. I have to do things on my own terms."

Luca gives me a small smile. "You're right. I'll back off. I can't promise Dom and Alex will, but I'll talk to them. What are you going to do with Stone, though?"

I smile widely, making Luca groan.

"I didn't mean that literally, Ari. Not *with* Stone. What are you going to do *about* Stone," Luca says as he covers his eyes in jest. "Honestly, I think he wants you, but he doesn't know how to come to terms with wanting Alex's sister. And, you know, the whole age thing."

"It's not that big of a deal. It's a decade. So what?"

"It may not be a big deal to you, but it obviously is to him," Luca comments.

I sigh. He's right. I hate that it's a big deal to Stone. So what am I going to do about him?

I'm not sure yet, but I know I'm not done with Stone.

He might claim I'm just a kid, and that nothing will ever happen between us, but there was no denying what I felt during this last kiss. He wants me just as much as I want him.

Stone doesn't stand a chance.

Chapter 3

Stone, 16 years ago

"Remind me why we're here?" I ask my best friend, Alex.

"My mom said I had to come. Luca got pushed up to the first line, and she said we all had to support him, or she wouldn't feed us dinner this week," Alex explains. Like many kids in Eternity Springs, his younger brother Luca has been in ice skates since he was barely walking. Now he's an ice hockey protégée with dreams of making it to the NHL.

"Dude. You're twenty. You don't even live there anymore. Hell, you're gallivanting around the planet. Pretty sure you can find your own food," I tease. Alex is in the Air National Guard. He joined right after graduating from high school. After attending basic training and tech school, he snagged an eighteen-month deployment overseas. This is the first time he's been home since we graduated. I'm almost a year older than him, but due to my October birthday and his July birthday, we were in the same grade.

"She's making her lasagna tonight, man. I haven't had it in two years."

I groan. Mrs. Santo makes the best lasagna I've ever had. She won't even share the recipe with some of her own family members.

Sofia Marino Santo was born and raised in Colorado, but she claims to have cousins still in Italy. Alex's father, Nick Santo, doesn't speak much about his family. Mr. Santo has never cared much for me. He's never come out and said it, but it's clear he thinks the entire Santo family is above my pay grade. I get it. Really, I do. I'm the son of a maid who got knocked up by a washed-up professional athlete. I was his punching bag more than once in my childhood, and if he hadn't left town when I was thirteen, I have no doubt the hits would have continued until I could overpower him. My mom still blamed me for him leaving, though.

"Any chance she has enough for one starving bartender?" I ask hopefully. Mrs. Santo took mercy on me so many times over the years. It didn't stop at making sure I was fed. I sat at the table with Alex and his younger brother Dominic, under the watchful eye of both parents, as we did our nightly homework. More than once, she'd shove leftovers and bags of necessities in my arms before dropping me off at my mom's trailer. Clothing, deodorant, non-perishable food, even money. I learned quickly to hide the money in the only place my mom wouldn't look: in the toilet tank. She may have been a maid at one point, but cleaning up the home she shared with her child was not high on her priority list. Although calling it a "home" is a stretch.

"You know she'll feed you, Stone. If I didn't bring you home, she'd probably yell at me," Alex says with a laugh.

Alex has been my safe space for as long as I can remember. My childhood was rough. I'm not going to sugarcoat it. More than once, my mom told me how she never wanted me and how she only wanted to "trap" my dad so she could quit working. Clearly, she didn't see how her world would change when he popped positive for banned substances for his major league baseball team and was booted from the team. He arrived back in Eternity Springs with no job, no prospects, and a checking account in the red, courtesy of a gambling problem my mom didn't know about. We were kicked out of our lovely apartment, and ended up living at the edge of town in a shitty one-bedroom trailer on cinder blocks. The only silver lining was that the move put me in a different elementary school, where I met Alex.

Alessio, or Alex, Santo clearly came from more money than me. Even my little pea-brain could detect that. I never questioned it. He was a good friend to me, and that's all that mattered. But I remember a teacher commenting once when Mrs. Santo showed up for *my* parent-teacher conference that "money couldn't buy class." I didn't understand that sentiment until I was much older. It wouldn't matter if my mom won the lottery. She'd still be trailer trash. And even if the Santos lost everything, they'd still have class.

Alex always held himself differently, a chip off the old block of his dad. He stood taller than our peers. His confidence and swagger were evident even then. I'll never know why he decided to befriend me all those years ago, but I chose not to look that particular gift horse in the mouth. We bonded immediately, and we've been best friends ever since.

I'm not the biggest fan of hockey, but I'll attend anything if it means I get to spend time with Alex while he's home. While he actively watches the action on the ice, I'm content to scroll my phone as we lounge up in the stands.

"Lexy!" I hear someone shout. It's a young, pint-sized voice. This means we only have a few seconds before ...

"Fuck," Alex mutters.

Before I can turn, a hand slaps my cheek, jarring me. Suddenly, a face is an inch away, dark eyes like molten chocolate peering intensely into mine.

"Tone."

"I know you can say my name correctly, Arianna," I remark dryly. Alex's youngest sister, all three and a half feet of her, has been the bane of my existence since she was born. The baby of the Santo family has everyone wrapped around her finger. Everyone except me. You know how people claim cats flock to those who don't like cats? That's how it is with Arianna. She knows I don't like her, so she won't leave me alone. Well, it's not that I don't like her. I just don't do kids. They're small, impressionable, and I don't know how to act around them. If only Ari would get the message and go bother someone else.

"You're Tone to me. Always will be," she says flippantly before slapping my cheek again. For a ten-year-old, she packs quite the punch. Her eyes narrow when she notices me jolt, and pops me again. She's called me Tone since she was a toddler and couldn't pronounce the ST sound.

"Dammit, Ari, stop that," I snap.

"Why? Am I hurting you?" she taunts. "You're ginormous, and I'm tiny. Can't take a hit from a girl?"

"Seriously? Alex, control the angry dictator," I tell him.

He holds up his hands in surrender. "Then she'll hit me. Sorry, man, you're on your own. I'm gonna go talk to my parents."

Assuming Arianna will follow her brother, I'm aggravated when she continues to stand in front of me, her hands on her hips.

"What?" I ask.

"Do you like my dress?" Arianna asks, taking one hand and motioning up and down her dress. It might look like a standard princess dress, but I do not doubt the Santo family had this custom-made, or shipped in from a specialty store. Nothing but the best for their littlest diva.

"Not especially, no," I say nonchalantly. Arianna growls at me, making me work hard to keep the smile off my face. Aggravating this little girl is just too much fun.

"You do like it. I can tell. Boys like girls to wear pretty things," she says with a glint in her eye.

"I'm not a boy; I'm a man. And men don't look at little girls' clothing, Arianna. It's gross and illegal," I respond.

"Illegal?" she asks.

Fuck. I don't want to get into this kind of conversation with a seven-year-old.

Eight? Wait. How the hell old is she?

"I'm ten, you dork brain!" she shouts.

Guess I asked that question out loud. And dork brain? Is that the big diss for tweens these days?

"Regardless, we're not talking about your dress. Don't you have a boyfriend your own age you can bug? Run along, Princess, and go find someone else to bother," I tell her, waving my hand down toward where the rest of the Santo family congregates near the ice.

"Princess? See! You do like my dress!" she says triumphantly, then grimaces. "And no, ew. Gross. Boyfriend? Yuck. Boys are disgusting."

I roll my eyes. "No, Princess. I called you that because everyone treats you that way. The baby of the family. You have everyone wrapped around your finger. You get everything you want out of life. You'll probably never know any hardship in your entire life, Arianna. And all I've known is bad times," I mutter.

"That's not true, Tone. Lexy isn't a bad time," she says assertively.

I sigh. "You're right. Your brother is a good guy."

Just about the only good thing in my miserable life.

"What does it mean to have someone wrapped?" she asks, jarring me from my negative thoughts.

"It means they'll do anything for you, regardless of the consequences."

"Oh. Then they are wrapped, Tone. My family loves me," she says proudly, spinning again.

"Arianna! Come wish your brother good luck!" Mrs. Santo calls, then gives me a warm smile and a wave.

"Better go, Princess. Can't leave your public waiting," I say, dismissing her as I pull my phone out of my pocket and open my text messages. Shaina texted, asking to meet up. She's my current fuck buddy, and she typically doesn't talk much at all. I could use a release and immediately text back asking when she's free.

I'm popped in the face again. "Jesus Christ, Arianna! Stop fucking hitting me!"

She gasps, her deep eyes as wide as I've ever seen them. "You said two bad words!"

"Huh?" I look at her in confusion. Two?

"You said the F-word and the JC-word," she whispers. "You're not a very nice person, Tone. You should know better. Lexy taught you better than that."

Now, it's my turn to growl at her. "I'm a grown-ass man, Arianna. I can speak however I want. You're a *baby*. Get over it. Now leave me the hell alone."

I wince as her eyes fill with tears. "Why are you so mean?"

She turns and flounces down the bleachers, running out of the arena. I'm tempted to go after her and apologize, but the entire Santo family is watching me. Mr. Santo glares, shaking his head in disgust. Alex shrugs as he turns his grandmother, Nonna, around to speak again to Luca. Dominic and Leo, Alex's other brothers, openly laugh.

"Fuck," I mutter. I didn't mean to upset Arianna. Sometimes, she just brings out the worst in me. I have no idea what it is about this girl, other than how much it aggravates me that she's getting everything handed to her. She won't know a hard day's work in her life. She'll undoubtedly be given a cushy job at the hotel the family owns, and she'll marry some rich prick who keeps a side chick in the city while Arianna does brunch with friends here at home.

"Stone? Are you alright?" Mrs. Santo asks quietly. I was so lost in my thoughts that I didn't hear her approach. "How has my youngest daughter upset you today?"

"Aside from her slapping my cheek more than once, nothing other than her usual activities," I explain.

"Slapping you? That's unusual," Mrs. Santo comments. "She's a violent one, sure. But it's never gone outside the immediate family before."

"She's violent at home?" I ask, a bemused smile on my face.

"Oh yeah. She and Luca go toe-to-toe all the time. It's remarkable how quickly she can bring him to his knees. What's it called when you kick someone's legs out from under them?"

"A roundhouse kick?" I guess.

"Maybe. Arianna will feign she's fallen, and she'll begin to cry. Luca will immediately go to check on her, and she takes him down. Every damn time. But my sweet *cocco* can't let his sister be hurt," Mrs. Santo tells me, an adoring smile on her face. What must it be like to have a mother love you like that? To have anyone love you unconditionally.

"I wouldn't know," I murmur. I don't know how to love like that, and I've certainly never been loved like that. I'm an only child — at least, that I know of — and my mom tells me every chance she gets how much she despises me.

"Oh, Stone. You'll find someone in the future that teaches you how to love, and that woman, whoever she is, will show you what it's like to be loved unconditionally."

I laugh bitterly. "There's no such thing as unconditional love. Sorry, Mrs. Santo. I get that you lucked out and won the lottery for your family, but you're the exception, not the rule. Everything is conditional."

Mrs. Santo smiles sadly at me. "One day, sweet boy, a woman will knock *you* off your feet. And you'll realize that unconditional love means many things. For one, it means you support that person in everything. But in another, even more important way, it means you see them at their best and worst, and you choose to love them despite it all. Because even your worst day with that person is better than your best day without them."

I think of her words for a moment before answering. "That's never going to happen to me, Mrs. Santo. Love, marriage, babies. I'm not cut out for all that shit — I mean crap."

"You're twenty-one, Stone. You're allowed to say shit in front of me. Just try not to drop the f-bomb in front of my ten-year-old, okay?" she says before smacking my cheek. Her eyes widen comically. "Oh my God, I'm to blame for the cheek-hitting!"

"Apparently, you are," I say, rubbing my sore cheek. Her light cackle makes me smile as only the Santo family members can. "What does that thing you call Luca mean? *Cocco*?"

"Technically, it means coconut," she laughs. "But it also means darling son."

"Wonder if I could call him that," I joke.

"I think he'll probably roundhouse kick *you* if you try. Oh, and Stone?" she says as she's halfway down the bleachers. "You're welcome for dinner tonight. But will you promise me something?"

"Sure," I answer, assuming it involves apologizing to Arianna.

"When you fall in love, you'll let me rub it in, right?"

I roll my eyes. "Sure, Mrs. Santo. But don't hold your breath."

She turns her head and watches Arianna walk slowly back into the arena, her cheeks clearly red, as she wipes her eyes. Arianna refuses to look in my direction, sitting quietly beside her Nonna and ignoring me. Mrs. Santo turns around to stare at me again. "I can't wait to watch this happen."

If only I knew then what I know now.

Sofia Santo is *never* wrong.

And Arianna Santo, much like her mother, is trouble.

Chapter 4

Stone, Present Day

If you would have asked me twenty years ago what career I'd have, I'd have probably said something ridiculous. Maybe military, or possibly construction. Sports. Definitely not a desk job.

Owning my own barbershop? Not even on my radar.

I came into it out of boredom, honestly.

I tried the college thing with one class at a community college near Eternity Springs. Wasn't for me. Thought about doing a trade school, but figured I'd take some time to pad my bank account before I had to pay for any schools or classes. Occasionally, I helped out at Everlasting since Alex was gone a lot and I was bored, but I wanted something with more hours.

Walking along the main drag of Eternity Springs, I saw a help-wanted sign in the local barbershop. Lloyd had owned it as long as I'd remembered. Maybe even longer than I'd been alive. He was old, bald, and would much prefer to shoot the shit with patrons than actually do any work around the place.

At first, I was hired for general upkeep and janitorial work. Then, I oversaw the phones, deliveries, and stocking shelves. For a small-town joint, Lloyd always kept a ton of products on hand for clientele. I learned quickly that the theory of a barbershop being just for men was a myth. Lloyd was trained in all aspects of men's and women's haircuts and haircare. Before long, he was taking me under his wing to show me different techniques and things he'd learned along the way.

While I was in school, it was rough going. The state of Colorado required fifteen hundred hours of schooling, or fifty credits, before I could work on my own, and handling those hours, plus regular work, was debilitating. Once I was fully licensed and could take on clientele, Lloyd was happy to hand over most of his clients to me. I purchased the shop entirely within a few years, and revamped it into Stone Cold Cuts.

Lloyd had always depended on locals and tourists who just happened to walk by and want a cut, but I knew the power of social media could help the shop grow. Within a year, I was able to hire two more barbers, a licensed cosmetologist to provide nail services, and an esthetician for facials and waxing. We've become a full-service shop, and I'm incredibly proud of what we've created since I took over.

Which brings me to today. Social media helped us grow, but it also brought a lot of chaos. Like teenagers who walk in and think we'll all have availability to do whatever they want.

I'm generally a go-with-the-flow kind of guy, and I don't put judgment on people for their decisions. With their hair, at least. But if I have one more teenage boy come in and ask for a perm today, I'm going to lose my damn mind.

"Bro, I asked for a perm, not what this is, yo," the kid moans as he picks up one corkscrew curl and pulls it off his head. Standing behind him and watching as he stares at his reflection in the mirror above my station, I'm forcing myself to breathe and remain calm. The quicker he gets out of here, the better. I have things to do. My station is a mess. I need to order some products, and clean the bathroom. Ownership has its perks, but also some downfalls.

"That is a perm," I mutter. Seriously, why don't kids do fucking research?

"But why is it so curly?"

"Because it's a perm. That's what it does; it makes your hair curly," I snap.

"I only wanted it like this," he says, showing me a picture on his phone of some weird kid flipping the peace sign at the camera, an old-school Farrah Fawcett hairstyle with flips of hair that look like wings sitting on his forehead.

"That's his natural hair, kid. That's not a perm, and it's not what you showed me when you walked in," I remind him. He showed me something reminiscent of Justin Timberlake's ramen hair of the late nineties.

"Whatever, I'm not paying for this," he says defiantly.

I smirk. "Oh yeah?"

"Yeah, brah." I went from 'bro' to 'brah' real fast.

"Well, brah, when you came in, I made you fill out an online form, and you put in a payment. I don't work for free," I explain. One of the best things I ever did was start requiring a deposit on services, or full payment upfront. Generally, if I know the client, I'll waive both of those concepts. But for some, and clearly in this case, pre-payment is needed.

"Are you fucking kidding me?" he shouts. "How much was this?"

"One hundred dollars."

"For this? Are you shitting me? My mom is gonna kill me!" he wails.

I shrug. Not my problem. Mom shouldn't give him a damn credit card then.

"Seriously, bro, you gotta refund me. I figured it was ten or twenty bucks," he pleads.

"You've been here for over two hours. You really thought I'd work for half minimum wage and pay for the products myself?" I ask in disbelief. Do schools not teach the value of money anymore?

"I don't know! I didn't expect this. I just wanted my hair to look different!"

"Well, it looks different," Sam, one of my other barbers, announces from his station. The guy he's working on coughs to muffle a laugh.

"Are you really not going to refund me?" the kid asks, a full-on pout crossing his face as he looks close to tears.

I sigh. I'm tempted to, just to get the brat out of here. But what will that teach him? If he whines and sticks his lower lip out, and I give him a discount or refund, he'll get what he wants. No. I refuse to be part of that problem. "No, kid. I'm not refunding you. Let this be a lesson to do your research before you spend money on something."

"You're an asshole," he mutters, ripping off the cape I've had across his shoulders and stomps out of the shop.

"Not the first person to tell me that today," I call after him, then chuckle as he flips me off.

"Wouldn't be a normal day for you if you hadn't made at least one person cry, right, Stone?" Sam comments wryly.

"It's what I live for. Especially when it's children," I remark. That gets a bark of laughter from Sam.

"You ever think of having kids, Stone?"

I shudder. "No. I'm not made for the parenting gig."

"Really? I think you'd be a great one, actually."

"Why?" I ask, intrigued, as I begin to clean up my station.

"Well, you wouldn't let a kid walk all over you. You'd be realistic with them, maybe to a fault. You wouldn't sugarcoat things. Part of the problem with these Gen Z kids is that they've been told they're God's gift, and everything should be handed to them. You wouldn't be like that. You'd want and expect your kid to have a backbone, but also respect others. You'd be a good dad, Stone," Sam explains.

Wow. That was not what I expected him to say. That was deeper than I imagined. "I figured you'd say something about teaching a kid sarcasm, and how to cut a fade properly."

Sam laughs. "Totally valid points, and I'm sure you'd do both.

You don't give yourself enough credit. A kid would be lucky to have you as a dad."

"I wouldn't know how to be a dad, Sam. My own didn't even stick around. How would I be a role model when I didn't have one?"

"Weren't you always with the Santos? I can't think of a better role model than Nick Santo," Sam says.

"Mr. Santo has never liked me. He put up with me because of Alex."

"I highly doubt that's the truth," Sam says. "Knowing what I know about Nick Santo, he doesn't do anything he doesn't want to."

"How well do you know Mr. Santo?" I ask.

"I love that you still call him Mr. Santo, and you're almost forty," Sam chuckles. "I'm only a few years younger than you. I hung out with Leo Santo quite a few times, and my parents always took us to Everlasting for events and things. I think my dad plays golf with Nick once a week nowadays."

"About ten years ago, I tried to call him Nick. If looks could kill, man, I'd be dead right now. He turned right around and growled, 'You call me Mr. Santo, boy.'"

"Ten years ago?"

"Yep. I already owned this shop, and he referred to me as 'boy.' I've never called him Nick since."

"Okay, maybe he did put up with you for Alex's sake."

I'm well aware.

✦ ✦ ✦ ✦ ✦ ✦

*O*nce I close the shop for the night, I head home. I have a house on the outskirts of town. Buying the shop took all of my savings, and only a couple years ago was I able to buy a home. It's an older property with four bedrooms, two bathrooms, and came with every outdated item you can think of. The brown carpet, reminiscent of the shag style from the seventies, was ripped out the day I closed on the house. Gold everything: light fixtures, outlet covers, and even gold trim around the mirrors in the bathroom. Weird paneling on every cabinet door, and the oldest refrigerator I've ever seen.

I'm slowly renovating it, so it leaves a lot to be desired. But the bones of the house are solid, and it sits on a half-acre, which is virtually unheard of in Colorado. Picturesque views out almost every window make the less-than-stellar setup worth it.

So far, I've gutted and rebuilt the kitchen. Cabinetry stained a horrid red color from the original kitchen, a good forty years old, was replaced with white cabinets. Granite countertops and a farm sink add charm and functionality. Fortunately, the kitchen was initially styled as an eat-in kitchen, and I could add a large island with a bar so I'd have more storage but still a place to eat.

Next, I tackled the main bedroom and ensuite bathroom. I don't need all the space, so I removed a wall to make one spare bedroom part of my closet and bathroom. While I'm the most masculine guy out there, I'll be the first to admit I love a bath. Self-care is important. When I've been standing on my feet for twelve hours, and then come home to work on renovations for another couple of hours, a bath is the perfect way to relax and unwind. So, I needed a huge bathroom with a massive soaking tub. I added a large tile shower. The closet has every built-in imaginable, and should I ever sell this house, I'm sure any woman would love the space. Because, let's be honest, no woman will ever move in here with me. I'm a lone wolf, and I know it.

I don't think any woman would put up with me and not hope — or expect — for me to change. I've had a handful of casual relationships in my adult life, and the women have typically had the same complaints. I work too much. I'm too set in my ways. I expect the worst out of women. I'm crabby. I find it hard to trust anyone, especially people with money. In fact, my ex-girlfriends have pointed out that I only trust Alex, but at the same time, I dislike his family having money.

It doesn't make sense, even to me.

I'm not altogether sure if the Santo family is as well-off as I've built up in my head. It seems like they pump quite a bit of money back into Everlasting and events like the Children's Hospital Gala I attended, where I ran into Arianna. I wasn't even supposed to go to that. Alex was going, but he got tasked with some kind of short-notice military thing. Fortunately, we're about the same size, and I have a key to his apartment, so I borrowed his tux. I'm glad I did because I'd been wondering what Arianna tasted like for years.

That kiss. Fucking hell, that kiss. I'll remember that forever.

I'd always considered Arianna as my best friend's annoying baby sister. I didn't interact with her too much as a kid. Honestly, she was in the hospital a lot growing up. I only found out about a year ago what actually happened to Arianna as a child. Suffice it to say, she was dealt a shitty hand.

And once Alex was gone with the National Guard, I had to depend on the rest of the Santo kids for information about the family, so I didn't have to interact with Arianna much. Sofia still encouraged me to come over for dinner, but it didn't feel right without Alex there. I felt like I was playing pretend family.

Plus, our interactions were relatively volatile after I made Arianna cry at her brother's hockey game when she was around ten. She just always brought out the worst in me. We began arguing about everything. If she said it was sunny, I'd argue it was dark. If I said hockey was the greatest sport, she'd argue it was football. I swear, when she turned eighteen, she voted opposite of me just out of spite, even though I knew her political views were actually on par with mine.

On her nineteenth birthday, I rescued a clearly trashed Arianna in Denver. Alex was home for a change, and mentioned Arianna was out celebrating her birthday. Should I have gone to find her? No. Do I regret it? Absolutely not. I carted her kicking and screaming all the way home. Someone was feeding her alcohol in the women's bathroom, and I couldn't do anything but watch and wait. The moment I carried her inside her house, making the mistake of smelling her hair, made me horribly angry with myself. I was at war with my own brain: the juxtaposition of seeing her as becoming a woman, while also recognizing her as my childhood best friend's baby sister.

And then, on her twenty-first birthday, when Alex joked that Arianna would need someone to follow her around Denver to make sure she didn't do anything illegal, or get drugged, I took it to mean he wanted me to follow her. It was that night, watching her, that I realized I was in trouble.

Or maybe it's just that *she* was trouble.

Because when I saw her on the dance floor, grinding against some douche, I saw her.

I *saw* her.

It wasn't that I saw the bratty little sister of my best friend.

She was a breathtaking creature, with legs I wanted to be wrapped around my waist, and luxurious dark brown wavy hair down to her waist that I could almost feel slipping between my fingers, or dragging along my thighs as she took my cock deep into her mouth. The fiery red dress, if you could call the tiny scrap of clothing she wore that night a dress, accentuated every perfect curve on her luscious body. I stopped dead in my tracks, watching the little minx as I got a boner in the middle of a fucking dance club.

And when Arianna saw me, she knew. She knew I was captivated by her, and she looked right at me when she kissed that douche. Even in the darkened confines of the club, I could see her chocolate brown eyes sparkling with mirth.

I about threw her over my shoulder and stalked out of there, ready to shout that she was fucking mine, and every man there needed to know it.

Instead, I kept an eye on the douche, watched him slip something in her drink, and then laid him out.

If I thought Ari would be happy, boy, was I mistaken. She lit into me, going as far as to push me away from her. Even after she knew the guy tried to drug her, she wouldn't thank me for stepping in. Arianna only yelled at me, telling me she was sick of her brothers trying to run her life, and that I better not tell Alex about it. I never told Alex, and if anything, it made her even more hostile toward me.

Now, here we are, five years later, and our relationship is even more volatile. I might have seen her in a different light on her twenty-first birthday, but she's always seen me as an overbearing big brother type. I might tease her about a teenage crush, but I know she doesn't feel that way now. It's straight venom seeping from her pores.

But ... that kiss.

That fucking kiss.

She kissed me back. She pulled me against her. Did she feel what I felt? Or was she able to turn on acting skills that quickly? I'm not even sure how I recovered to interact with her ex. No clue what she was doing with him. No one in the family liked him, not even her mom. Sofia likes everyone. She gives people the benefit of the doubt and typically gives them way too many chances to redeem themselves. It seemed like he was good at his job, and maybe they put up with him in Arianna's life because of that. I've never talked to anyone in Arianna's family about her dating life. It's bad enough that I think about who she dates. She's always given men more opportunities than she should. I'm more of a "strike one, you're out" kind of guy.

As I finish my project on a guest bedroom for the night, I find myself imagining what a night with Arianna might be like. Would she fight me like she usually does, or would she let me take control? Hell, would I let her take control? Doubtful. As my imagination begins to take flight, I know I'm in deep trouble.

Not only is she a decade younger than me, but she's my best friend's sister. I've never been one to have set parameters for what I will, or won't do, but that's a line I vowed never to cross with Alex's three sisters. I don't even think we've ever discussed it. Some guys would need to verbalize their rules, but Alex never did. I think he knew I'd respect him and his family.

I probably shouldn't have kissed her. I could have pretended to be her man without that display. But I felt this feral need to claim her, and had her wrapped in my arms before I realized what I intended to do. And now Alex is mad at me, her whole family thinks we've been dating behind their back, and I can't even be in the same room as her without putting my foot in my mouth. So much for being a knight in shining armor. I made everything worse.

But now that I've kissed her, I wonder if she'd be worth it.

*A*rianna

I'm a wimp. I called in sick, which I *never* do. It's my family's hotel, for crying out loud. I knew they'd all be like vultures, swooping in to get the gossip. Yelling at me, or chastising me. Something.

I just couldn't handle it today. I know how everyone will react.

My mom will want details. She'll try to act casually, but she'll be busting at the seams to find out how long it's been going on. Even if I tell her the truth, she won't believe me. She's a romantic, and she's desperate for all of her kids to find their person. You'd think she would feel vindicated when Dom's marriage failed, since she made it obvious how much she disliked Dom's ex-wife, Savannah. But she didn't. She believes Dom will find his perfect match, even though he has made it perfectly clear he's never getting into another relationship.

How my mother, the romantic, married my father, the pragmatic, is beyond me. He won't approach me. He'll give me that disappointed shake of his head. Just as my mom didn't like Dom's ex, our dad has never liked Stone. He'd be aggravated with me for a public display of affection, but even more so about it being with Stone.

My sister Isabella, the introverted baker of the family, won't want any details. She probably wouldn't even want to talk about it. She's never been comfortable gossiping, or doing the whole sister talk thing. On the other hand, our sister Gianna thinks gossiping is an Olympic sport. It's really too bad she just had a baby, and I can't call her to chat. The last time we talked, my nephew Carson puked down her shirt, and she screamed so loudly I thought she'd perforated my eardrum.

It's a good thing Alex is overseas because he'd probably show up and drag me to Stone's, just to berate us both at the same time, or some other bullshit like that. Alex means well, but he's over the top with his big brother role. He's the oldest, but chose to join the military instead of taking over the hotel. Then, when his wife was killed in a car accident, leaving him a single dad, things got worse with his big brothering from afar. He takes his role a little too seriously.

Dom isn't much better. Fortunately, he's too busy with the hotel to take our Saturday morning conversation about Stone any further.

Which leaves Luca. He at least knows the situation with Stone isn't all that it's cracked up to be. But I know he won't leave me alone about it. Luca knew all about my crush on Stone growing up and how often Stone would hurt my feelings. I don't even think Stone knows how often he made me cry. But, in all honesty, it helped me develop a thicker skin. I just wish I could stop comparing every man I date to Stone.

I'm totally screwed now that we've kissed. No way anyone is topping that anytime soon.

Since I haven't wrapped my own head around it all yet, I'm avoiding my family. I've even called in reinforcements via my friend Natalie, who should be dropping off food any minute now.

And when a knock is followed by a faux falsetto voice shouting, "housekeeping!" I know she's here.

"I'm only giving you the goods if you explain why the site has you and Stone secretly engaged and knocked up," she announces as she steps into my apartment. We don't even list the town gossip site by name anymore. It's just "the site."

"What?" I yank my phone off the coffee table and bring up the link. For fuck's sake.

How long has this been going on? Stone Dixon was seen outside Dr. Mansfield's office early this morning, carrying a paper bag. Unnamed sources suggest he was inside picking up prenatal vitamins for his decade-younger paramour. If that is the case, we can only assume Stone and Arianna Santo have been secretly dating for much longer than we know. Does this mean while Bradley Wetherington was two-timing Arianna, she was doing the same? Pulling on our best Jerry Springer accents, but who IS the father?

"Who's the father, Ari?" Natalie asks. She sets our lunches on my kitchen counter and removes containers as I pull out plates and flatware.

"Jesus. I'm not pregnant, Nat."

"You sure about that? The site is hardly ever wrong," she points out.

"Well, considering I just had my period, I'm pretty sure. And since Stone and I have definitely not had sex, he's not the father of my imaginary baby."

Natalie actually looks sad. "Bummer. His eyes, your hair, and his lips? You'd make a gorgeous baby."

I don't answer her. I don't need to. She knows I've had a thing for Stone. There may have been a drunken night a few years ago when we found a website where you can add pictures to determine how your future children might look. Stone and I would have incredibly photogenic babies, but that's beside the point. It's never going to happen.

"In any case, I'm super bummed I wasn't there to witness the kiss," Nat comments. "Was it as good as you imagined?"

"Better," I admit. She squeals.

"Seriously?"

"God, yes. It was so good. I can't stop thinking about it."

"Have you talked to him since?"

"Yeah, he showed up here the following morning."

"No fucking way!" she shrieks. I can tell by the look on her face that she thinks it's a good thing. She's positively giddy, her eyebrows almost touching her hair line as she jumps up and down while clapping. It's hard to be sad or depressed around Natalie. She's protrudes sunshine and joy.

We take our plates into the living room to sit comfortably on my couch. Natalie didn't even ask what I wanted but showed up with my perfect comfort food from our favorite soup and sandwich place. Today, she got me a chef's salad and baked potato covered in cheese, and a Caesar salad and soup for herself.

"Get whatever thought is whirling in your head right out of there. He showed up here so he could tell me that Alex knew we had kissed and didn't believe Stone was trying to help me save face in front of Bradley. Then, he immediately launched into a wonderful conversation, reminding me that we would never happen."

"Seriously? No. That can't be it."

"Well ..."

"I fucking knew it!"

I can't help but giggle at her all-consuming glee. "We may have kissed again. And it was even better than the first time. If my jackass brother hadn't shown up, I don't think Stone would have stopped."

"Which one?"

"Stopped everything. Kissing. Touching. Sex. You do know how that works, right?"

"No, smartass. I mean, which brother showed up?"

"Oh. Luca."

"Does he think you're really dating Stone?"

"No. Luca knows me too well. Called me out on it immediately.

Alex and Dom really believe it, though. Alex called me, too. He's pissed at both Stone and me."

"Oh, whatever," Natalie says, waving her hand in annoyance. "He's always been a freaking hothead. Yell and zing accusations first; ask questions later. That's nothing new."

"True."

We pause for a few minutes, focusing on eating our lunch. I'm lost in my thoughts as I revisit the second kiss with Stone. If Luca hadn't shown up, I wonder what might have happened.

"Isn't he deployed or something?" Natalie asks, jolting me from my walk down memory lane.

"I guess. He never tells us anything. He takes the whole 'top secret' thing very seriously."

"What job does he have again?" she asks.

"Girl, I don't know. I don't pay attention to that stuff. I have too many brothers as it is, and two of them are in the military. I'm lucky I know what branch they're in," I joke. But honestly, I don't really know. The military confuses me. A lot of times, Alex will start out with one "job" but end up doing something completely different. All I know is he doesn't actually fly aircraft. His trying to explain that to my tiny brain when he joined the Air National Guard after high school when I was only around seven years old, was comical.

"So what happens now?" Natalie asks.

I grab our now empty plates and walk to the kitchen. "Nothing, I guess. Same old, same old."

"What does that mean?"

"Business as usual. We hardly interact, and when we do, it's mostly testy and passive-aggressive comments back and forth."

"I highly doubt that's how it's going to be, especially if he kissed you here when no one was here to witness it," Natalie says. She has a point, but I refuse to get my hopes up. I was confident after Luca left Saturday morning, truly thinking that I could put the moves on Stone and he'd eventually fall for my charm. But sitting with every-thing that has happened has made me second-guess it all.

"I don't want to think something might happen, Nat. It's easier for me to expect the worst, and hope for the best." I return to the living room and sit beside her.

"But that's not you, babe. That's not your personality at all. You've always been a glass-half-full kind of gal. You want, and expect, the best out of everyone. I swear you've made things happen just by believing in them. If you want Stone, now is the time to go for it."

"I just don't know if it's worth it —" I get interrupted by a knock at the door. Immediately, I motion for Natalie to be silent. It's likely one of my siblings, and I'm in no shape to talk to any of them.

"Babe?"

"What the fuck?" Natalie shouts as I jump up and fling open the door, finding Bradley and a bouquet of flowers.

"What the fuck are you doing here?" I ask.

"I heard you were sick. Wanted to bring you some flowers and check on you," he says with a lopsided grin. That grin is what did me in months ago. What prompted me to finally agree to date him. Look how well that turned out.

"Asshole, you need to go!" Natalie shouts, attempting to grab the door from my hands and shove it into his face.

"Why is she here, and not your boyfriend?" Bradley sneers.

"Her boyfriend has a job, asshole. I just stopped by for lunch," Natalie retorts.

"Oh, really? I was just at his place, and it's closed today," he says innocently.

"Okay?" I comment with a shrug. "Could be a lot of reasons. Maybe he's sick too. Maybe he's doing a training or special event somewhere."

"If you're his girlfriend, why don't you know where he is?" he asks.

"Because I don't have to keep tabs on him to believe in him, Bradley. I can trust him. Besides, I'm heavily medicated. It's possible he told me, and I just forgot."

"Would you look at that?" Natalie says, grabbing my vibrating phone off the coffee table, "Her boyfriend is calling her now."

Lo and behold, Stone is actually calling. "Hey, boyfriend."

He chuckles painfully. "That is obviously for the benefit of someone. Is your ex bothering you at work?"

"No, at home."

"What?" Stone says sharply.

"Since I wasn't feeling well today, I stayed home. Bradley showed up here with flowers," I tell him.

"I'll be there in five minutes. Fuck that. I'll be there in two," Stone says before ending the call. I wait a minute before removing the phone from my ear. Is it wrong of me to want to see another interaction between Bradley and Stone? It was fucking hot how Stone fought for me at the gala. Maybe I'll get another kiss out of it.

"Bradley, why are you here?" I sigh.

He has the nerve to smirk. "Well, I saw the news on *The Eagle Has Landed*, and figured I should check on you. See how you're feeling."

"How I'm feeling?"

Bradley's eyes dip to my stomach. "I mean, babe, if you're ... with child ... it's probably mine."

For fuck's sake. "We had sex once. I'm on the pill, you used a condom, and I'm pretty sure you pulled out before you came. That means we essentially used three different types of contraception. Oh, and I've had my period since then, so I'm definitely not pregnant with your unfortunate offspring."

"No need to be uncouth, Arianna. I had to check. You understand," he says condescendingly, then has the nerve to chuck me under the chin.

And with that, I'm done. My eyes look up triumphantly at Bradley.

"My boyfriend is on his way here. Are you going to wait?" I ask.

Bradley has the decency to look slightly horrified at another run-in with Stone. "Uh, no. I'll see you at work, Arianna."

I call out after him as he quickly jogs down the apartment stairs. "What about my flowers?"

My answer is the sound of the exterior door slamming against the wall as Bradley runs outside.

"Bummer. I like lilies," I pout.

Natalie laughs. "Tell Stone to get you some."

"Please. I doubt Stone has ever given a woman flowers."

"I have, actually. It's rare, but I have," Stone says, panting as he climbs the staircase. "Obviously, you're fine. I'm pretty sure I made your ex pee himself a little, though."

"What I wouldn't give for that to have been recorded," I sigh. I could show it to people at work and send a copy to his virtuous fiancée.

"Now that I know you're in capable hands, I'm going to go," Natalie says, grabbing her phone and keys. "Thanks for having lunch with me."

After a quick hug, I call out, "Thanks for bringing my favorites!"

Stone slips into my apartment and waits for me to close the door.

"What are your favorites?" he asks.

"Of what?"

"Lunch."

"Today was a comfort food day. Chef salad and a baked potato covered in cheese," I explain as I walk past him to clean up the leftovers.

"Why didn't you go to work today?" he asks.

"Mental health day," I mumble.

"Must be nice to be the princess," he responds.

"What does that mean?" I ask sharply.

He shrugs. "Most people can't take a mental health day, Arianna. You get away with a ton because of who you are, and where you work."

"Are you kidding me? Why aren't you at work, Stone? People in glass houses," I counter.

"Good to know you don't pay any attention, Princess. My shop is closed every Monday," he tells me.

I stare at him. "So?"

"You didn't know."

"Well, why would I know that?"

"Because on Mondays, I'm typically helping out at the hotel."

"No — no. You're no — no, you don't. You aren't there every Monday," I say, my mind frantically scouring the last few months of Mondays, trying to find any clue that he isn't there.

"I'm there every Monday. Sometimes, it's just to have lunch, but mostly, I do odd jobs around the place. Especially whenever Alex is gone."

"But why?" I ask.

"Because your parents have enough on their plate when taking care of Alex's kids. When Alex is home, he does a lot of the maintenance around the hotel and grounds. If I can remove a few items from their to-do list, I'm happy to do it," he tells me quietly.

"I had no idea," I confess. "I didn't know you were doing that, Stone. That's incredibly thoughtful of you."

He shrugs, looking down at the ground and stuffing his hands in his jeans. I take a moment to study him. Scuffed boots lead to form-fitting jeans that are molded to his thick thighs. A dark blue Henley stretches across his sculpted shoulders, and I notice a smudge of dirt across his cheek. Without thinking, I reach up and swipe at it. He flinches momentarily before subtly leaning into my hand. "You have some dirt, I think."

"I was cleaning out a couple of the fire pits," he says absentmindedly, his eyes latched on mine. I leave my hand on his cheek, the heat of his skin sending a direct route through my veins.

"This is the first time I've ever called off work," I confess. "I love my job, and I love my family. I wouldn't leave them in a bind."

He winces, his eyes scrunching closed, and I drop my hand from his face. "I know you wouldn't. I shouldn't have said that."

"No, you're right. You help out just as much as I do. You had a right to call me out on it."

"Did you really need a mental health day?" he asks.

I nod. "I wouldn't have gotten anything done at work today. They all mean well, but my family wouldn't have left me alone. They've all been texting and calling nonstop as it is."

Stone clears his throat. "Have you heard from Alex?"

"Everyone except him," I whisper. Alex is either more upset than I thought, or he's on a mission and can't call to yell at me some more.

"I haven't either," Stone admits.

"He's probably on a mission," I tell him. He gives me a pained smile and nods almost imperceptibly.

"You're probably right. Well, I should get going. Let me know if Bartlett shows up here again. I'll try to remember to record the inter-action in case he pees."

I giggle. "It's Bradley, not Bartlett."

"Whatever."

As Stone approaches the door, I say, "Thanks for coming to ensure I was okay."

He nods. "We may not always see eye to eye, Princess, but I'll always make sure you're okay. That's what fake boyfriends do, right?"

I giggle, but it hurts. "I guess so."

He gives me a slight wave before walking out.

I wonder if it's as apparent to him as it is to me that I'd give anything to make him my actual boyfriend.

Arianna

I was right to take the day off and avoid my family.

Tuesday, bright and early, they attacked.

"You looked a little too cozy with him, *paperotta*," my mother says. "Especially those pictures on the site. Like little lovebirds."

"We're not in love," I grumble.

"Maybe not yet, sweetheart. But you could get there."

"Seriously?" I exclaim. "I *just* broke up with my boyfriend, or whatever it is you want to call it, and you're trying to pawn me off on Alex's best friend. We have such a weird family."

"I'm not pawning you off on him, Arianna. I honestly think the two of you would be good for one another," Mom shrugs. We both turn as we hear a throat clearing, and my father stands at the entrance to my office.

I haven't even had a chance to take off my coat.

The fact that both of my parents came to my basement office tells me they would have been waiting yesterday as well. Usually I have time to grab a cup of coffee. Water my variety of low-light plants, and admire the windowless office that I've made my own. Clearly not today, as my parents are set on discussing things with me, whether I like it or not.

It really is remarkable that only one of their seven children is in a successful marriage. My parents look at one another with adoration. It's what we all witnessed growing up. Their devotion to each other is what fairy tales are made of. Forty years of marriage. They've consistently told us that we need to find a partner that loves us out loud. Find a partner that makes you want to shout it from the rooftops. The person who makes you strive to be a stronger woman. One who knows all your faults, and still chooses you.

My parents aren't perfect. I've witnessed some horrid arguments between them, mostly about my dad's health, where they've both said some things they've regretted. But they've always taught me to keep the lines of communication open. My mom says she waits for my dad to work through his thoughts before she talks to him. My dad needs time to process things. He's not one to express his emotions well, and my mom knows it. She waits him out.

"Can I help you with anything?" I say snottily. Dad's eyes narrow.

"Drop the attitude, Arianna."

"Just say what you need to say and get on with it, Dad. I have things I need to catch up on."

"If you had come to work instead of cowering in shame, this would have already been done," he says.

"I wasn't cowering in shame," I mumble.

"Yes, you were."

"Okay, fine. Cowering? Yes. Shameful? No. I did nothing wrong. I just didn't want to have to explain myself to all of you throughout the day when I barely understood it myself."

"All of us? Who else would you be expecting?" Mom asks. My cell phone chimes with a text as if on cue, and then the hotel phone rings.

"Well," I say, looking at both screens, "Gianna just texted, and Hannah is calling."

When I pick up the hotel phone, Hannah peppers me with questions. "He showed up again? What did he say? Did he kiss you again? That kiss was hot, by the way. I don't appreciate being ignored all weekend, Ari. If you say I'm your person, then you better treat me as such. Were Natalie and Claire notified? What did Alex say? I bet he's totally pissed. Do you know where he is?"

"Hannah!" I shout. Good lord, she really does ramble when she's excited or nervous.

"Sorry. You know I get going," she mutters.

"I know. I'll answer your questions so everyone can hear, and then I'm getting back to work."

"Everyone?"

"My parents are here."

"Oh."

I sigh. "Stone came to check on me Saturday morning. Yes, he kissed me again, but followed it up by saying that nothing would happen between us because I'm too young, and he respects my family too much. I ignored everyone, not just you. I needed to ... escape for a day or two. It was a lot to deal with emotionally."

"Do you think you can stay professional with Bradley working here?" Mom asks.

"I don't really have a choice, do I?"

"It's a pity he can't be fired," Hannah comments.

"I cannot fire him based on your feelings being hurt, Arianna," Dad says.

"I never asked you to fire him, Dad. Jeez. But thanks for that amazing vote of confidence in my ability to do my job."

"It's not that we doubt you, *paperotta*. I certainly would find it hard to maintain a mature appearance around him if I were you," Mom says.

"Me too, and keeping quiet is in my DNA," Hannah mutters.

"*Cara*, I didn't say I wouldn't fire him, just that your feelings being hurt can't be the reason why. I will handle this by-the-book, and you will not get involved. Understood?" Dad says resolutely.

"Okay, well, we all agree that this sucks, but I should keep doing my job. Great. Mom and Dad, thanks for checking in on me. I'm fine. I'll continue to be fine. Can I get to work now?" I ask exasperatedly.

My dad tilts his head to the side as he studies me. "Of course. However, we need to have a quick word with Mr. Wetherington to ensure he keeps his distance from you."

"Dad, that's really not necessary. And why are you doing this instead of Dominic?"

"Because Dom is ready to murder your ex-boyfriend, and we'd prefer if he stayed out of prison. I will handle a quiet investigation into Mr. Wetherington, while Dominic continues his current job and family responsibilities."

"That's because they don't want to have full custody of his kids," Hannah whispers, and I stifle a giggle. She's not wrong. Dom's youngest daughter, Aspen, alone is a handful, but it's a mutiny when all three of Dom's kids get going.

"I heard that, Hannah," Mom calls out, and Hannah swears under her breath. "Heard that too. I thought southern ladies didn't use so many f-bombs."

"You fucking thought wrong!" Hannah bellows, causing me to wince and pull the phone away from my ear. My mother cackles with glee before she gives me a hug. Dad kisses my temple, and they both leave. "Are they gone?"

"Yeah," I sigh as I sit heavily in my office chair. Today, I'm wearing my favorite pair of Jimmy Choo knee-high black leather boots, a gingham tweed high-waist skirt, and a black turtleneck. I felt powerful when I got dressed this morning, as if somehow my clothes could give me the strength to handle almost anything. Now, however, I just feel drained. Like I've been sent through a meat processor, ground up, and spat out.

"So he kissed you again?" Hannah asks quietly.

"He did."

"Was it as good as the first time?"

"Better, actually."

"Really?"

"Yep."

Hannah hums noncommittally as we both sit quietly with our thoughts. That second kiss did a number on me. I don't have a lot of experience with men. Granted, I've been on tons of dates. I've had countless first kisses. Sex? Not so much. Thinking back to so many kisses, and they all paled in comparison to my two kisses with Stone.

"How was it better?" Hannah whispers.

"It just — was," I state. "At the gala, it was amazing. But he was calculated in how he kissed me, I think. He was restrained. When he kissed me in my apartment ... I've never experienced anything like it, Han. He consumed me."

"That's how I felt when Luca first kissed me. I know you hate hearing details, so I won't say anything about the actual kiss. But everything faded away, and it was just me and him. I didn't know it could be like that until Luca."

That's exactly how I feel. I've compared men to Stone my entire life. It's as if I knew he was the gold standard. And now that I know how it feels to be wrapped in his arms, how his tongue tastes as it circles mine, I don't know how I'm supposed to go back to accepting dates from subpar men.

"What are you going to do?" she asks.

"I don't know," I sigh. "Luca thinks Stone actually wants me, but he's too scared to admit it. He thinks I should try to seduce Stone."

"I agree with him," Hannah replies.

"But ... but what if he shuts me down again?" I ask quietly.

"If he shuts you down, you'll know if he's *really* shutting you down. I mean, he looks at you when he thinks no one is watching, Ari. I've barely even met the guy, and I can tell he wants you. So I can assume we'd all know if he truly didn't want to be with you. And then you can move on."

"I don't know if I'll be able to move on," I confess.

"You don't give yourself enough credit," Hannah says. "If Stone doesn't want to be with you, then he's not the man for you. You'll know that, Ari. You'll move on because you'll want to find the man who is the perfect partner for you. If Stone doesn't see how amazing you are, he doesn't deserve you anyway. Someone out there will."

"I don't think I trust my own damn judgment anymore," I mutter.

"I know. I felt that way too. I certainly had no intention of anything happening with your brother. But he just barreled his way through my walls like a bull in a china shop," Hannah says with a light laugh. "Listen, I have to go. Christmas parties are up the wazoo right now, and we've had multiple servers call in sick for tonight. The banquet rooms aren't going to set themselves up."

"Text me if you need help. My schedule isn't too heavy today." Some hardcore guests will still access the hot springs in December, but most don't. No matter how often I tell them how peaceful it is to watch the snow fall while shoulder-deep in warmth, they don't believe me.

After hanging up with Hannah, I check my cell phone to find a handful of messages from Isabella.

> Belly: I gave you the weekend. I expect answers now.
>
> Belly: Don't ignore me.
>
> Belly: It's past breakfast. I didn't bug you earlier because I know you don't people until you've had caffeine.
>
> Belly: Come on, sissy. Answer me!

Grrr. She only calls me sissy when she wants to aggravate me.

> Belly: Mom just texted that you already had a visit from the parentals, and that Hannah called. So, potential sister-in-law trumps real sister? Nice.

Me: Oh, shut up. I can't talk to Hannah and text you at the same time, although it might have been nice to get this conversation over quicker that way.

Belly: She's alive! But seeing as how your mood isn't the best, either you haven't had any caffeine yet, OR you didn't convince Stone to give you a workout this weekend.

Neither one, actually.

Me: Nice, Belle.

Belly: Come on. I know you've had a thing for him for years. How was the kiss?

Me: Better than I anticipated. MUCH better.

Belly: Knowing Stone, he freaked out at some point.

Me: Yup. Showed up at my apartment Saturday morning at the crack of dawn, complained about my lack of Stone-acceptable pajamas, told me we could never be anything, then promptly threw me up against the wall and kissed me again.

Belly: I'm sorry…he did WHAT???

Me: I said what I said.

Belly: He threw you?

Me: Okay, no. Slammed me against the wall? Pushed? I don't know the correct term. All I know is my back is surprisingly sore from where my spine hit, and I wouldn't be surprised if there was an indent in the paint. I need to look when I get home. Might frame it for a memorial.

Belly: "Here lies the place where Stone gave it to me good."

Me: Something like that. And if our fucking brother didn't cockblock, I bet Stone would have really given it to me good.

Belly: Which brother?

Belly: Forget that. It has Luca written all over it.

Me: Yeah. Dom is pissed too. Stone showed up as Dom was leaving.

Belly: Jesus. Three guys within thirty minutes? Bet that old hag downstairs thinks you're one hell of a harlot.

Me: Undoubtedly. She hits her ceiling with something when she thinks I'm being too loud.

Belly: Bringing on the Friends reference. What was the landlord's name?

Me: Heckles.

Belly: It worries me how quickly you answer trivia about Friends.

Me: It's my show.

Belly: I know that, sissy. Still concerning.

Me: I'm sorry that I like actual comedy, Belle. Not everyone is dark and sinister with the vampire and werewolf shit.

Belly: I'm on trend. You're somehow the oldest of all of us. Were you even alive when the show aired?

Me: Yes.

Barely. I never saw any of it live. Only reruns.

Belly: Watch something current this
weekend. Challenge yourself.

Me: Nah.

Belly: You'll have time. Not like you'll be
hooking up with Stone anyway.

Me: Below the belt, sis.

Belly: At least someone is getting below your
belt.

Sigh.

She's not wrong.

While Bradley and I dated for six weeks, we only actually had sex once, and it was early on in our relationship. That should have been a red flag. Why would he get it and then not try to get it again? And honestly, I felt more between my legs from both kisses with Stone than I ever did with Bradley. Red flag number two. Actually, it's probably red flag number one hundred. I ignored everything because I was jealous of my brother and sick of being single.

I hate when I have hindsight anger. Anger at the things I should have said in a situation. When Bradley's fiancée insinuated she knew I was just a fuck buddy, I should have told her I'd only slept with him once, and that it had been weeks since that happened. I should have told her how he seemed to be wooing me. Bradley bringing me flowers yesterday wasn't the first time he'd shown up with a bouquet for me. I think I got caught up in the stereotypical romance of our relationship. The dates, the gifts, and the thought of someone. Focusing on those things allowed me to ignore the voice of reason in my head.

I turn my phone to silent so I can focus on work. While I told Hannah my workload wasn't too heavy, that's only partially true. I need to finish all the paperwork for the gala, write up thank you cards for all the volunteers, and tally all the donations so I can make a social media post.

I've never been able to run this event, but Hannah let me have free rein on a lot of the aspects she didn't understand. And as soon as she realized why the gala is so important to me, she was all too willing to hand it over.

When a hospital saves your life from a rare illness, you want to give back.

Chapter 7

Arianna, Age 6

"I don't wanna be here again."

"I know, *paperotta*."

"Maisie's party was today, and she told me there was a real princess coming, Mommy," I pout. Mom sighs. She sighs a lot.

"Yeah, well, I don't want to be here either," Luca grumbles.

"Meanie," I snap. I watch as Luca throws a hockey puck into the air. All my brother thinks about is hockey. "Why are you even here anyway?"

Luca shrugs.

"Because Daddy had to take Isabella to her cooking class, and everyone else had after-school activities, we can't leave Luca by himself."

"I would be fine, Mom. It's not that big of a deal," Luca replies.

"Luca, we left you alone for fifteen minutes, and you almost burned down the house."

"How was I supposed to know you have to put water in with the rice to cook it?" Luca asks defensively.

"And that's why we specifically told you *not* to touch the stove. When we feel you'll follow directions and not try to burn down the house, your father and I will discuss whether you're mature enough to stay home alone. Today is not that day," Mom says.

I stare down at the tube resting against my arm, watching my own blood go to the machine on my left. "What's this called again? What I'm doing, I mean. Die-days?"

"Dialysis."

"I don't like it. I don't like coming here."

"I know, sweetheart. I don't like it either," Mom says quietly. I see her chin tremble a little as her eyes get glassy. Mom cries a lot these days. Ever since I got sick the first time. Now I'm in and out of this hospital.

"What's the name of the thing I got that made me so sick?"

"Hemolytic uremic syndrome."

"And it messed up something inside me?" I ask.

"It damaged your kidneys when you were so sick, Arianna."

"But I feel better. I'm not so sick anymore."

Mom sighs again. "Today, yes. But yesterday, you took two naps. And your legs and tummy are swollen. And you're barely eating anything these days."

I frown. "But ..."

"No buts. I know you don't want to be here, *paperotta*. This keeps you healthy, or as healthy as you can be, until we can get you some new kidneys."

"How do I get new kidneys?" I ask.

"Well, someone could donate one, or it would be when someone dies and is an organ donor."

I gasp, horrified. "I'd get dead organs?"

"That's both gross and cool at the same time," Luca comments, loudly smacking his gum as he tosses the puck in the air. Mom throws out her arm and smacks the puck in midair. "Dang, Mom."

"You got your hand-eye coordination from me, not your father," Mom snaps. Turning back to me, she gives me a soft smile. "They aren't dead organs. When someone dies, anything still in perfect condition can be donated to someone who needs it."

"What does donate mean?" I ask.

"It means to give."

"So, someone gives me a kidney?"

"Yes."

"How much longer do I have to wait?" I ask impatiently.

"It's harder than you'd think. The doctors have to find the perfect kidney for you, and it has to meet a lot of criteria as a match."

I look down again at the tube funneling my blood into the big white machine. "I missed show and tell again today."

"I know, sweetheart. I'm sure your teacher will let you do show and tell tomorrow."

I don't want to be here. I spend more time in hospitals than I do at home. When I had that hemolytic thing Mom talked about, I had to sleep in the hospital for a week. I couldn't even get up to go to the potty.

"I don't want to be here," I grumble again.

* * *

Age 8

Everything hurts.

I guess I thought I'd be better immediately after getting my new kidney. Instead, my body just can't handle any germs. Mom told me it was my immune system. All the dialysis, then the transplant, took a beating on my body. I didn't understand what she meant until now. I feel like I've been beaten.

The transplant went well. My whole family was tested to see if anyone was a match, but a donor kidney became available that was a perfect match for me. The doctors didn't tell me anything about the donor, but I overheard Mom whispering to Dad on the phone. A ten-year-old girl died in a car crash. The doctors tried to save her, but said she was brain dead. I'm alive because a girl died, and I don't know how I feel about that.

Mom tells me the cold I got somehow turned into pneumonia. I don't know how; I haven't gone anywhere, or done anything. Luca says I'm a hermit, whatever that means. All I know are hermit crabs. I guess that makes sense? They live in their shells and hide a lot. I basically live in my room ... or the hospital. It's no fun.

It hurts to breathe, and during this hospital visit, they put me in the Intensive Care Unit. I don't like the ICU. It's loud. Nurses wake me up all the time. Something happened in the room next to mine, and I could hear a mom crying. I know it was a mom because she sounded like mine.

All moms sound the same when they think their kid is dying.

When I hear a sniffle closer to me, I force one eye to peel open and see Mom wiping her eyes. I hate that she's wearing a mask. Mom's smile makes me happy, and I can't see it now.

"Mom," I croak, not recognizing how hoarse and raspy I sound. I attempt to clear my throat, but it feels like there's a gallon of goo stuck in there.

"Oh, baby," Mom gasps, lunging toward me and slapping something near my head. "Hold on. The nurse will come clean you out."

I was afraid of that.

The suction.

I try even harder to clear my throat, not wanting to feel the pressure of the vacuum in my nose and throat. I hate it, but it works.

My nose itches, and I swipe at it, only realizing a second too late that the oxygen tube is what is tickling me. I accidentally yank it off, and the tube pulls against the IV in my arm. I cry out, gasp, then launch into a coughing fit. The coughing fit seems to help clear my throat, and I spit something out onto my hospital gown. When I'm done, I look at my mom and find her crying hard. She immediately hits something next to my head again.

My dad walks in at the same time as a voice speaks out above my head. My dad shouts, "Help!" as the voice asks what we need. Only then does my brain recognize what I'm seeing: I'm covered in blood.

"Oh my," a nurse says as she swiftly walks into the room. "No worries, Mom and Dad. This happens with pneumonia. Why don't you step outside while we get Arianna cleaned up?"

"I'm not leaving my daughter!" my mom snaps.

"Just outside the room, Mom. I promise nothing bad is happening here. I'll clean her up, and you can come back in. Okay?"

"Come on, Sofia. Let's give them a moment," Dad murmurs.

Once they are gone, I peer up at the nurse. My mouth is full of an unfamiliar metallic taste, but I remember Luca telling me about it when he got hit in hockey last year. It's blood. "Am I dying?"

"No, ma'am, not on my watch," the nurse announces as she unties the hospital gown behind my head and pulls it off. "This happens sometimes with pneumonia. Your poor body has been through a lot, Arianna. It is trying to build back up to what it was before you got sick."

"I don't want to be sick anymore," I confess, my chin trembling as the nurse carefully wipes my face, neck, and shoulders with wipes. "I just want to be normal. This isn't fair."

"I know, sweet girl," the nurse sighs. "It's not fair."

The nurse cleans me up, lets my parents back in the room, and then brings her lunch to eat with me so we can play a game together. She encourages me to sit up, walk around the bed, and eat food. She even creates a secret handshake for us at the beginning and end of her shifts.

Nurse Amy was amazing. She found the good in every situation and made my month-long hospital stay so much better. She was the last nurse to hug me once I was finally discharged, and I saw her tears of joy as my parents pulled away from the hospital.

At that moment, I decided I'd do whatever it took to help the hospital, which was such a major part of my childhood.

*A*ge 18

"*I*'m an adult now. You should let me help out more," I pout stubbornly as my sister Gianna rolls her eyes. "G, I've been helping you for five years. Why won't you let me take on more responsibility?"

"You just graduated from high school, Ari. Take a breath. Live a little. I've got this," Gianna says gently.

"I don't want to take a breath. I want to run the gala."

A few weeks after the last long hospital stay, I approached my parents with a list of ideas for ways we could give back to the children's hospital in Denver. The distance proved to be a significant issue, however. Without traffic, it can still take sixty to ninety minutes to get from Eternity Springs to the part of town where the hospital is located. Not only was I clearly well under the legal age to drive myself, but my parents had to take into consideration the rest of my siblings. Alex had just graduated high school, and Dominic was right behind him. Leo and Gia were involved in after-school sports, and Luca had an insane hockey schedule. Isabella and I were the two with hardly any activities.

Mom suggested a fundraiser, and together, we started planning. Our first year was incredibly small. By the time I was twelve, we had graduated our tiny fundraiser into a dance at the high school. By age fifteen, it was held in Denver at a small hotel. Gianna was in charge that year, her first year as the events coordinator for the hotel. I'd been bugging her ever since to give me more responsibility.

My parents wanted me to attend college, but I did not desire that. College wasn't for me. I knew I wanted to be in charge of the hotel spa and patiently waited until that position became available. Until then, I did whatever was needed around the hotel, bugged my sister as often as possible, and tried not to stare at Alex's best friend, Stone, whenever he was around.

I'd hoped he'd see me, now that I was a bonafide adult, but that wasn't happening.

A few weeks ago, he called me pipsqueak.

I cried for two hours.

"Seriously, G. I don't want to just be a greeter or someone who takes coats. I want real responsibility. Give me something," I complain.

Gianna sighs. "Fine."

I perk up. "Really?"

"Yes, if it gets you to leave me alone."

I jump up and down, clapping my hands with glee.

"See, this is why I don't want to give you any real responsibility. You do shit like that and remind me you're basically still a child."

"Not gonna dignify that with a response. Oh, how adult of me," I tell her haughtily. "What's my job? Calling donors? Picking out china? Oh! Can I be the liaison with the hospital?"

"Good God, no," Gianna chortles. "Baby steps, Princess."

I narrow my eyes and growl at her. "Don't you dare start doing that."

"But you are the baby, baby sister. And you basically are a princess," Alex says from behind me. I whirl around, my eyes widening when I see Alex and Stone, and some girl wrapped around Stone. I've seen her around before, probably for some community event in town. I think her name is Amber. She sneers at me when she sees Stone watching me.

"I. Am not. A princess," I snarl.

Stone chuckles, his voice husky and deep. It's somehow deeper than the last time I saw him. I notice a new tattoo on his arm, and Amber reaches out to trace the lines when she sees my focus. "Sorry, Princess. Everyone knows it except for you. Your sister won't even give you things to do because we all know you'll probably fuck it up."

Alex bristles. "Hey, that's too much, man."

Stone winces. "You're right. I apologize."

"Wow," I comment, attempting to control the tremor in my voice, "I didn't know you *could* apologize. Did that hurt?"

Stone's eyes narrow. "Nowhere near how much it must have hurt you when you had to tell your dad you totaled your car."

"There was black ice, and you know it!" I shout.

"On a clear day? Hardly," Stone laughs.

"A building blocked the sun, and I didn't see the ice until it was too late," I answer.

"Are you even old enough to drive?" Amber pipes up, a look of pure malice on her face. "Shouldn't you be running off to a babysitting job or something?"

Stone laughs awkwardly, and attempts to extricate himself from her arms wrapped around his waist, but she tightens her grip as she stares at me. "I've heard about you, you know. The Santo princess. The stories Alex and Stone have told me ..." she trails off, laughing before shaking her head. "I honestly don't know how you show your face around here. A fucking embarrassment. He's never going to go for you."

"I don — I don't know what you're talking about," I stammer.

Her gaze is intense and doesn't falter. "Yes, you do."

I glance between her and Stone, a wave of mortification heating my body as he refuses to make eye contact with me. Turning away, I feel the first hot tear slide down my cheek as Gianna tries to stop me by grabbing my hand. I pull away from her and quickly exit the area outside the front desk.

Christmas trees decorate the lobby, and a roaring fire fills the stone fireplace. I laugh wryly at the pun. Stone.

I've never felt so unseen before. So trivial.

I've crushed on Stone for as long as I can remember, and he's never seen me as an equal. Not even as a friend, or potential partner. Never acknowledged me as anything but his best friend's annoying little sister. Seeing him with Amber today felt like a calculated attack, as if he had brought her just to show me what he really wanted. But if that was for my benefit, does it mean he knew about my crush?

Whatever the reason, I can't keep on like this. I'm sick of the princess comments. Sick of everyone assuming I can't be an adult.

From now on, I'm making changes.

Age 25

"How did it go today?" Alex asks as we sit by a fire pit at the hotel. His two kids, Abbie and Ben, are lounging on a blanket nearby.

"Fine. It was just my yearly checkup."

Every year, I have to see a transplant surgeon for a checkup. On average, a donated kidney lasts fifteen to twenty-five years. The transplant team recommended I contact my nephrologist, or as my family refers to him as the 'kidney doctor,' since I just had my second transplant.

"Was this the transplant dude or the kidney dude?" Alex asks before taking a long drawl of his bottleneck beer. He looks tense today. Tired. Like the world is weighing heavily on his shoulders.

"Are you okay?" I blurt out.

Alex chuckles before cocking an eyebrow at me. "Redirection?"

"No, not really. You look … sad, Alex. I don't know," I shrug. "I'm worried about you."

Alex sighs. "I'm fucking tired, Ari."

"Tired of deploying?"

"Yeah. No. I don't know. Just tired." He looks over at his kids, who are giggling at something on an iPad, and manages to smile at them. "Get back on track, ma'am. Which doc did you see?"

"Princess needs a doctor?" A voice pipes up behind me, forcing my spine to straighten. Stone.

I hate how his voice, no matter the distance, always feels like sandpaper against my skin.

I hate how my gaze always dips to his full lips, and I wonder how they taste.

And I really hate that I don't hate him at all.

"She's just telling me about her yearly checkups."

"This family shares some weird fucking things," Stone murmurs. "Checkups? Plural? How many docs do you have, Princess?"

"Jesus, Stone, simmer down," Alex says, his hands up in a defensive gesture as he prepares to referee. "She has to get the checkups after her transplants."

Stone's gaze zeroes in on me, his expression darkening. "Transplants? Plural?"

"Damn, dude. You're intense today," Alex comments. "Don't you remember how sick she was as a kid? In and out of the hospital?"

"I'm not sure," Stone mutters. "When was this?"

"I first got sick when I was around six, and then had the first transplant when I was eight."

"What kind of transplant?" he asks. The intensity of his gaze is unnerving. Typically he ignores me, or his face is covered with an ever-present smirk. This look of complete focus, all of his attention on me, is making me incredibly self-conscious.

"Kidney."

"Why?"

"The illness I had destroyed my kidneys. I was on dialysis for a while, but the damage couldn't be repaired. My immune system was shit, and I got really sick after the transplant. I was in the hospital for a good month," I explain quietly.

"How did I not know this?" he asks suddenly. Stone's hands grip the arms of the chair tightly, as if he's so tensely coiled he might explode into the sky.

Alex clears his throat. "When she got sick, you were around

seventeen. We were on the football team. I remember that taking a lot of time. Don't you remember how we always had to walk back to my house after practice? Everyone was busy or at the hospital with Arianna."

"I didn't think to ask," Stone murmurs. "I was just glad I didn't have to go back to the trailer."

My heart constricts as I think about how Stone's childhood must have been. Alex hasn't told me much, but I know Stone's home life sucked.

"And when she had the transplant, I was deployed, so word probably just didn't get back to you," Alex adds.

"Why didn't you tell me?" Stone says, his tone accusatory as he glares at me.

"Seriously? I was eight, asshole! My priority was walking from the bed to the bathroom. Calling my brother's best friend who basically only tolerated me was not on my daily to-do list."

"Well, you could have told your mom to talk to me. I still came by here every now and again."

I shrug. "I didn't think about anything else, Stone. I couldn't fully comprehend why I got sick, and why my mom cried a lot. I'm sure you'll tell me how self-involved I've always been, but I thought I was going to die. Telling friends of my brother wasn't anywhere on my radar."

Stone has the decency to look chagrined as he takes in my words. "Then you had another transplant? When?"

"Another kidney transplant. A little over a year ago," I tell him.

"Why another one?"

"Transplanted kidneys have a shelf life, for lack of a better explanation," I tell him, and he chuckles. "I got a transplant from a deceased donor, and those only last fifteen to twenty years. This past transplant was from a living donor, so it should last me longer."

"A year ago? I was in and out of the hotel all the time. I never noticed you absent from there," he murmurs.

"I didn't need to take too much time off. My mom and Gianna

covered a lot. And since it was more preventative than due to a diseased kidney, I was healthier. I think that had a lot to do with how quickly I bounced back."

"You said it was a living donor. Family?"

"No. I don't know who it was, actually," I admit. "An anonymous donation. Whoever it was said they didn't want to be identified. They said they were paying it forward."

"What caused the kidney failure? The disease you had." I'm slightly unnerved at the intensity with which Stone is bestowing upon me.

"It's pretty rare. Hemolytic Uremic Syndrome."

"I've never heard of that. It's a syndrome? Doesn't that mean it's genetic?" he asks. I'm surprised he asks that, and it must show on my face, because he chuckles. "I'm not completely incapable of reading, Princess."

"It's not genetic. It's a complication of an infection. The doctors never knew exactly where I got it."

"So it's not something you'll pass on to your kids?" he asks.

"No," I answer, again surprised at his questions. Most people don't want to know how my childhood illnesses have impacted my life. Stone looks genuinely interested in learning about it, surprising me once again as I stare at him quizzically. Could this be the turning point where Stone and I can be cordial?

"That's good. Your spawn will have enough trauma coming from you, won't they," he tells me with a malicious grin.

And now we're back to our regularly scheduled programming.

Chapter 8

I almost kissed her again.

As soon as I found out her ex-boyfriend was at her apartment, the rage that filled my veins propelled me to her in record time. I wanted to obliterate him when I saw the little jack-off walking out of her apartment door, holding what appeared to be a relatively expensive bouquet of flowers. What angered me even more was the fact that I realized pretty quickly I'd never be able to give her that kind of bouquet. Not only would I not know how to do that, but I just don't have the money. Yeah, I could buy her a cheap bouquet from the grocery store, but the one Bartlett showed up with? That was easily over a hundred bucks.

I love my job and my home, but I live paycheck to paycheck. Arianna is basically Eternity Springs royalty, and she should be with someone who understands that lifestyle and can support it as well. No way would she be interested in a barber who still wears a pair of jeans from high school. Most of my income goes back into the barbershop or into renovating my house. I could probably save a lot of money by learning how to cook, but that's not going to happen anytime soon.

It's been a week since I rode to her rescue, and I haven't spoken to any Santo family members since. I shouldn't have given Arianna trouble about calling in sick on Monday because I also didn't go to the hotel. The dirt on my face was probably from my own house. I couldn't deal with the prospect of nasty looks from her dad and open-ended inquiries from her mom. I don't know what prompted me to drive into Denver, or what made me call her at that moment. I can count on one hand how many times I've called Arianna, but I'm sure as fuck glad I decided to that day.

So when Luca and Sofia strolled into my shop on Saturday, I knew my time was up.

"Looks like you can fit us in for some cuts, my man," Luca says boastfully, extending his arm to survey the empty shop. My last two clients canceled, and it's been relatively quiet. Winter months aren't the most popular for Front Range towns like Eternity Springs. Without a ski resort, people typically only stop here on their way into the mountains. I'm not too concerned, as I've done this long enough. I know how to build this lull into my budget. The busy time in the summer more than makes up for weird, quiet days in the winter.

"Sure. What do you want done?" I ask as Luca sits down. Sofia comes to give me a hug, and I kiss her cheek. Sofia has always been the mom I desperately wanted and needed as a child. My own mother is still a waste of space.

"I just need a trim. Mom wants something frilly," Luca says, gesturing at his mom.

"It's not frilly, *cocco*. It's also called a trim for women," Sofia says, rolling her eyes.

"Whatever. You knew what I meant," Luca shrugs with a grin. I get busy with Luca's cut as mother and son chat amicably about anything but the massive elephant in the room.

The elephant by the name of Arianna.

Not that she's an elephant. She's fucking perfect. Legs a mile long, with dark hair long enough to touch her waist. When she smiles, I feel it in my soul. And because I can count how many times she's bestowed that smile on me with one hand, I think it's a life-altering smile.

Once I've finished Luca's cut, he walks to the mirror to admire my work. "This is why I get my hair cut here, Stone. You made this gorgeous mug even gorgeous-er."

"That's not a word, son," Sofia says as she sits in the chair.

"What would you like done?" I ask.

"Just a trim. Can we do a shampoo, though? You give the best scalp massages."

"Sure."

"Wait. You give scalp massages? How come I didn't get that treatment?" Luca asks.

"Because you didn't ask. And the last time you were here, you made fun of women in general for self-care practices, so you don't get any extras."

"Luca!" Sofia says, clucking her tongue in disbelief.

"I was just teasing Ari."

"And? What is wrong with taking a moment for yourself?" Sofia asks as she sits in the shampoo chair.

"Nothing wrong with that, I guess. Hannah is all for self-care. I just didn't know men did that kind of stuff," Luca says.

"You should get a pedicure. Take Hannah. I bet she'd like that for one of your unusual dates," I say. Luca told me recently that he's been taking Hannah anywhere that would be considered a hole-in-the-wall restaurant, or activities that only locals and natives know about. Those of us who were born and raised in Colorado are considered natives. Everyone who moved here is a transplant.

I didn't come up with the names. All I know is we had a small community twenty to thirty years ago, and then the population exploded.

"Have you ever had a pedicure, Stone?" Sofia asks.

"Yes, I have."

"Really?" Luca asks, a look of complete shock on his face.

"Why are you looking at me like that?"

"Because you're — you. You're all growly and serious, stubborn, and masculine. I just didn't imagine you'd be out there with pink polish hidden beneath your scuffed-up boots."

"I don't have polish on, you moron. It's nice to have someone remove the calluses and dead skin. I'm on my feet all day. Your feet are probably much worse than mine, cramped in skates all the damn time."

"Shit, I never thought about that," he says quietly. I continue washing Sofia's hair as Luca looks lost in thought. He absentmindedly rubs his lower lip as he stares off toward the front door. Arianna does the same thing when she's thinking. I wonder how many of the Santo clan have the same move. Finishing the shampoo and conditioner on Sofia, I move her back to my chair and brush through any tangles.

"I'll never forget the first time I took Arianna to get a pedicure," Sofia blurts out suddenly, throwing her head back in laughter, knocking the brush from my hand. "She was so excited but could not sit still to save her soul. She accidentally kicked the gal in her face."

"I remember that! Wasn't that right after she had pneumonia? Your special treat to her for getting out of the hospital," Luca says. Jesus, she had pneumonia?

"When did she have pneumonia?" I ask, bending down to retrieve the brush.

"When she was eight or nine, right?" Luca says. "Right after ..."

When Luca's phone dings with a text as I begin Sofia's trim, he grunts and laughs loudly. "Well, this is going to be interesting. Mom, Ari is on her way here."

"What?" I blurt out.

Luca chuckles, his eyes alive with mischief. "She needs help. I told her we were here. She's just down the street grabbing lunch for the banquet staff."

"Why is she grabbing lunch for them?" I ask.

"She started doing it a year ago, I think. Once a quarter, she treats everyone to lunch. They can eat for free at the hotel during their shift. Still, it's a way of giving them something different and establishing a community amongst the staff," Sofia explains.

"That must cost the hotel quite a bit," I comment.

"She pays for it, not the hotel."

I stare at Luca incredulously. "You can't be serious."

He nods. "Pretty sure Dominic tried to convince her to write it off and just take petty cash for it, but she refused."

"She doesn't even work in that hotel section," I murmur. Out of her own pocket? How much does that cost her? Why is she doing it? I have so many fucking questions. Arianna Santo is proving, once again, that I might have judged her too harshly.

"Her job might focus on the spa and hot springs, Stone, but Arianna is a fixture across the hotel. In fact, she's known for giving quite a bit of time and money in various ways. She's known all over the place. Not only in Eternity Springs but even in Denver. Everyone loves her," Sofia says.

"That I can believe," I mutter as the front door opens and the object of my most recent dreams comes tearing into my shop. I believe that everyone loves Arianna. The part about dropping money on others? I'm not so sure about that.

I'm about to make a snide comment about shopping, until I see her tear-stained cheeks and drop the scissors I'm holding to go to her. My hands cup her face as her pained eyes stare up at me. "What happened?"

"Stone," she whispers, tears filling her eyes as her lip quivers. "I just got evicted. I have forty-eight hours to get out of my apartment."

"What?" Luca shouts. "How the fuck can they do that? You pay them every month, right?"

"Of course I do! They said the entire complex has termites. When they started doing treatment for the termites, they found asbestos. My building was built in the seventies. They want everyone to move out so they can fully renovate everything," Arianna says quietly, her eyes never leaving mine.

I'm still holding her face, and I can't seem to move away. I've seen this pain in her eyes too many times, most of which were caused by me. And this time, I want to take away her pain. Her worries. I want to hold her close and promise her the world. Watch her give me that breathtaking smile as if it's reserved just for me. But I know that's not going to happen.

So I do the only thing I know will help. "You can move in with me."

"What?" she breathes.

"I have extra rooms. I just renovated the guest room. You'd have your own bathroom. I'm working on other areas of the house, so it isn't perfect, but it would just be temporary."

"That's ridiculous. Ari, you can move in with me and Hannah," Luca announces, grabbing Arianna's hand and pulling her away from me. Ari's face screws up in disgust.

"And listen to you two go at it? No, thank you," she says. She turns to Sofia. "Are there any rooms at the hotel?"

"No, *paperotta*. We're booked solid through New Year's," Sofia says softly. She catches my hand and squeezes it, and when I look at her, she winks almost imperceptibly. Lord almighty. Is she trying to force Arianna and me to be in the same house?

"I can call Natalie or Claire and see if they can take me in for a bit," Arianna says uncertainly.

"Don't they live further into Denver than you do? Your commute would be worse," Luca points out. He gives me a small smile, and I think maybe he's also trying to work this for me. He doesn't seem upset at the prospect of Arianna living with me, even though he did offer a room to her as well.

Holy shit.

I always assumed the entire Santo family would oppose anything between Arianna and me, but they're giving me looks as if they'd support it.

Is this my chance? Would Arianna even welcome a romantic relationship with me?

"Princess," I whisper, and Arianna turns to me. I step closer to her and take her hands. "Your commute would be much less. Half of my house is renovated, and I have a two-car garage, so your car would be covered for the winter months. I don't have any living room furniture yet, so you could bring anything you want. Everything you need. It's not much, but it's home, and I'd be honored to give you the sanctuary you need."

Arianna studies me, a mixture of confusion and worry evident in her eyes. "Okay," she finally whispers.

"Really?" I ask, an unusual smile covering my face. She returns the smile with a giggle. That unforgettable smile that haunts my dreams.

"Yeah, really."

"Fuck yeah," I whisper. "So you need to be out by Monday? Want me to rent a truck?"

"We have a truck at the hotel you can use," Sofia pipes up. I jolt, having forgotten Luca and Sofia are watching this entire interaction. I almost leaned down to kiss Arianna again.

"What can I do to help?" I ask.

"Heavy lifting," Arianna says with a light chuckle. Her eyes have cleared slightly, and her bright and shiny personality shows through again.

"Anything you need, Princess," I say, squeezing her hand.

Arianna and Luca converse as I'm drying Sofia's hair. As soon as I'm done, Sofia jumps from the chair.

"Luca, let's go to the hotel and get the truck. *Paperotta*, we'll text you when we're heading your way in the morning," Sofia says.

Once they've left, Arianna turns to me. "I don't know how I'll repay you. Can I give you a room and board rate or something?"

"Fuck no," I swear. Arianna looks stunned at my vehemence at her giving me money. "You can cook dinner each night. It's been a while since I've had a home-cooked meal."

"You don't cook for yourself?" she asks quietly.

"Most recipes call for massive amounts. I'm just me, and I don't like leftovers. It's easier to eat takeout, fast food, or freezer meals," I admit. "I like to grill, so that's what I do if I cook at home."

"My mom taught all of us how to cook, so I can definitely contribute there. I'm not the best cook, but I can manage some things without burning down the house."

"If you say you know how to make her lasagna, I'm never letting you move out," I blurt out.

Arianna gives me a half smile with a breathy giggle, and I'm tempted to tell her I'm not joking. "I know how to make all of Momma Santo's specialties. Although I'm pretty sure the lasagna recipe comes from Nonna."

I groan a little, thinking of the last time I had Nonna's cooking. These Italian spitfires know how to cook, and I salivate thinking about whether or not Arianna can be on par with them. "How old is Nonna these days? I can't imagine anyone lets her in the kitchen much."

"She's eighty-three, but her age isn't why she's not allowed to cook."

"Oh, really? What happened?" I ask, intrigued.

"There was an incident with a spider."

"What, did she break the smooth top of the stove trying to kill a spider?"

"No, she threw a lit candle at the smooth top of the stove, breaking the glass and setting fire to the curtains behind the stove. Then, instead of using the fire extinguisher to put out the fire, she fanned the fire with a stack of takeout menus, which also caught fire."

"Jesus," I swear. "Did she call 911?"

"No, the lit curtains caught the eye of the neighbor, who broke into Nonna's house and found the fire extinguisher. Nonna didn't even tell us about it until Mom went over and saw the damage to the cabinets and walls, then noticed the busted stove top."

I can't help but chuckle. "Nonna sure does keep things interesting, doesn't she."

"That she does," Arianna says, scratching at her scalp. She's consistently scratched her head since she walked in here, which is unusual for Arianna. She's more likely to twirl a lock of hair than scratch. And yes, I know how pathetic it sounds that I know that. I may have considered her off-limits for five years, but I'm not blind.

"What's going on?" I ask, pointing toward her head.

"Oh, it's nothing," she says, waving me away. "I used a new shampoo, which irritated my scalp."

"Sit down, let me look," I tell her, patting my empty chair. She hesitates for a moment before sliding into the chair. As soon as my hands dive into her hair, I hear her quick intake of breath, and I feel the same way. Arianna has beautiful hair. I've always thought that. Hell, the entire Santo clan could take part in shampoo commercials. But Ari's hair, in particular, is phenomenal. The thick chocolate tresses have a soft and natural wave that I bet pisses off a lot of women. Absolutely exquisite. I take my time examining her scalp. I uncover a few freckles, a small beauty mark she might not even know she has at the base of her hairline, and try to memorize how her strands feel wrapped around my fingers. Because right now, all I can think about is how spectacular she might look on her knees, my cock in her mouth, and her hair wrapped around my hand while I rut against her. Clearing my throat and stepping away from her, I motion toward the shampoo bowl. "Whatever it is, your scalp is irritated. Let's wash it out, and then you will hopefully be good to go."

"I didn't stop in here for a blowout, Stone," she jokes, and I cough to cover what is now a revolving door image in my mind. Blowout ... blow job ... my mind can't differentiate between the two things right now. I need to wash her hair, count back from a thousand — *for fucks's sake, Stone, avoid thinking of anything that ends in sixty-nine —* and get her the hell out of here.

"Come on, let's just do this, and then you can go," I say, strain evident in my voice. It sounds like I've suddenly regressed into puberty again, my voice quite a bit higher than it was before.

"Are you okay?" Arianna asks as she sits, one eyebrow cocked as she looks up at me.

"Uh-huh, I'm great," I tell her, but then I recline the chair quickly, forcing Arianna to brace, and all four limbs go up in the air. I don't ask if she's okay. I just turn on the water and attempt to drown her as water shoots across her forehead and down onto her face. As she continues to flail, I dump an excessive amount of shampoo on her locks and get to scrubbing. I start absentmindedly humming a song, not thinking about what I'm doing.

When you do the same tasks repeatedly, it's easy to start performing them on autopilot. Shampooing is one of those things for me. I have quite a few female clients, and many guys will book a more thorough cut so they can have some of the treatments. Arianna remains silent, and I can dissociate and get out of my head for a few minutes. Only when she reaches up and grabs my forearm do I realize what I'm doing. I've already moved past the conditioner and on to the final rinse ... while *singing*.

I was clearly singing — not humming, *singing* — *You Were Always On My Mind* by Elvis. Before that, I hummed *Hit Me Baby One More Time* by Britney Spears. Why? Who the fuck knows. Did I hum *Touch Myself* by Divinyls? I might have.

"I think my hair is clean," Arianna whispers.

"Let me get you dried then," I tell her, wrapping her hair tightly in a towel.

"Um, no. I think I'm going to go," she stammers.

"Princess, it's thirty degrees outside. You can't go out there with sopping wet hair."

Her eyes narrow, and I hear a low growl. I chuckle. I'm not sure if anyone on this planet frustrates Arianna more than me. And that's fine with me right now. She walked in here a fraction of her usual boisterous and larger-than-life self. If antagonizing her gets a little bit more of her fire back, then I'm happy to do it.

"Fine," she huffs. "But hurry up. And you better not pull my hair."

"Trust me, Princess. One day, you'll be begging me to pull your hair," I tell her with a wink, and her mouth drops open. For fuck's sake. What is happening to me right now? "Shit, Ari, I'm sorry, that was so fucking out of line, and I don't know what happened, so I'm going to shut up now."

Her shocked expression makes me almost lose it. I turn on the hair dryer and spin the chair so she can't stare at me in the mirror, thus also hiding my own embarrassment. While Arianna and I have fought or bickered for more than half of her life, I've never blatantly spoken to her like this. Until recently, I didn't know what she tasted like either. There's a surge of heat in her eyes that tells me she's interested in whatever is going on between us. Knowing her mom and brother seem to support a future for us, I wonder if this is the start of something new.

Arianna bolts from my chair as soon as her hair is mostly dry, only stopping when she's at the door. Turning, she says, "You know you can't talk to me like that once I live in your house, right? We're roommates now. Whatever happened, or was happening, can't happen anymore."

As she pushes open the door and quickly rushes down the sidewalk, I'm the one left speechless. I might be thinking about something with her, but she's clearly not on the same page. It makes me think about that night six months ago when something almost happened. I don't know if I'm grateful nothing happened ... or if I regret holding myself back. Now that I know how she tastes, I wouldn't have been able to stop at just a kiss when we were alone in a hotel room with only one bed.

Arianna, Six Months Ago

I hate him.

I hate how he makes me feel.

I hate wishing he could see me as more than just an annoying little sister.

But mostly, I hate that I can't stop thinking about him.

And now that I'm stranded on the side of the road at close to midnight, and none of my family are answering their phones, he's a last resort. I tried to call the friend I was visiting up here, but she didn't answer. I could call a rideshare service, but I don't want to leave my car. My dad warned me to pay for roadside assistance, and I blew him off. I wouldn't need that. I only go between Eternity Springs and Denver. What could go wrong?

Two flat tires, that's what.

And this time, I'm up in the mountains, surrounded by storms with tons of lightning, and I'm getting scared.

Stone is my last hope, and I know he's going to lecture me for pretty much forever, but I just want to go home. Bringing up his number in my contacts, I take a deep breath to calm my nerves.

"Arianna." God, his voice. How he can sound so frustrated with me, and it still turns me on, remains a mystery.

"Are you — are you busy?" I ask quietly.

"What did you do?" he snaps.

"I didn't do anything, dammit."

"You calling me at midnight tells a different story, Princess. Too scared to call your family?"

"No, I called everyone before you. No one answered."

Stone is silent for so long that I check my screen to see if we're still connected. My service up here is spotty.

"Are you there, Stone?"

"Yeah, I'm here," he says, clearing his throat. "What happened that made you call everyone?"

"Um, well, I was visiting a friend, and I think a truck must have dumped some construction material or something because I think I have two flat tires."

"Two?" Stone shouts. "Jesus, Arianna. Only you would manage that."

"How in the hell was I supposed to see nails on the highway in the goddamn dark, Stone? Quit being a jackass. Can you help me or not?" I snap in return.

"Fine," he sighs. "Where are you?"

I hesitate, knowing he's going to be pissed. "Can you promise me you won't be angry?"

"No."

"Come on, Stone. Just promise." I don't know why I'm making him promise. I know he's going to be furious, but I still find myself asking for some semblance of patience and understanding from him. As I wait for him to answer, I nervously tap my foot against the floorboard of my car while chewing on my lower lip.

"I promise not to be *too* angry. I assume you're in Denver?"

"Um, well ... no."

Stone swears under his breath. "Just tell me where you are, Princess."

I take a deep breath and blurt out, "I'm sorry, but I'm up by Vail. I was visiting a friend who is on vacation here, and honestly, I didn't realize how far that actually is because I'm always the passenger, and typically Luca, or someone else drives, and my cell keeps going in and out of service, and I'm scared."

"God dammit, Arianna. And you were driving home at midnight? And you wonder why I call you Princess. You don't have a fucking clue about anything," Stone snarls, but I hear him ruffling around in his house, presumably getting dressed. "Send me your location. I'll get there as soon as I can. Turn off your lights and hazards, lock the doors, and don't open it for anyone."

He hangs up before I can answer him.

Relieved someone is coming to my rescue, I feel that bubble of emotion clog my throat as tears fill my eyes. I hate how everyone thinks I'm clueless and incapable. My siblings tease me about my supposed ineptitude, but no one more so than Stone. Almost every time I'm near him, he comments on it. Even knowing he'll remark on things, I'm still unprepared for it each time. That is probably why I never can respond in a civil or composed manner. I've heard people say good relationships are like fire and ice, where one can douse the flames and calm the other person down. Stone and I are fire and fire. We just explode.

About ninety minutes later, someone pulls up behind my car. Stone texted me that he would flash his lights at me three times, and I breathe a sigh of relief when the car behind me does. Only a handful of cars have driven past, but I reclined my seat to try and hide from any gawkers, or criminals trying to score a quick buck. My SUV isn't the best out there, but it has great ratings for traveling in the snow, and I got a great interest rate on it a few years ago.

I watch as Stone turns on a flashlight and walks around my car. I see the moment he checks out my tires, and hear the loud sigh of annoyance he lets out. Even with my windows closed, I hear him. I always hear him.

Stone briskly walks around the car and taps on the window. When I open the door, he barely looks at me. "It's three tires."

"Three?" I gasp.

"Yep. Nothing we can do about it now. We'll have to wait until morning. Let's get some rooms somewhere, then I can find a repair shop. Looks like you drove on them for a bit, so there might be damage. What the fuck were you thinking, Arianna? Didn't you see the gauges go down telling you your tires were getting low?"

"It all happened so fast, Stone. It was like the tires just deflated. And I don't have gauges like that."

"All new cars do."

"My car isn't new. I'm not even the first owner."

Stone looks momentarily confused. "Oh. Get your stuff. Let's go."

I debate on arguing some more, but I worry Stone might just leave me here. Who am I kidding? He'll probably wait for me to lecture me some more. I don't think there's anything Stone loves more than telling me all the things he feels I do wrong.

I'm right.

He bitches the entire car ride to a hotel on the outskirts of Vail. I feel myself sink further and further into the seat of his car. First in an attempt to disappear, then it's to get closer to the worn fabric on the passenger seat because it smells like Stone.

He pulls up to a rather dilapidated building. The large fluorescent hotel sign where the "h" and "t" blink sporadically, tells me this hotel is more of a motel. Stone sees me staring at the sign, and he sighs loudly. "Closest and cheapest. You picked a costly town to break down at, Princess."

"I didn't pick to break down here," I grumble. Stone is acting like I did all of this just to make him miserable. That's an added benefit, but I certainly didn't want my evening to end with a Stone lecture.

"This was the only place with a vacancy that was within my budget, so ..." he trails off. My head whips to his.

"I'm paying for the rooms."

"The hell you are!"

"It's my fault we're in this predicament, so I should pay for your room."

"If you're with me, I pay. End of discussion." Stone turns off his SUV and gets out.

"Hold up! You don't get to pull that end-of-discussion bullshit on me, Stone. I'm not your daughter. Stop acting like a Daddy." I quickly leave the car and round the front to stand before him, hands on my hips in defiance and determination. "I'm paying. It's not the Stone Age. A woman can pay for things."

Stone growls at me and rolls his eyes. "As if you're the one paying for this, Princess. Bet your Daddy pays your credit card bill."

"For fuck's sake, Stone! He does not!" I exclaim, stomping away from him in exasperation. I'm so sick of his comments about money. I'm sure my parents gave me more things than my siblings at the same age, but all parents do that with their youngest child. But I've been paying my way since I was nineteen, and I'm done with Stone suggesting otherwise.

Flouncing into the hotel lobby, I'm surprised to see it's well cared for and quite comforting. Big couches surround a gas fireplace, and a small refrigerated section houses snacks and drinks for guests to purchase. Large plants dot the area, and a woman smiles warmly at me from behind the counter. "Mrs. Dixon, I presume?"

I startle, first at her knowing Stone's last name, and then at the thought of me being married to Stone. As a teenager, I had a notebook full of doodles with our initials, my first name attached to his last name, and tons of hearts. Even when we argued like cats and dogs, I still wanted him. He was my first crush. Being called Mrs. Dixon tugs at my heartstrings a little too much.

Stone arrives behind me, his hand briefly on my lower back, and a very obvious shiver overtakes my entire body. Without looking at me, he smirks, aware of my reaction to his touch, and I want to slap his hand. Instead, I roll my eyes and follow him to the reception desk. Subtly, I slide a credit card out of my wallet. I'll be damned if Stone is going to pay for this.

"I'm sorry, sir, but since we spoke, almost all of our rooms have been taken. We have one room left, and I'll honor the rate we discussed on the phone," the woman says.

"It's fine." Stone's mouth falls into a firm line, showing how it clearly isn't fine that we will be forced to stay in the same room. Hopefully, there are two beds.

As Stone prepares to pay, I throw my credit card at the woman. She squeals in surprise, and Stone tries to grab it. "I said I'd pay, Arianna!"

"No," I grunt as I grab his arm and hold it down. Wrapping both arms around his, I squat to keep my weight down. I don't know who is more surprised when he lifts his arm, and me, into the air. My feet dangling off the floor, he grabs his wallet from his pocket and thrusts his card across the counter. He sets me down carefully without making eye contact.

"Use this card, please. My *wife* is mistaken," he snaps. The woman places my card on the counter and hurriedly swipes Stone's. We're walking down the hall to the elevators within a few minutes.

I don't speak as I think about what just happened. I've never touched Stone. Well, I've never touched him like this. I felt every defined muscle of his arm as he lifted me. His bicep flexed, and his tee shirt slid upward so one of my hands touched his skin. His hot, smooth, veiny skin that I've dreamed about.

When we arrive at our room, Stone says, "I forgot to ask if this has two beds. If not, I'll sleep on the couch or the floor."

"No, I will," I say firmly.

"Why do you argue about everything?" Stone asks, looking at me for the first time since we exited the car. "You and I both know you won't sleep on the floor. Have you ever even been camping, Princess?"

"Yes, I've been camping! God, why are you such a dick, Stone? Open the damn door."

Stone unlocks the door and pushes it open before beckoning me to go before him. "After you, Princess."

Holding my head high, I strut into the room, hoping Stone is looking at my ass and not the expression on my face. Looking over my shoulder, I see that's the case, but at the same time, we both realize there's only one bed, and no couch.

"Fuck," Stone breathes.

"What size is that? It looks so small," I whisper. I don't splurge on much, but I have a decent mattress at my apartment. I'm a shitty sleeper, and if the mattress is uncomfortable, I don't sleep. My apartment is tiny, and my king-size bed takes up most of my bedroom, but it's worth it if I sleep well.

"Can't be more than a double," Stone comments.

"Everlasting used to only have double beds. Did you know that?" I ask, turning toward him. Stone shakes his head, and I continue. "My grandfather refused to upgrade the mattresses. It was one of the most common complaints on guest surveys. My dad started the upgrade when he took over, but replaced the mattresses incredibly slowly. Dom pushed for the full overhaul about ten years ago. Not only are they almost all king-size mattresses now, they're nice ones. None of that Sleep Number bullshit."

Stone chuckles. "Did you have any input into what mattresses were allowed at Everlasting?"

I shrug. "I have a lot of trouble sleeping, so I went with Dom to test some out."

Stone sits on the edge of the bed and bounces carefully. "I really doubt this will pass your inspection."

I move to sit next to him, choosing to sit fairly close to him. Not only because I'll be able to smell him, but I know it'll also unnerve him, which makes it fun for me. I immediately grimace when I can feel every single coil pushing against my thighs. "Wow. This is awful. We might both be sleeping on the floor."

"Our cars would have been more comfortable than this," Stone comments.

"Yeah."

We're silent for a moment before Stone speaks up again. "You said you have trouble sleeping?"

"Yeah. Always have."

"Why?"

I glance at him, expecting to see his ever-present smirk as he waits for a reason to poke fun at me, but his expression shows interest and concern. It's like we're having an actual conversation where Stone wants to get to know me, and I'm not sure how to react. My plan to unnerve Stone has backfired.

"Um, I've always had trouble with anxiety. It's hard to calm down my brain at bedtime. I keep thinking of everything I need to do, or things that could go wrong. Things happening to my family and stuff."

"And you have to worry about Leo and Alex," Stone says quietly, and I nod. I worry about them nonstop. They tell us nothing about their deployments, which means they are probably in danger a good chunk of the time. "Can I ask you a question?"

"Sure," I respond.

Stone hesitates, his mouth opening and closing multiple times before speaking. "Do you take medicine for your anxiety?"

"I do." I've never hidden the fact that I'm on medication. I'm not embarrassed about needing a little assistance there. The biological components of my brain are different, and medication mutes the anxiety enough that I can function.

"Do you have anxiety attacks?" Stone asks.

"Sometimes. I haven't had one in a while, though."

"What's it like when you have one? I mean, what happens? How do you feel? Do people know you're having an anxiety attack? How do people help you? Shit, how have I never known this? I'm around you enough, and I never knew you struggled with anxiety." I force myself to listen to his tone of voice so I don't let my defenses take over. He sounds curious. Interested. Concerned.

"It's not like I advertise it. And my family doesn't. My brothers probably don't even know I'm on medication for it."

"So what happens when you have one?"

"Well, they can be different, but typically, I start to almost hyperventilate. I can feel my blood pressure rising, and I get hot. Sometimes, it's as if the world around me falls away. Like a weird tunnel vision, I guess. Sometimes, I sort of pass out, but it's not like I'm fully unconscious. It's like I tuck into a part of my brain and stay there for a bit."

"Jesus, Princess. That sounds like a seizure," Stone murmurs.

"It's not. Trust me, my parents had me tested for it when I was younger. I was tested for everything ..." I trail off. I don't know how much Stone remembers about my medical history. I only have fleeting memories of my times in and out of the hospital, and I don't remember him ever visiting. He might have, though. He and Alex were inseparable for as long as I can remember. Honestly, I'm surprised he didn't join the military with Alex so they could stay together.

"We should get some sleep," Stone announces, startling me from my thoughts. "The closest repair shop doesn't open until ten, but the hotel stops serving breakfast before that. I don't know how long we'll be at the repair shop."

"You can just drop me off and go home," I tell him. "There's no reason for you to stay here. I'm perfectly capable of waiting for my car alone."

"No."

"Stone," I whine exasperatedly.

"Arianna," he mimics.

"You know, you tell me often that I'm a princess and that my family caters to me, and then you turn around and won't let me be an adult. Pick your fucking lane and stick to it," I snap.

Stone's eyes widen in surprise at my animosity. "It's not that I don't think you're an adult. I know Alex would kick my ass if I left you up here. Once I know your car is fixed, I'll be out of here."

"Fine."

"Fine," he mimics before pulling the covers from the bed. I don't know why I'm bothering to try and sleep. I know I won't be able to. I won't get comfortable in my clothes. And knowing other people, people I don't know, have slept on these sheets? Just ew.

"What's wrong now?" Stone asks with a sigh.

"I just wish I had some more comfortable clothes," I tell him with a bitter laugh. I'm wearing a skirt and a somewhat tight corset top.

"You do look like you were out clubbing," he replies. "I'm sure your friend appreciated the outfit."

"Considering *she* is completely heterosexual *and* married, I don't think appreciated is the correct word," I retort. "But I guess that's your way of giving me one hell of a backhanded compliment, so thanks."

"Sorry," he mutters. "I just assumed —"

I cut him off. "Yeah, you assumed. I don't even date that much at home, Stone. I'm certainly not going to drive hours into the mountains for a date."

Suddenly, he rips off his shirt. "Here."

"Huh?" I can't keep my eyes focused on his face. God, his pecs and abs are spectacular. I want to rub my face through his chest hair and trace his abs with my tongue. For being in his mid-thirties, he has a phenomenal body.

"You can sleep in my shirt. It's long enough to cover all your ... important parts," he murmurs. He tosses it to me, hitting me in the face with it. "Shit, Ari, I thought you'd catch it."

"It's okay." My senses are overwhelmed with his scent. I'm two seconds away from having a mini orgasm.

"Uh, I'll just go change." I walk briskly into the attached bathroom, averting my eyes from the somewhat gross shower, and close the door. Bringing his shirt up to my nose, I take a deep inhale. I quickly strip out of my skirt and shirt, breathing a sigh of relief when the corsets are loosened. They look adorable, but they hurt like hell. I throw on Stone's shirt and walk into the room, stopping when I see Stone studying the floor with a look of apprehension. When he looks up at me, I give him a hesitant smile. "You okay?"

"Yeah, but this floor looks disgusting. I'd like to share the bed if you're okay with it. I'll sleep on top of the covers."

"Okay," I whisper. He motions for me to climb under the questionable bedding. I try to control my breathing as my mind whirls with thoughts of bed bugs, bacteria, and unexplained stains. I quietly slide under the bedding and try to relax.

"You're shaking the bed," Stone says quietly next to me. I turn onto my left side, so I'm facing him. He's studying me with an introspective expression, almost as if he doesn't trust his own thoughts about me. And maybe there's some truth to that.

"I don't like sleeping in hotel beds," I confess. He chuckles as I continue. "Ironic, right? I work for a hotel. But I know the cleanliness standards we have at Everlasting. I don't know what they do here. It makes my skin crawl."

"You're overthinking it, Princess. I'm sure they use washing machines just like Everlasting," he says with a hint of a smile. "Did you always want to work at Everlasting?"

"Yeah," I tell him with a yawn. "I always knew. I even knew I wanted to be in charge of the spa."

"If anyone would know about beauty treatments and shit, it's clearly you," he chuckles.

"That's not even it, Stone. I get to help a tired mom feel a little better about herself. Watch a family introduce their baby to the hot springs. Give a woman suffering from PTSD an hour of self-care to remind herself that she's absolutely worth it, and that she's not defined by her trauma. Don't trivialize what I do as just being surface level."

"You're right. I'm sorry," Stone says after a moment, clearing his throat immediately.

"Did that hurt?"

"What?"

"Apologizing to me. Admitting you were wrong."

He doesn't reply, and as I listen to his steady breathing, I fall asleep much faster than I thought I would.

I awake with a jolt as a very vivid dream about Stone makes me moan out loud. Opening my eyes, I find I'm still on my left side, but I'm in the center of the bed, suctioned against Stone. His arms are wrapped tightly around me with his nose in my hair, and I wonder if he's breathing me in as he sleeps.

My right leg is sandwiched between his thighs, and my hands are pressed against his chest. When I realize that, I become acutely aware of *his* hands and arms. One hand is buried in my hair, and the other cups my ass. As I'm wearing a thong, I realize his hand is on my bare skin, and I almost come on the spot. His hand twitches, sliding against my skin, and he groans ever so quietly. His other hand tightens in my hair as his arms squeeze me closer. His scent surrounds me, and I feel like I'm in heaven.

I know the exact second he wakes up because his body stiffens. The hand on my ass squeezes again, and he curses quietly under his breath. Stone's body subtly melts into mine for a moment before he takes one extra-long inhale against my hair. He then begins carefully extricating himself. He quietly goes into the bathroom, and I let out a held breath. He couldn't have known I was awake. Stretching luxuriously, I silently squeal. He held me as we slept! That has to mean something, right? I can't wait to tell Natalie, and our other bestie, Claire, about this.

"Arianna."

I open my eyes to find Stone standing by the bathroom door, and I know he's not happy.

"Let's get this show on the road." His expression is cold and callous. Everyone else can get smiles, but this look is reserved just for me. He barely speaks to me as I retrieve my clothes and get dressed, or when I give him back his tee shirt. He's silent while driving from the hotel to the repair shop and as we follow a tow truck back to my car. Once back at the repair shop, he doesn't acknowledge me as we wait for my tires to be patched, stepping out to take more than one phone call while I stay inside. I catch a glimpse of him throwing back his head in laughter, but as soon as our eyes meet, the cheerful smile on his face drops.

We don't speak as I pay for the tire repairs, or when we walk to our cars.

I call out to him as he's about to get in his SUV without a word. He stops but doesn't turn around. "Thank you for rescuing me."

His head subtly nods before he enters his car. He waits for me to start my car, and then follows me home. The entire drive, he's in my rearview mirror, a scowl of epic proportions on his face.

So much for thinking the night changed things.

Arianna, Present Day

I'm an emotional mess, but even I recognized the sexual undertones to everything Stone said in his shop. I was unprepared for how it would feel for him to say those things, or how it would feel when he wrapped my entire head of hair around his fist and pulled. Don't even get me started on the songs he hummed and sang. *I Touch Myself?* Really?

I'd never heard Stone sing before, but damn. The grittiness in his tone made me feel it everywhere, especially between my legs. Honestly, I'm surprised I can walk without sounding like a container of milk being shaken. I don't think I've ever been this wet, and definitely never this turned on by a blowout.

I giggle when I think about how clearly he reacted to my use of the word blowout. Obviously, he was already thinking inappropriate things.

Nothing can happen now. I don't know how long I'll need to stay with Stone, so we can't start anything. We never should have crossed the line — lines — we did. He's Alex's best friend. If, or when, things end badly, it will be incredibly awkward when Stone comes around.

He's basically been a member of my family since before I was born. He's like a ... brother.

Gross.

He's not a brother. He can't be a brother. I certainly wouldn't have imagined him in my wildest fantasies if that were the case. Right? God, a therapist would have a field day with me right now.

But since I chose years ago to not go the route of conventional therapy, I do the next best thing and send out an SOS to my friends.

Me: 911! 911!

Claire: The last time this happened, there was a suggestion of major felonies. I need to know immediately if it's in the same ballpark.

Natalie: Whatever it is, I'm in.

Kate: It's been a shitty day, so I'm in too. Three hots and a cot would be a break from your batshit crazy family members. No offense, of course.

Me: None taken. You nanny for Dom again?

Kate: Yes.

Me: Which kid did your head in?

Kate: Not them. YOUR FUCKING BROTHER did my head in. Controlling bastard.

I can't help but giggle. Dominic is insanely type-A, so it doesn't surprise me that he's irritating Kate. She's a free spirit. I bet she let the kids pick the activities today, and Dom expected a military academy-style learning experience.

Kate is our almost-cousin. She shares a dad with our cousins Matt and Zane, who are cousins on my mom's side. When she was really struggling to make ends meet after her dad went to prison, Matt brought her to visit us, and we basically adopted her. She works all kinds of odd jobs, but recently has been helping Dominic with nannying his three kids.

Hannah: Considering I just heard from Luca how there were some HOT sparks at Stone's barbershop, I can safely say this 911 text relates to fewer crimes of law, and more crimes of passion.

Natalie: Ooooooooo yes, girl, get you some old man!

Hannah: He's not that old.

Kate: He's got a decade on most of us, so that makes him old.

Hannah: I hate that I'm the oldest in this chat, and I haven't even hit thirty yet.

Claire: Watch it, Grandma. We turn real fast on the newcomers.

Hannah: Noted. Anyway, Arianna, is it about Stone?

Me: Yes.

Kate: We need more information than that.

Me: I feel like this conversation would be better suited over lots of wine and as many appetizers as we can find. Hannah, would Luca mind if we all swooped into your house for the evening?

Hannah: He's meeting a friend for drinks, so I think that's fine. Is everyone okay with BYOB? Luca doesn't have the alcohol setup here like he has at his apartment, so it's slim pickins.

Me: Sounds good. Everyone bring an appetizer or two.

Claire: Girls night!

Natalie: Woohoo!

Kate: Turning off my phone now so Dominic doesn't call me back for some ridiculously minor infraction. Can't wait to see everyone!

With my spirits lifted, I head to the grocery to pick up ingredients for my favorite cheese dip and a meat and cheese platter. I can't wait to see my girls.

Natalie, Claire, and I have been friends since high school. We bonded immediately over our love of fashion, being baby sisters to hockey players, and our ability to pick an exceptional wine. All three of our brothers play in the NHL. We didn't go to the same high school, but we met while Luca played in a summer league while he was in college. My parents dragged me to the games after catching me attempting to sneak a guy into our house once. Fortunately, Natalie and Claire supported their brothers at the same summer games.

Honestly, other than having similar personalities, we're incredibly different. Natalie is an elementary teacher working in an urban district of Denver. She makes hardly any money, but her heart is so invested in helping the kids who really need it. Claire, on the other hand, is an accountant. She's told me more than once how she loves working with money because it's black and white. When looking at budgets, checks and balances, and investments, there is no gray. One plus one is always two.

Kate has worked herself to the bone since her mom died. Finding her dad in Colorado Springs, she discovered she had two half-brothers, my cousins Matt and Zane, who had no idea she existed. Unfortunately, that also led to her father getting arrested on various charges. After thinking she'd found another parent after losing the only one she had, she was used by him. Ever the optimist, Kate cultivated a relationship with her half-brothers and their mother before being introduced to our family. Now, before you think she can't be an almost-cousin, she really is. Zane and Matt's mom is my mom's sister. Kate's dad is their dad. That's why we call her our almost-cousin, but our family accepted her immediately. She's worked various jobs at the hotel, mostly bartending and working as a concierge. Recently, Kate has been helping Dominic with his three kids after his regular nanny moved out of state to be closer to her family.

And lastly, Hannah. The southern belle, the one who finally taught my brother Luca that it's okay to give your heart away. I've honestly never met a more compassionate and empathetic woman before. Hannah will give the shirt off her back to almost anyone. To see her with my brother makes my heart so happy. She's perfect for him.

As I roll up to the house Luca bought just a few months ago on the outskirts of town, I see Hannah waving gleefully at me from the front door. She might have needed this night as much as me. We see each other throughout the week at work, but our jobs don't intersect as much as I'd like.

Hannah hugs me when I get to her, and she ushers me in before closing the door. As a lifelong Eternite, as we like to refer to ourselves, I can typically tell when we're due for some crappy weather. There's a moistness to the air. A bite to the wind, and I swear I can smell the snow coming. As if my phone knew what I was thinking, I get an alert that we've been put under a Winter Weather Advisory for the next eighteen hours.

"Dang, they're forecasting six to eight inches ..." I trail off as my eyes adjust to Hannah staring at me expectantly. "Holy shit, Han."

A roaring fire in the fireplace casts a beautiful glow on five seats Hannah has moved in a horseshoe. Tables stand between each chair, and the chairs all have thick blankets. She has soft music playing, and as I look further into the kitchen, I see an entire table of snacks.

"I, um, I wasn't sure what I was supposed to do," she says nervously.

"What do you mean?" I ask.

"I've never hosted a girls' night. Did I go overboard? I think I might have, but I didn't know, and the only thing my mom ever taught me about events was to make sure there was more than enough food and comfortable seating, but never actually to sit down, but that seems dumb because who goes to a girls night and doesn't sit?" she rambles.

Luca told me Hannah doesn't have a filter, and rambles when she is nervous. This is the first time I've witnessed it in person, and I'm tickled that she went to such trouble for me. "This is wonderful, Han. Thank you for hosting and doing all of this."

She beams at the praise and skips to the door when the bell rings. It's Kate, moaning about how Dominic tried to track her down by sending one of the grounds workers to her apartment because he didn't like a coloring sheet she provided for his youngest daughter, Aspen. She looks mutinous, and I think if I suggested murdering my brother, she'd be on board immediately.

"Hey," I say, but she holds up a hand to stop me.

"I'm mad at you."

"Why?" I ask.

"Because you're related to him, and so you're in trouble too."

"If I agree with you, does that get me off your hit list?"

She nods. "Yes. But I'm not talking about it. Your brother is an asshole, and I hate him."

"Alright. Dom definitely has the asshole thing going for him," I respond.

"He's lucky I love his kids," she mutters. "Then he was pissed because Savannah showed up, and somehow that was my fault too."

"Oh shit, The ex-wife is here? No wonder."

Kate looks at me. "What's the deal there?"

I hesitate. "Listen, Kate. I'm all for supporting you in your 'I hate Dominic' campaign, but I'm not going to gossip about him and his ex-wife. It's his story to tell. The only thing I'll give you is this: don't believe a word that comes out of Savannah's mouth, and don't let her try to steamroll over you. And don't, under any circumstances, let her befriend you. She's not a good person."

Kate pales. "So the fact that she friended me on Facebook and I accepted is pretty bad?"

I groan. "Yes. Unfriend. Immediately. Bad, bad, bad!"

Savannah is miserable. She's dog poop on your shoe. A popcorn kernel stuck between your back molars. The sun when it's in between your visor and the steering wheel. I never understood how she latched her claws into my brother. I can only assume she must give really good blow jobs, and he was orgasm drunk when she convinced him to get married.

Kate doesn't reply as the doorbell rings again, signifying Claire and Natalie's arrival. I'm assuming they're together. Generally whenever they come into Eternity Springs, they carpool. Since they live further away, I figured they'd be the latest to arrive. Everyone quiets when they notice Hannah's spread.

"Dang, girl. You can host girls' night anytime you want," Natalie comments before giving her a one-armed shoulder squeeze.

"Seriously. This is amazing!" Claire exclaims.

"It's too much, isn't it? I went overboard. Luca told me it was fine, but he'll say anything to keep me happy ..." she trails off. I stifle a giggle as I think of my pussy-whipped brother. I have no doubt he'll say anything to keep Hannah happy, but I also think he wouldn't know if this was too much or just right.

"It's perfect, Han. It's exactly what I needed," I tell her. She lets out another relieved exhale before taking everyone's coats and encouraging us to add our hors d'oeuvres to the table. Once everyone fills up a plate, we relax by the fire, and I explain everything that happened. The eviction, ending up at Stone's barbershop, and the blowout. I leave out the part about him singing. For some reason, I want to keep that part of Stone for me.

As expected, Hannah says I can stay with her and Luca, and I graciously say no. Not only do I want to avoid listening to all the sex, but also they are too disgustingly sweet with one another. I don't want to be around that nonstop. Kate is currently renting a basement bedroom from a family in town, but she said I could stay on her couch if I wanted. Claire just got a new roommate, and Natalie is living with her sister.

"It's okay. I think I have something worked out," I say quietly.

"Where?" Kate asks, and I see a look of understanding dawn in Hannah's eyes.

"That's why Luca and Sofia got the hotel truck," she says, and I nod.

"I'm, um, going to stay with Stone for a bit," I blurt out. Every pair of eyes whips to mine as silence overtakes the group. Finally, Claire speaks up.

"Stone? Stone Dixon? The guy you've crushed on since you were in diapers?" she asks.

"Okay, that's just a bit of an exaggeration," I say, rolling my eyes. "Since I was a teenager, yes. But not my entire life."

"But you've known him all your life."

"Well, yeah. He's my brother's best friend. I don't remember much of him when I was super young, but definitely, once I got into the upper elementary grades."

"He's like forty or something?" Kate asks, scrunching her nose.

"No," I giggle. "He's thirty-seven."

"Same difference," she mutters.

"You got a thing against an age gap, Kate?" I ask, raising a brow and looking at her directly.

"No, but those older guys are just rude. They're set in their ways, and no one can tell them otherwise. You're going to get hurt here, Ari."

"I said I was moving into one of his spare bedrooms, not that we were going to have a sexual relationship. I know I'd get hurt, which is why I already told him nothing would happen. Especially after that kiss in my apartment," I say.

"Hold up. You kissed him in your apartment? When the hell did that happen?" Claire shouts. Natalie gives a smug grin, and I'm honestly surprised she didn't gab to Claire about the gossip already.

"The day after the gala. He showed up at my apartment to tell me he was just helping me save face with Bradley and that it would never happen again. Then we started sniping at each other, and suddenly I was against the wall with his tongue down my throat."

"Damn. The old man has game," Kate comments.

"How did you all know that I call him that?" I ask. Natalie said it earlier, but I brushed it off as a slip of the tongue. When Kate looks confused, I explain. "I've called Stone 'Old Man' for as long as I can remember."

She lets out a loud cackle of laughter. "No way! I had no idea. Ironic, huh."

"Anyway," Hannah says, trying to get us back on track, "Ari, how does your apartment having asbestos and termites end up with you living with Stone?"

"I called Luca to complain because he gets all riled up and angry, which typically makes me feel better. And he was with our mom, getting haircuts at Stone's shop. So I walked in, feeling all sad and lonely. Stone took one look at me, dropped everything, and had my face in his hands to wipe my tears. I could barely get all the details out before he asked me to move in with him."

All four women stare at me, making me feel extremely self-conscious.

"Wow," Natalie whispers.

"That's sexy as hell," Claire comments.

"Yeah," Kate agrees.

Hannah is silent, but I can see the wheels turning in her head. She opens and closes her mouth a few times before finally speaking. "Will you be signing a lease? Is there a specified amount you'll be paying? Are you allowed to have guests, or gentlemen, over if you begin dating anyone? How will you feel if he has a female spend the night? Are you supposed to stay in your room all the time, or are common areas open for you?"

"We didn't discuss all of those things yet, Han. This literally happened today."

"But if you need to be out of your apartment by Monday, you

need to move your things tomorrow. Shouldn't you have discussed these details? Are you even sure of the kind of man Stone is, Arianna? What if he's different than you expected? You seem to bicker quite often with him. How will that change when you're in each other's spaces all the time? What if he becomes volatile or even angrier?"

Hannah's voice has risen, and her cheeks have reddened since she began speaking, making me wonder what is going on beneath the surface. She's only a month out from her ex-boyfriend assaulting her, and from the few snippets Luca has given me, the ex wasn't a nice guy to Hannah during their relationship.

"Han," I say gently, "Stone and I bicker because we've always argued. He's a worthy adversary who doesn't back down and doesn't just let me run over him. But he's also one of the most loyal men I've ever met. Regardless of my crush on him growing up, I trust him. And I know my brother trusts him. I'm safe with Stone."

"Are you sure?" she whispers, her voice breaking.

"I am. Did you know he goes to the hotel on Mondays and does odd jobs to help out? He said he wants to do anything that can help my mom and dad since they're the guardians of Alex's kids while Alex is deployed. I had no idea Stone did this. He said he's been doing it for years, even when Alex is here."

"I've seen him around, but didn't realize he was working on things there," she sniffs. "I just worry about you, Ari. You have such a genuine heart, and I'd hate to see someone stifle that in any way."

"I know, Han. I'd never let anyone do that to me."

"You say that, but it happens more easily than you think. It's so slow you don't even realize you're changing. I'm thankful I looked in the mirror one day and didn't recognize the person I'd become. If that moment hadn't happened, I wouldn't be here today. With my little family," she says shyly, pressing her hand to her abdomen.

"Hannah Ann Beauregard, are you telling me you're making me an auntie?" I screech. She nods with a tearful giggle. I scream, grabbing her and giving her a massive hug. "Oh my God, I'm so happy for you! Is Luca excited? I can't believe he hasn't told me yet!"

"I asked him if I could tell you tonight. He's over the moon," she gushes. I move out of the way so the other ladies can congratulate Hannah. "But don't tell anyone in your family yet. Luca wants to be the one to tell them."

"Of course."

A new baby. Another Santo baby.

I'm thrilled for my brother. Truly. He will be a phenomenal father.

But my heart hurts just a little because I'm acutely aware that I'm nowhere near having that for myself.

S tone

$\mathcal{I}$ have no idea how I became DD to the Santo clan tonight, but that's what happened.

I wasn't lying to Arianna when I said I don't cook much. When I finish my dinner at a local bar, I see Dominic and Luca Santo walk in with a couple other guys I recognize from town. When Dom sees me, he waves me over to join them. Since I'm driving, I stick with water and one Scotch, but that doesn't stop them from imbibing quite a bit. After an hour, one guy leaves, leaving me with Luca, Dominic, and Sebastian Garcia.

Luca is a giddy drunk, and I'm reminded of how similar he is to Alex. On the other hand, Dom is having a bad day, or he's an angry drunk. The scowl on his face only gets more pronounced as the evening goes on. Granted, I know he has a lot on his plate. Running the hotel, dealing with an aging father who still likes to stick his head in where he's not needed, a geriatric grandmother who wants to meddle way too much, and sole custody of three kids. That's a lot for anyone.

I've learned that Sebastian went to school with Dominic, but is also friends with Luca. He's calm and reserved, steadily drinking

Mezcal, a Mexican tequila with a smoky taste like whiskey. I nursed one scotch all night, watching the guys as they continued getting louder. Luca must be used to his brother's attitude, because it doesn't seem to faze him at all.

"Savannah is back in town," Dom announces, and Luca spits his drink across the table. Dom has barely spoken all night, choosing to sit next to Luca with his broody and growly attitude, so I'm surprised when he suddenly speaks about his ex-wife. I only knew of her in passing once she married Dom, as she didn't grow up in Eternity Springs.

"Seriously? She run out of money or something?" he asks once he regains his composure.

"I don't fucking know. She showed up at the hotel and tried to give Aspen a hug. Aspen screamed bloody murder. Kid doesn't even recognize her own mother," Dom snarls. Damn. Poor kid. No preschooler should have their mother run out on them.

"What are you going to do?" Luca asks.

"I don't know. Wait and see what happens, I guess. She doesn't stay long. Just long enough to fuck shit up for me," Dom says with a dark and bitter laugh. I can recognize the sentiment. My dad would come into town just long enough to get my mom's hopes up, then he'd leave again. He only lasted a handful of months living full-time with us after he was booted from the league, and then he was gone for good. It's been two and a half decades since I've seen or heard from him. I only wish it had been as long for my mom, but she likes to show up like Dom's ex and make my life a living hell as often as she can. It's a pity she still lives in the same trailer I grew up in because it means she's still here in Eternity Springs.

"Do you think she'll try to get back together with you?" Sebastian slurs. He may seem very relaxed, sitting lazily in the booth next to me, but his eyes are hooded and focused as he watches everyone around the bar.

"No. I made it clear the last time she rolled through that any relationship between us was done. Once she admitted to fucking with her birth control, I knew I couldn't trust her," Dom admits.

"No fucking way," Luca says quietly. "When did she do that?"

"You mean which time?" Dom asks, and Luca nods. "All of them."

"Fuck," I mutter. She's a piece of work.

"I don't regret my children. I fucking love them. But their mother is a conniving bitch, and I despise her," he snarls.

"I don't doubt it," I tell him. "How do your kids feel about her?"

"Aspen doesn't remember her at all. Savannah split when Aspen was only a few months old, and she's only come back a couple times since then. Carter remembers her, but not a lot. He's generally apathetic about her. He's content with our family now and doesn't care for a flighty person who comes in and out of our lives whenever she sees fit. His words, not mine."

"Smart kid. How old is he now?" I ask. I'm horrible with remembering ages. I just know he's in elementary school.

"He's only seven. Fucking hurts that he recognizes her for who she is, but I'm glad he does."

"Chip off the ole block, Dom," Luca teases.

"How so?" Dominic asks.

"From what Mom says, you were the same way as a kid. You could read a person at a young age, and you didn't put up with bullshit."

Dom chuckles. "Then my boy definitely has that going for him."

"How old is your other daughter?" Fuck me if I can't remember her damn name or age. I really should pay better attention when I'm with the Santo family. But I typically end up focused on Arianna, and miss everything else going on around me.

"Sienna. She's nine, and she's been the hardest to deal with. She wants a mom so badly. When Savannah leaves again, Sienna will be the most heartbroken."

"Is Kate helping?" Luca asks.

"Who is Kate? Girlfriend?" I ask innocently. I've been around Dominic and Kate enough times to feel the sexual tension oozing from their pores. They're going to hate fuck at some point, I can just tell.

Luca laughs while Dom grumbles. "Not my fucking girlfriend. She's an almost-cousin."

"What the fuck is an almost-cousin? I know Alex mentioned something about a cousin in Colorado Springs having a fucked up family life, is she related to them?" I ask. I know Kate isn't technically related to the Santos by blood, but I've never heard them refer to her as an almost-cousin.

"Yeah, she is the half-sister of our cousin on our mom's side. Our cousin and Kate share a dad, so she's actually not blood-related to us at all. But we basically adopted her and put her to work at the hotel," Luca explains.

"So why is she helping with Dom's kids?" I ask.

"Availability," Dom grunts.

"Jesus, Dominic. That's nice," Luca says, motioning the server for another round. I'm gonna need to force them to eat some appetizers to soak up all this booze.

Dominic shrugs. "Tell me it's not true? My regular nanny quit, and Mom is the guardian for Alex's kids while he's deployed, so I can't use her. God knows Aspen is a handful anyway, so it had to be someone who could take on the kids full-time. Kate was already working a bunch of weird hours at the hotel, so it was easy to just transition her to full-time with my kids."

"She's also really good with them, which helps," Luca says.

Dominic grunts again. "I wouldn't go that far. She's average at best."

Luca laughs. "You're just saying that because you want to fuck her, and now you can't."

"I do not want to fuck her!" Dominic shouts.

I see Luca wince as he looks over Dom's shoulder. "Shit. Incoming."

Turning, I see a rough-looking blonde approach the table. "Who are you fucking tonight, baby? You play your cards right, I can certainly arrange an encore with your wife."

"*Ex*-wife, Savannah. Ex. And I can guarantee we'll never have sex again," Dominic growls.

"Oh, hush. You'll always be my husband in my heart, Dominic. And never say never, baby."

"Well, thankfully, according to the state of Colorado, you won't always be my wife."

The woman giggles while eyeing Sebastian and me. "Boys. Does anyone want to buy me a drink?"

Sebastian rolls his eyes. "Hard pass."

She shrugs before looking at me. "What about you, hotness?"

"No." I bite my tongue to hold in my initial reply that I'd rather not have to get tested for all the STDs out there just by being in her periphery.

"Whatever. I'd rock your world," she spits out. Dominic laughs loudly as she walks away.

"What the hell did you ever see in her?" Luca asks.

Dominic shakes his head. "I literally just told you she fucked with her birth control to get pregnant every time. Why do you think I married her?"

Luca shrugs. "I assumed you were in love. You didn't need to marry her just because of a baby, Dom. You could have just paid child support."

"First of all, I don't believe in love. And secondly, it was drilled in my brain from a very young age that you man up and take responsibility. I didn't realize she messed with her birth control until Carter was born. I thought we could make it work. Savannah thought she could force me to fall in love with her. Looks like neither of us got what we wanted, which leads me back to the first point. True love is a fucking myth."

"Don't tell Mom that. She'll wax poetic about true love and the woman of your dreams knocking you on your ass. She's convinced you were in love with Savannah and that Dad was devastated when you divorced."

Dom snorts. "Dad wasn't devastated. He doesn't believe in true love either, except for Mom."

"If you knew about her tampering with her birth control after the second kid, how'd the third one happen?" I wonder.

"A fifth of bourbon and a very bad judgment call," Dom deadpans.

I have a vague memory of Sofia giving me the true love speech, the one about true love knocking a man on his ass, almost verbatim, fifteen years ago. Good to know she's still up to the same tricks.

Sebastian has been quiet, and I notice he's on his phone. He looks up at me and shoves his phone in my face. "You made the site again," he says.

Fucking gossip site.

Recent lovebirds Arianna Santo and Stone Dixon are moving up in the world! Or are they just moving? After Arianna found out she'd be evicted due to mold, termites, and holes in the floor of her apartment in crime-ridden urban Denver, she ran right into Stone's arms at his work. He immediately offered up his home, and she accepted. Santo family members were seen picking up a truck from Everlasting to help the couple move Arianna's things into Stone's renovated home. How much time do we have before we hear wedding bells? Or the pitter-patter of little feet?

Fucking hell. How much could they get wrong here? Holes in the floor? And she lives in a nice fucking suburb, not "crime-ridden urban Denver."

"Are you fucking kidding me, Dixon?" Dominic seethes looking up from his own phone. "Thought I made myself very fucking clear that you were supposed to stay away from my baby sister!"

I roll my eyes. "Was I supposed to tell your sister to live out of her car? And seriously, how have you not heard about this yet? Your family phone tree is faster than the speed of sound."

"She has other siblings she could stay with," he counters.

"I'm aware. I offered, and I didn't think she'd accept. But she did. Deal with it."

"You're an asshole."

"Because I offered her a place to stay? Then I guess I'm an asshole. Jesus, Dom. You're overreacting."

"No, I'm protecting my sister. You're taking advantage of her," he says.

"How are you protecting her exactly? I'm the one who came to her defense at the gala. I'm the one that just so happened to call her when her ex was at her fucking apartment last week and got over there so fast he left tire treads on the parking lot cement. And I'm the one that took one look at her face today and wanted to do anything to take away the tears. So yeah, great job protecting her, Dominic, but she's obviously not coming to you for shit."

"Her ex was at her apartment? Bradley Wetherington?" Dominic says quietly. He speaks so quietly that I almost don't hear him, and it's the kind of quiet that lets me know Dominic is lethal at this moment.

"Yeah, I guess that's his name," I respond. "Doesn't he work for the hotel?"

"Not for fucking long," Dom growls. He motions like he will stand up, and Luca and I grab his wrists simultaneously. Sebastian looks on with an amused smile.

"Where do you think you're going?" Luca asks.

"Gonna go introduce Mr. Wetherington to my fists and then fire his ass like I should have last week."

I slam my hand down on his shoulder, forcing him to stay seated. "You know that asshole will sue you and the hotel for discrimination and wrongful termination, or some other kind of shit. You have to be patient and wait for him to fuck up so the firing sticks, man."

"How can you be this calm? If she's supposedly your girl, why aren't you ready to burn down his house?" Dominic asks as he takes a shaky swig of his drink.

"Because I already threatened that Leo and Alex would dump his ass in a lake in the mountains where no one could find him," I admit. Sebastian lets out a loud bark of laughter before slamming his hands down on the table.

"And you claim you don't want her," he says with a smile. "I barely know you, my guy, and I can tell you want in her panties."

"I don't," I lie. "Arianna is generally a menace to society, and someone has to keep track of her while Alex is gone."

"She's not a menace," Luca says. "You need to stop with that shit. You've claimed that for years. Ari is one of the strongest and most driven women I know. And Sebastian, don't you *ever* fucking talk about any of my sisters like that again."

"I didn't even say anything that bad," Sebastian sputters, throwing his hands up in mock surrender.

"I know what you're thinking, man. And I know what you want to do with a certain Santo woman," Luca says, his eyes narrowing as he stares Sebastian down. Dominic looks on with interest.

"You're the one that wants Isabella? Over my dead fucking body," he barks.

"Excuse me?" Sebastian says.

"You heard me. We don't need you pulling some bullshit on her. Isabella won't like ..." Dominic trials off as his brow furrows, then he throws back his head in a raucous bout of laughter. "Fuck me. Isabella is going to eat you alive. Go for it. This is gonna be fun to watch."

I don't know how to handle these Santo siblings, and I've asked one to move in with me. What the hell was I thinking?

I roll my eyes. "So anyway, back to Arianna. Agree to disagree on the whole menace thing."

"Why are you with her then?" Dom asks.

"Man, you seriously have to believe me. I was helping her out. Her ex was belittling her, and I watched her just whither. The only thing I could think of was to step in and act like her boyfriend to shut Bartlett up."

"Bartlett?"

"The ex. Whatever the fuck his name is. I don't know. Baker? Bart? Bill? Something."

"Bradley," Luca and Dom say simultaneously with laughter, making me smile.

"Whatever. I don't give a fuck what his name is. He's not important. Giving Arianna some confidence back is what's important. So yeah, I kissed her. And if she needs me to play pretend again to help her, I'll do it."

All three men look at me with varying stages of expression. Dom studies me with a glare while Luca thoughtfully nods. Sebastian chuckles silently while shaking his head. Yeah, I know I'm fucked. It's just a matter of which of the guys believes me most now.

"*O*h shit, they're all still here," Luca mumbles before belching and laughing at himself.

"Who?" I ask, noticing three cars along the side of Luca's driveway. I'd already dropped Seb and Dom off at Dom's house, but Luca lives the farthest. Since it's in the complete opposite direction of my house, and the snow is really coming down now, I'm hoping to quickly get him inside so his girl can deal with his drunk shenanigans.

While I didn't mind all the tales Luca and Dominic told me about growing up in the Santo household, most of which I hadn't heard before, I really wanted to be home hours ago. Arianna's room isn't fully ready yet, and Mrs. Santo texted me to say they'd be bringing over furniture Sunday afternoon. Mr. And Mrs. Santo wanted Arianna's furniture to go into storage so it would be easier to move her in this weekend. Mr. Santo clearly pointed out that I should expect Arianna to stay in my home only briefly. They had an extra bed and couch they wanted to get rid of and asked if I'd like them. I read between the lines and figured this was a weird sort of dowry for giving Arianna a place to stay. I'd already said I wouldn't charge Ari rent, and in true Santo fashion, they've stepped in to save the day for her again.

Arianna might claim she's not a princess, but she clearly is. Parents don't act like this. They don't drop everything to help their kids out. Right? Wait. Do they?

"You coming inside, man?" Luca slurs, opening the passenger door and immediately falling out of my car. The immediate cackle tells me he's fine, as does the comment, "Tone! Come make a snow angel!"

Jesus Christ. I haven't been called Tone in well over a decade. Hell, I think that time Alex dragged me to Luca's hockey game, when Ari was around ten, was the last time she ever called me that.

I turn off my car, round the trunk, and find Luca happily flailing his arms in an attempt at a snow angel.

"Did I do it?" he asks.

"No, dude. Your feet are still in my car," I tell him. "Come on. Up you go."

I grunt as I help Luca up, as he's got a couple of inches on me and at least fifty pounds of solid muscle, before helping him slide to the door. He is giggling like a lunatic as the front door swings open.

"Pixie!" Luca calls out, and Hannah beams at him. I hear a rather loud hiccup from someone, and I swear under my breath. The sound of more women giggling makes me realize I'm walking into a girls' night, and they're probably all drunk. I don't want to be DD for all of these girls because one is likely to puke in my car. I'm honestly surprised none of the guys puked.

Luca collapses against the door and pulls Hannah to him, nuzzling her neck. She shrieks as snow hits her skin, but doesn't let go of him. I have no idea how she's supporting his weight because she's a good foot shorter than him, but before I can say anything, a blur launches into my arms.

"Tone," Arianna whispers against my neck, her arms tight around my shoulders and her legs wrapped around my waist.

"Princess," I murmur, taking a moment to bury my nose in her hair and breathe her in, my arms wrapped snugly around her waist.

I hate how perfect she feels in my arms.

I hate how my pulse slows when her heart is next to mine, and how I desperately want to drag her home to my bed right now.

But mostly, I hate that I know I can't have her like I want, and can't be what she needs.

"I think I'm drunk," she mumbles, making me chuckle.

"I think you're right."

"How am I supposed to get home to my bug-ridden and stinky apartment?" she moans.

"Come back to my house, baby girl." I've never been one to use pet names with women. But with Arianna, it just feels right.

"Like that."

"What?"

"Baby girl," she mutters, and I still when I feel her tongue dart out and touch the side of my neck. "Wanna hear you call me that when you're fucking me six ways to Sunday. Or is it six ways to Bevin Kacon? No, wait. That's not right. Kevin Bacon."

I groan as my cock twitches. It agrees. With the fucking, not with the Kevin Bacon.

"Princess," I warn.

"What?" she says, yawning, then latches her teeth on my collarbone.

My dick is no longer twitching. It's fully saluting. I imagine her naked and riding me. Her head tipped back in bliss, her hair tickling my balls as she finds her pleasure. Bringing me to my own orgasm. I already know she'll be the best I've ever had, and once I've had her, it'll break me.

Hannah clears her throat, jolting me from my thoughts of what I want to do to Arianna. "The rest of the girls are staying here until they can sober up. Do you want to stay?"

"Uh, no. I'm fine to drive home."

"Arianna?" Hannah asks.

"Hmm?" Arianna replies, her head still buried in my shoulder. One of her hands has found my hair, her nails delicately dragging up and down my scalp.

"Do you want to stay with us?" Hannah says loudly. Arianna lifts her head, her eyes fully meeting mine, and I see the unbridled lust in them. The desire.

I don't know if I have the willpower to say no to her. If she asks me to fuck her, I'll want to. Desperately. Consequences be damned. If she gets in my car, I may not be able to hold her at arm's length.

For a moment, I see hesitation in her expression. But then her grip on me tightens, and she sighs as she settles into my embrace.

"Take me home, Stone," Arianna whispers.

My resistance is shot. The last layer of defense against the pull toward Arianna is crumbling around me, standing in the doorway of Luca's house. But I know if I take her home, and subsequently into my bed, I don't think I'll be able to come back from it — from her.

Who am I kidding? Arianna has already ruined me.

Arianna

I don't know what I'm doing.

I told Stone earlier today that nothing could happen between us, and I meant it. Too many glasses of wine, and four women harping in my ear that I needed to "take the bull by the horns" made me impulsive and frivolous. The fact that the girls kept saying horns as a pun for horny made me crave sex like never before. I can only assume that, given how off the charts the kisses have been, Stone knows how to use his tongue, and therefore, probably knows how to use every other appendage to make me feel all the things. And while I enjoyed the one time with Bradley, it definitely wasn't the best I've ever had.

I can tell Stone will rock my world.

Have you ever seen a guy who exudes confidence and sex appeal? Like the kind of guy who walks with swagger, but not because he thinks he's hot shit. The guy that exudes confidence as it seeps from his pores. A guy who understands the difference between cocky and confident. The guy who understands the female orgasm and takes pride in knowing multiple ways to make a woman come.

That's Stone.

I've never met a woman he's actually dated, and I honestly don't know if he's dated anyone long-term. I've interacted with some of his fuck buddies, and I've overheard some women gossiping about his prowess in the bedroom. Nothing quite like trying to enjoy breakfast at a local diner and listening to two women compare their experiences in the bedroom with the guy you've crushed on for years. Suffice it to say, if he doesn't change his mind before we return to his house, I won't regret tonight at all.

Stone is silent as I gather my belongings, but he frowns as I approach the door. Assuming he's going to change his mind, my heart falls. That is, until he mutters, "fuck this," and bends down to throw me over his shoulder. I barely make a sound as he strides out the door and hustles to his car. He opens the door and carefully places me in the passenger seat, not even allowing me to put my seatbelt on. However, his eyes won't meet mine, and he's quiet as he eases into the driver's seat.

He shakes his head as I open my mouth to ask if he's okay. "Don't talk. I won't be able to focus if you ask me anything, and I'll be damned if I wreck on these roads and I don't get you home safely."

I'm tempted to ask questions anyway, which has always been our give-and-take. I push, and Stone pushes back. But something tells me I shouldn't push Stone right now. Maybe it's how tightly he grips the steering wheel, or how a vein pulses on the side of his neck. He doesn't glance at me once during the drive to his house, and I find myself tightly squeezing my hands together as anxiety weaves its way into my brain.

Due to road conditions, it takes double the time to get back to Stone's house, allowing me much needed time to gain a little sobriety. As I study his profile, I realize I don't feel any differently about Stone right now than I did an hour ago. Or a day ago, or even a week ago. I've always wanted him.

Stone turns off the engine when we arrive in his garage, but doesn't get out of the car.

"Last chance," he whispers.

"What?" I ask. He turns to me, and his look is intense. Feral.

"I can back out of here. Take you to your apartment. Act like nothing happened. Move you in tomorrow, and continue doing what we've always done."

"What have we always done?" I ask quietly.

"Avoided this. Acted like this chemistry didn't exist. Like we haven't thought about each other and wondered what the other tastes like, and how we'll sound when we come together. If you open that door, baby girl, you're mine. There's no going back from this. If you open that door, Princess, it's game fucking on."

His hand creeps toward mine, and I realize I've been slowly reaching for him since he pulled into the driveway. Before he can grab my hand, I reach up to touch his face. A day's growth of stubble covers his skin, rough against my palm, and I shiver, imagining it against my core. Stone's eyes, his pupils blown wide with lust, stare intensely at me, awaiting my response. He moves his head to kiss my palm before sucking just the tip of my forefinger into his mouth. The pressure around my finger, along with his tongue skirting along my skin, makes me gasp.

"Answer, baby girl," he says deeply.

I don't answer.

I just open the door, leaving it slightly ajar, but giving Stone the sign he needs to understand I'm ready to play.

The responding smile I get from Stone is wicked. He's out of his door and next to mine within seconds, ripping the door open and yanking me out of the car before throwing me over his shoulder again. He quickly enters the house, bypassing darkened rooms barren of furniture, before entering what I assume is his bedroom. I'm unceremoniously thrown onto the bed, bouncing twice while I let out a breathy giggle until I notice Stone waiting. His stance above me is possessive and commanding. I might have thought he had swagger before, but this is on another level.

"We need some ground rules, Arianna," he grounds out as he begins to unbutton his shirt. I barely noticed his clothes before I launched myself at him at Hannah's house. Jeans that showcase his thick thighs and scrumptious ass lead to a fully buttoned flannel over a tee shirt. Once he finishes unbuttoning the flannel and removes it, I salivate at gorgeous forearms, one arm with quite a few tattoos. A wolf covers one bicep, and I've always wondered what the symbolism is as to why he chose a wolf. I've been fascinated with wolves since I was young, even having a birthday event at a wolf sanctuary when I turned thirteen. I volunteer when I can, and have raised funds for the sanctuary on multiple occasions with hotel events.

I wonder if Stone knows these things.

As my eyes track lower, seeing a sliver of skin above his waistband, I sit upright and reach toward him. I need to touch him. Feel his skin. Ground myself before I lose focus.

"Ground rules, Princess," he says again.

"What?"

"Look at me," Stone snaps, drawing my attention to his face. He gently grips my chin with his thumb and forefinger. "My house, my bed, my rules. Do you understand?"

"Your rules? What does that mean?" I ask, sobering up quite quickly. I've never known a man to have rules in the bedroom. What does Stone have in store for me?

"It means I like to control things here, Arianna. I'll decide if, and when, you come. How often. I'll set the pace."

"What if I don't like something? Or what if I get nervous, or frightened, and I don't want to continue?" I ask.

"Then tell me." The wicked gleam in Stone's eyes has been replaced with a wary attentiveness as he waits for my next response.

"So you'll stop? If I ask you to?"

"Of course I will." Stone pauses, studying me. "Have you ever been in a situation where someone didn't stop after you told them you didn't like something?"

I hesitate before nodding.

"Christ," Stone swears, squeezing his eyes closed and swiping a hand over his face. "Who. Tell me his fucking name right now."

"It doesn't matter."

"Yes, it does."

"No, it doesn't. I handled it."

"You probably didn't handle it the way I would, so tell me his name, and I'll make sure he never fucking touches another woman without remembering me."

"Stone, it's okay. I get that you want to solve this, but it was handled. I'll admit, it's pretty hot; you going all growly alpha hole right now, but trust me. The jerk got what was coming to him."

Stone stares at me, cocking his head to the side as he formulates his response. "I think I'm going to need some more information, Princess."

"Can you sit with me?" I ask, patting the bed next to me. He does, and I grab his hands. "I want you to take a breath and promise me you'll listen to everything."

He nods. "I promise."

I take a deep breath, waiting a moment before beginning my story. A story that no one, not even my mother, knows. "I was on a first date. I brought him back to my apartment because I thought the date had been going well — don't growl at me, dammit — and we kissed on the couch. He pushed me down and tried to take off my shirt. I started getting freaked out and told him to stop. He said he deserved to get some because he had bought me dinner."

"Give me his fucking name," Stone rumbles.

"You seriously need to stop growling at me. Let me finish. He ripped my shirt, and that really pissed me off because it was my favorite shirt at the time —"

"Which shirt?" Stone interrupts.

"I don't know why that's important, but it was this rainbow ombre button-up that I loved —"

"I remember that shirt. You wore it all the time until a few years ago ... until you didn't wear it anymore," Stone says flatly.

"Yeah. So anyway, when he tried to get my pants pulled down, I started grabbing anything I could find and hitting him with it. For some reason, I had a bucket of pens next to the couch, and one just so happened to be open, and I stabbed him with it. In the neck."

"You stabbed him with a pen?" Stone asks incredulously.

"I did. And then when he got up, he slapped me —"

"That motherfucker hit you?" he bellows.

"Well, not really hard, but yes —"

"Give me his fucking name!" he shouts, his eyes wild.

"He stood up, and so I stabbed him in the dick," I blurt out.

Stone's mouth drops open in shock. "What?"

"I, uh, I stabbed him in the dick. With the pen. And then I called the cops."

Minutes go by as Stone processes the information.

"Stone? Are you okay? You're making me kind of nervous."

"You stabbed a rapist in the neck and dick with a pen. Ballpoint?"

"Uh, gel, I think."

"And the cops arrested him?"

"Yeah."

"Did he go to prison?"

"No, not that time. But he did it again, to another girl, and then he went to prison. He got out six months ago, and his parole officer called to tell me he was moving to Pueblo."

"Thank fuck," Stone breathes, closing his eyes and resting his forehead against mine. "Holy shit, Arianna. How did I never know this?"

"No one knows," I confess.

"Why?"

"Because I was embarrassed. And the family was going through so much at that point. Alex's wife had died, and Dom was going through his divorce. I didn't want to add stress."

"You were assaulted, Princess. That's not stress. Your parents would have been there to support you."

I shrug. "It's okay. I was lucky, and like I said, I handled it."

Stone chuckles. "That you did. You never cease to amaze me, baby girl. Just when I think I know the person you are, you surprise me again."

"What does that mean?"

"I guess I had you lumped into this princess category where you were always waited on hand and foot. I mean, everyone is wrapped around your finger, but you're stronger than I ever realized."

"I don't have everyone wrapped, Stone. That's a ridiculous thing to say."

He looks surprised. "I've said it to you more than once, and you've always agreed with me. Hell, you even agreed when you were only ten years old!"

"That's what you're basing this on? What I said when I was ten?"

"Well, yeah. You make it sound awful when you say it that way, but yeah. You bragged about how you had everyone wrapped around your finger."

"Again, I repeat, I was ten. Most ten-year-olds do have their parents wrapped around their fingers, and I was the baby of the family. Plus, adding in all my health scares, yeah. I was catered to as a kid. Most kids are."

"I wouldn't know," Stone murmurs and my heart drops. So many memories growing up include Stone, and it is easy to forget he had a much different family dynamic at home. I've always lumped him into our family like he didn't have parents. I'm sure there were many times he wished that were true.

"Okay, let's meet somewhere in the middle here. Yeah, I probably got away with more as the baby. But Luca got away with a ton, too, and Isabella is younger than him. Gianna got away with a ton, but Leo, her *twin*, never even tried. It's safe to say every kid is different, and my parents dealt with us as needed. But I've worked my ass off to get where I am, Stone. I wasn't given this position at the hotel. I started in banquets as soon as I could legally work. I only snuck into this position because the previous manager quit when her husband's job relocated. I know I'm lucky to have my family. I do. But I don't take them for granted."

"I know you don't," he says softly. "I'm sorry I insinuated you were this prim and polished princess. I think the only reason you're on this pedestal in my mind is because I put you up there myself."

He leans forward and presses a soft kiss against my lips. As I'm about to deepen the kiss, he yawns, which makes me yawn.

"I always get tired after alcohol," I whisper.

"It's been a long day for both of us. Let's get some sleep," Stone says, standing to push the comforter down. He motions for me to scoot under the covers, but I hesitate.

"Do you … do you want me to sleep on the couch?" I ask. He laughs.

"I don't have a couch, Princess. It's here or the floor until we get the furniture delivered from your parents."

"I can sleep on the floor. It's not the first time I've done it."

"It's a big bed, Arianna. I assure you we can both fit," he comments wryly.

"Well, I don't want to cramp your style. We arrived here with a different plan in mind, and now I feel awkward and self-conscious —"

Stone interrupts me. "There's nothing to feel self-conscious about. This will give us both more time to think. I want you to be sure about things because once we cross that boundary, there's no going back. We both need to think."

I sigh. "I know."

As he climbs under the comforter with me, he turns toward me but refuses to look me in the eyes. "But if it's okay with you, I'd really like to hold you tonight. If either of us changes our mind, I'd like to at least have this."

A relieved exhale escapes before I can hold it in. "I'd like that too."

He turns off the lamp before pulling me toward him, his arms tightly around my shoulders and stomach, as he spoons me perfectly. He buries his head in my hair, and I feel him tremble against me. Somehow, he feels different all of a sudden.

"Stone ..." I trail off. He doesn't speak, only tightens his arms around me, sliding one leg between mine.

"Go to sleep, Arianna," Stone finally says, his whisper a far cry from his normal gritty voice. I know something is wrong. He's in his head again, but I'm petrified to ask him anything.

As I slowly drift off, I feel Stone press his lips to my hair.

I only vaguely hear him say, "I can't do this to you, baby girl. I won't let you settle."

When I wake up alone, I immediately know things are different. Stone's side of the bed is cold, telling me he pulled away hours ago. I remember Alex mentioning how similar Stone and I were because neither of us liked mornings. When I check my watch and see it's not even seven, I know he's distancing himself again.

After using the bathroom and brushing my teeth with toothpaste and my finger, I search for Stone. I find him in a spare bedroom, applying light gray paint around a large window. His jaw is clenched, his entire body taut with tension, and I know he's already decided. He won't look at me when I clear my throat to announce my presence.

"My mom texted and said they'll be here after lunch with the furniture. Can you take me to get my car, or would you prefer I call a rideshare?"

"Whichever," he replies. His tone is cold. Tone. My Tone is long gone this morning. This Stone is a fraction of the man from last night.

Pulling out my phone, I open the rideshare app and find a car ten minutes away. I retreat back to Stone's bedroom and lock myself in the bathroom. I should have fucking known. It's been one step forward and ten steps back for five years with Stone. Anytime we agreed on something, he'd freak out and backpedal so fast. If we had a moment where this insane chemistry bubbled over, he'd treat me like shit right after. You'd think I'd learn, but here we are.

And I need to be done.

At this exact moment, getting the wool pulled over my eyes yet again, I realize something very pivotal about my feelings for Stone. It hasn't been just a crush. It wasn't an infatuation or attraction. I've been borderline in love with Stone for as long as I can remember, and each time I thought we were on the way to something different, I had to pick up the pieces and try to move on. Then he'd pull me back in somehow. My nineteenth birthday, and then my twenty-first birthday. Both times, I could see the desire on his face. The want. The need. And then he'd change. Guilt, disgust, or something. I don't know.

But it ends now.

When my car arrives, I bundle up and trudge outside. It looks like six or seven inches of snow fell. As I reach the car, I hear Stone call my name. I debate on ignoring him, but turn around. He doesn't speak, only looks at me. His expression is as closed off as I've ever seen, and I force myself to do the same. Without a word, I break eye contact and get into the car.

"Rough night?" the male driver asks.

"Something like that," I mutter.

"Walk of shame?" he teases.

"No, I live here. Just need to go get my car at my brother's house."

"Your boyfriend didn't look too happy," he comments.

Tears fill my eyes as I attempt to respond. "Not my boyfriend."

I text Luca that I'm on my way so he doesn't freak out when my car is gone. I plan to drive to my apartment and continue boxing up my belongings, then swing by a storage facility to drop off as much as possible. I'm taking the bare minimum to Stone's. I don't want his house to feel like home. It's just a layover right now. I'll find somewhere else to live, because I don't think I can live in such close proximity to him. If I'm going to move on once and for all, I need to get as far away from him as I can. My heart can't take it.

S tone

J stayed up the entire night watching Arianna. I couldn't help it. I wanted to wake her up and beg her to help me find a way to be together. A way that made sense somehow. But she deserves someone better. Someone put together with a good family, and a nest egg for them to build a life together. She doesn't need to deal with me and my idiosyncrasies, and she sure as shit doesn't need to interact with my mother at all. Arianna deserves someone who can give her the world, not just another reason to need therapy.

I know some people probably think I'm a success story, owning my own house and having a successful business, but I'm not. It took me over ten years to save up enough for the down payment on this house, and I'm barely affording the mortgage. My business is doing okay, but it's fucking expensive to own a business. I do as much as I can myself so I don't have to hire anyone else. Why would I want to chain Arianna to that? Would she be happy when I fall asleep at the dinner table because I've been on my feet for twelve hours? Or when I cover Sam's shift when he's sick, meaning I can't go to some Santo event with her? Tip of the iceberg for all the reasons why I know I'm not the one for Arianna. She deserves someone who will worship her.

Someone who will put her first no matter what. As much as I'd like to think I can put her first, I don't know if it's realistic.

While it hurt to watch her climb into that rideshare, I knew it was for the best. No twenty-something beautiful woman should attach herself to someone like me.

I threw myself into getting her room ready, then shoveled the driveway and sidewalk to prepare for the Santos to arrive with Arianna's donated furniture. Arianna isn't sure if her furniture will be salvageable once repairs and renovations are done at her apartment, but I think she wants to move closer to home anyway. I know her parents intend for me to keep their donations, but I don't think I'll want to. Once Ari moves out, I'll strip everything out of here that reminds me of her. It's bad enough that I see her fairly often. I'm bound to run into her at birthday parties, holiday dinners, and other events.

Maybe living with her is a blessing in disguise. I can see all of her bad habits and get over this crush I've had. I've thought about her as more than my best friend's sister for over five years, and I need to get over it.

When the doorbell rings, I shout for Arianna to open the door. I forgot to give her a key, and I'm scrubbing the remnants of paint out of my paintbrushes in the sink.

"You just letting anyone waltz in here, motherfucker?" I hear called out, and I immediately drop the brushes and jog into the living room to see Alex giving me a shit-eating grin.

"What the fuck are you doing here?" I ask, a wide grin breaking across my face as I stride toward him and hug him.

"Got sent home," he says, his voice muffled.

"That's not normal," I comment.

"No, it's not. I'm home for a few months, I think, and then they might send me overseas," he tells me. "You move fast, *Tone*. Shacking up with my baby sister? You sure you're ready for that?"

"Alex," I warn, but he chuckles and holds up his hands.

"I know. You're just helping out. You aren't really dating. I got the whole story from my mom and Abbie." Abbie is Alex's ten-year-old daughter. His seven-year-old son, Ben, is the spitting image of Alex.

"Abbie told you about this?"

"Ten going on twenty-five, that one. Abbie is too invested in a possible romance story for her aunt. Plus, she's been bugging me to set you up with anyone for years. She wants to be a flower girl, and I don't think she cares which wedding it takes place in."

"Shouldn't she just bug Luca into getting married? Seems like a safer bet," I comment.

Alex shrugs. "Who knows. You ready for the furniture? Mom and Dad should be here any minute, and I grabbed the suitcases Ari wanted to bring."

I frown. "Just suitcases? I assumed she had more crap than that."

"She's getting a storage locker for everything else. She said she doesn't plan to stay here for long, just until she finds an apartment."

Well, that hurts. I'm not surprised, but it hurts. Apparently, I'm not the only one who can make quick decisions.

"Is she not coming now?" I ask after a moment.

"No."

Damn. I really did a number on her.

"Does she need help moving anything?" I ask, willing my voice to stay calm.

"No. Luca and Hannah are helping her. Not sure what you did to piss her off, but she looked mutinous."

"Difference of opinions. It'll be fine once Arianna gets settled."

"Not Ari, man."

"Huh?"

"Hannah."

"*Hannah* is mad at me?" I ask incredulously. Hannah, the quiet and sweet southern belle who manages to calm Luca down with ease? I shake my head in disbelief.

"Yup. Considering you assumed it was my sister, it's a safe bet you did something stupid, and Ari talked to Hannah about it. My future sister-in-law looks tiny and adorable, but she's got a vicious streak." Alex looks weirdly proud about this fact.

I don't respond. I don't know Hannah well, so Alex is probably correct. But I know what I'm doing is in Arianna's best interest.

Alex's parents arrive a few minutes later, and we move the couch, coffee table, bed frame, mattress, and nightstand into my house. It's actually a nice set. I assumed it would be an unusual pattern on the couch or the bed frame would be scratched up, but everything is in excellent condition. Alex's dad barely looks at me the entire time, only grunting occasionally when I say Arianna's name. I find myself saying her name more and more just to fuck with him.

After they leave, I ask Alex if he wants to grab a beer.

"Can't, man. I have to get my kids from Dom's house. Last time they had a sleepover, Aspen convinced Abbie she knew how to braid, and it took my mom two hours to get the knots out of Abbie's hair."

"Okay, first of all, no five-year-old knows how to braid. And secondly, why didn't your mom bring her to me? I would have gotten the knots out in ten minutes, tops."

Alex sighs. "Abbie wouldn't let her."

"Why?"

"Fuck if I know, man. Abbie is hormonal. Every day is an adventure with her right now. Ben has started creeping past her room because he's afraid she'll tear into him for something dumb, and then she'll burst into tears. He's seven. He doesn't know how to handle female tears."

"I'm thirty years older than him, and I don't know how either," I remark.

"And yet you're letting the most dramatic woman in Eternity Springs move in with you. You're about to get one hell of a crash course in hormones and crying, Stone. I wasn't even living at home when she was a teenager, and I still have scars from the stories I've heard."

"Lovely."

Alex looks down at his phone and curses. "Shit. Dom just said

Abbie is sobbing about something, and he can't understand her. I gotta go. Text me when you're available this week for a beer, okay?"

I nod as he dashes out the door. Left alone in my quiet house, I wonder when Arianna will finally come here. Come home. Can I call it her home if she's only intending for it to be a brief stopover? I decide to bite the bullet and text her.

> Me: When will you be home?

> Princess: I have a dad and don't need another one.

> Me: I wasn't trying to be a dad, Princess. You don't have a key, and I need to be here to give you one.

> Princess: Just leave the door unlocked, Daddy.

Fucking hell. That is way hotter than it should be, making me feel even worse about my attraction to her.

> Me: That's not how I do things, Arianna.

> Princess: What's the big deal? This town is tiny. Nothing bad happens here. I highly doubt some dastardly criminal will look at your run-down house and think, "Yes! This joint certainly has all kinds of jewels and high-tech things!"

> Me: The attitude is unnecessary.

> Princess: The condescending tone is unnecessary.

> Me: Fine. Sleep in your fucking car then, Princess.

> Princess: It'll be better than sleeping in your fucking house, old man.

"God dammit!" I shout. That is not how I wanted this conversation to go. Arianna manages to infuriate me and turn me on simultaneously, even when she calls me old man. Makes me want to take her over my knee and turn her ass red. God knows she'd probably enjoy it, and then she'd taunt me constantly to see how far she could push me. Arianna is the quintessential brat. She would invariably find joy in setting me off, knowing it would ultimately benefit her.

As I'm about to lock the doors, turn off the lights, and force her to eat crow, another text comes through.

> Princess: I'm sorry. Everything this morning hurt me, and I'm taking it out on you.

> Me: Hurt by everything?

> Princess: I knew as soon as I woke up that you had changed your mind. I should have known better, but I got my hopes up.

Shit. I was so focused on how Arianna would feel in the future that I didn't even think about how she would feel right now.

> Me: I'm sorry. I should have handled that better. I think, given time, you'll realize this is for the best. I'm not the man for you, Princess. You deserve better. I'm just trying to look out for you.

> Princess: I'm well aware of what you think of me, Stone. But I had no idea you have such a shitty opinion of yourself.

> Me: I told you I had you up on a pedestal. My opinion of myself is a different story.

> Princess: Has it ever occurred to you that I might have YOU on a pedestal as well?

> Me: Haha. Very funny.

Princess: It wasn't a joke. I don't know why you think poorly of yourself. Anyone in my family will tell you that you're one of the strongest people we know. You've given so much of yourself to everyone around you. We might fight, and I might occasionally curse your name, but even I'm not dumb enough to act like you aren't a good person. My parents never would have let you stay with us so often. And my dad is an excellent judge of character.

Me: Your dad hates me. He just growled at me while setting up your furniture and only answered with grunts.

Princess: That's because he knows how I feel about you.

Me: How you feel about me?

Princess: It doesn't matter. I'm staying at Luca's tonight, so I can pick up a key tomorrow.

Me: I'll stop by the hotel and drop one off for you around lunchtime.

When she doesn't respond, I sit back on the new-to-me couch and ponder the text exchange. That is possibly the first time Arianna has ever apologized to me on her own. More than once, she's been goaded into an apology, typically by her mom, and I could always see her heart wasn't in it. For her to apologize first is new.

The comment about her dad knowing how she feels about me stumps me. I knew she had a crush on me growing up. I get that. And I lumped her actions yesterday into her being inebriated and around her friends. But I don't know if there's anything there past the off-the-charts sexual chemistry that could ignite a rainforest.

After heating up a frozen pizza and doing some laundry, I collapse into bed. I immediately groan as the scent of Arianna's perfume wafts around me in a painful embrace. Twenty-four hours ago, I had a different view of my life. It's really remarkable how quickly things can change.

Sleep eludes me, forcing me to angrily rip the sheets off the bed and throw them in the wash. After remaking the bed, I assume I'll finally be able to relax and sleep. But her scent erodes my senses. Since I was with Alex when he bought her the Marc Jacobs perfume two years ago for her birthday, and have since smelled it every time I venture into a store that sells it, I know the almond and daffodil notes. More than once, I've dreamed of tasting it on her skin. Tonight will be no different.

I'm incredibly crabby after less than five hours of sleep over two nights. When I arrive at Everlasting Inn and Spa to be told Arianna isn't available, I lose my temper. The poor teenager working at the concierge desk looked on the verge of tears after my outburst, where I demanded to see Sofia. When Sofia approaches me carefully, her look of understanding makes me even angrier.

"Give your offspring my key so she doesn't complain that I kicked her out," I spit out.

"I did hear that you told her to sleep in her car," Sofia teases.

"Well, she pissed me off."

"It wouldn't be a normal day if she didn't piss you off."

"That's the fucking truth," I murmur.

"Have you had lunch yet, Stone?" Sofia asks, motioning for me to follow her. "I'm starving. Come sit with me."

When she turns away without waiting for an answer, I give up and follow her into the hotel dining room.

Some guests feel the main lobby has the best views, while others enjoy their room views. I've always been partial to the dining room windows. Because the lighting in the dining room is always dimmer, the mountain peaks seem brighter and taller from here. My favorite time of day is twilight when the sun behind the mountains casts an ethereal glow against the peaks.

While the hotel offers a full menu, it's known for the buffet. The breakfast buffet is my favorite, but the lunch and dinner buffets have excellent selections. Once we are seated with our food, I patiently wait for Sofia to begin asking questions.

"Did you know I was in labor with Arianna for almost forty hours?" she asks, and I drop my fork loudly onto the plate. She giggles before continuing. "Most moms will tell you that every delivery gets a little shorter, and after my labor with Isabella was only a few hours, I thought Arianna would be a breeze. But, in true Arianna fashion, she came at her own speed. All of my babies were born with their faces scrunched up and wanted nothing to do with the world except to sleep, poop, and eat. But not my little *paperotta*. She wanted — no, *needed* — to see everything. I had to give up on breastfeeding because she demanded to be facing outward during feedings. It didn't surprise me when she crawled by five months and walked by eight months. She had things to do! Siblings to chase after, and discoveries to find."

"That sounds like her," I say, smiling.

"Did you know what her first word was?" she asks.

I chuckle. "Knowing Arianna, probably something like shoe, or lipstick."

Sofia doesn't laugh. "It was Tone."

"What?" I breathe, shock settling into my core.

"Her first word was Tone. She doesn't remember you much, but she was fascinated by you from the first moment you held her. She gave you her first smile, too. Not me. Not even Luca, who has always been her favorite sibling. It's always been you."

I'm incapable of responding. I remember Arianna's birth. I was eleven. I vaguely remember her parents having me hold her a few times, but I certainly don't remember a smile. But I do remember that first time in the hospital. She was the first baby I'd ever held.

Sofia must see that I'm struggling with my thoughts, because she quietly eats for a few minutes before bringing up another memory. "Do you remember the kid who accidentally pushed her down on the playground? She was two, I think."

That I do remember. "It wasn't accidental. The little fucker bragged about it to his little bitch friends."

Sofia smiles amusedly. "And he was around five or six at the time because Luca was one of his friends."

"I don't remember that part," I murmur. "Arianna screamed like she'd been shot."

"And you came to her rescue."

"Well, I wasn't going to let her sit there and be hurt," I say defensively.

"I'm not saying you should have treated the situation differently. I'm just reminiscing. You and Arianna have been interwoven in each other's lives longer than you think. I know you both remember that fight at Luca's hockey game fifteen or so years ago, and that's one of her earliest memories of the two of you. But you don't. You remember much more. I think that impacts how you both view your current relationship."

"There is no relationship, remember?" I say quietly, looking around. I'm suddenly aware of this being where her ex-boyfriend works. "Does that douche Bradley still work here?"

"For the time being, yes," Sofia responds.

"He on the way out?"

"As soon as we can legally have him removed, yes. But he's a weasel, and he will undoubtedly sue if we don't do everything by the book. I have seven children and six grandchildren. I don't have time for a lawsuit."

I bark back laughter at Sofia's expression, and Bradley appears as if he knew we were talking about him. "Mrs. Santo. How was your lunch today?"

"Excellent as always, Mr. Wetherington. You've met Arianna's boyfriend, Stone, haven't you?" Sofia asks, a vindictive glint in her eye.

Bradley coughs before extending a hand to me. "I have. Good to see you again, Stone."

I stand, moving a few inches closer to Bradley, and detect his withering posture. I have a good three or four inches on him, but he appears to shrink under my gaze. "You may call me Mr. Dixon."

"I'm glad you enjoyed your lunch, Mr. Dixon. Please, it's on me. Enjoy your day," he stammers before scampering away. Sofia bursts into laughter.

"Mr. Dixon? Really? How did you scare him this much?"

"He showed up at Arianna's last Monday. I happened to call her, and when she said he was there, I drove to her place. Caught him as he was trying to leave before I got there. I might have threatened that Alex, Dom, and I knew of a few places to dispose of a body," I tell her.

"Lord, that is perfect. You are so perfect for her, Stone."

"No, I'm not."

"You are. I know you think you're beneath her, and beneath us. That's so far from the case. Arianna needs someone who will challenge her, but fight for her at the same time. Someone who will let her control her own life, but will show up when she needs him. Call her out when she's being ridiculous, but still love her for her beautiful personality. It doesn't matter what your childhood was like, Stone. Yeah, your birth mother has always been a pain in the ass. But I raised you better than that. I raised you to be a strong man."

"You did do that," I whisper.

"Alright then. Arianna should be back in the next twenty minutes or so. She had to do the monthly Costco run for some supplies we ran out of early. I have to get back home. Nick has Aspen, and they've probably made a huge mess somewhere," she tells me before patting my hand and getting up from the table. She leans down and kisses my cheek. "You're enough, Stone. I need you to believe that."

As Arianna's mother walks away, I look out at the picturesque mountain view and ponder her words. Maybe someday I will believe her.

It's just not today.

Arianna

When the hotel staff tells me Stone had lunch with my mother, I'm both relieved, and disappointed to have missed him. Relieved that I didn't have to put on an aloof attitude and brave face. That I don't have to act like his actions didn't break me. But disappointed because my heart still wants him.

When I find a key on my office desk, I'm relieved that I can at least sleep in a bed tonight that doesn't include listening to Luca and Hannah go at it. Seriously, do they know how loud they are? I get it. You're happy and together. Wear a muzzle when you have guests.

I glared at my brother when he passionately kissed Hannah as I waited for my coffee to brew, too aggravated to recognize a goodbye kiss. Then Hannah told me Luca is off on a road trip for a week, and the marathon sex made a little more sense. I'm still pissed they kept me up all night, but at least I understand their actions now.

Mondays tend to be quite busy for the hotel. Weekend events are finished, and most guests have checked out. Lots of housekeeping tasks across the property, including my weekly tally of all consumable products for the spa, the status of washable products that might need replacing, and any required maintenance on the spa space or the hot springs. Typically, our grounds crew takes care of maintenance. Still, I always do a weekly walk-through to ensure I'm well-versed in areas that need to be closed for maintenance, when to schedule things, and what I can do to keep things running seamlessly.

While most people who frequent the hot springs are overnight guests, we sell day passes for tourists who are just in town for the afternoon, and season and yearly passes for Eternity Springs residents. Some pass holders even live in western parts of Denver, or small towns further up in the mountains. Our hot springs are well-known around Colorado, and we keep a good pace of visitors who wish to enjoy the water.

Ironically, I can't remember the last time I stepped foot in the springs past my knees. I've been known to retrieve an item for a guest, or grab debris slowly floating away, but it's been years since I've fully immersed myself in the springs and relaxed. Once I hit my twenties, I no longer found it as enjoyable. Most of my friends love the springs, but they also love to take bubble baths. I much prefer a shower. Get in, get out, get on with my day. I can read a book just as well in bed as I can in a tub, but without the awful wrinkle effect.

When Hannah frantically calls me requesting assistance with a Christmas event, right as I'm getting ready to leave for the night, I hesitate to offer up my help. It's not that I don't want to. But I'm tired. And I give every ounce of my life to this hotel. I want to pick up some greasy fast food, and go eat it in bed. Instead, I sigh, push up the sleeves on my floral puff blouse, and march as quickly to the ballroom as my pencil skirt and stilettos will allow.

As soon as I enter the ballroom, I'm thrown into chaos. Loud music makes it impossible to speak to anyone, and I'm worried about the multiple people I see dancing on the tables. It's barely dinnertime, and these people appear three sheets to the wind. How long has this party been going on?

Spotting the sound system, I root around until I find the main cord, and unplug it. The room is plunged into silence, barring one very loud and very drunk woman screeching to a song that must be in her head. It reminds me of the first night I met Hannah, and we did drunk karaoke to eighties songs.

"Oh, thank God, you're here," a breathless Hannah cries out as she collapses in a chair near me.

"What the hell is going on here?" I ask.

"Both bartenders called out sick, and when I couldn't find any replacements, the guests decided to help themselves. I'm pretty sure they pre-gamed before they got here because we don't have that much booze in here for how they're acting."

"This is an office Christmas party?"

"Accounting firm. I had the one banquet employee run to the concierge so they could call the police, because I don't think we can clear them out of here without some law enforcement present."

"Jeez. It's always the smart ones," I mutter as a man approaches us carefully, his shirt unbuttoned and his tie tied around his forehead.

"Lord have mercy," Hannah murmurs when he sways and almost sits in her lap.

"Why'd ya turn off da tunes, bitches?" he slurs.

"I beg your pardon!" Hannah gasps.

"Awe, shit. Hot bitches? Imma get in trouble, ain't I? Fuck."

"You are so out of line, Mr. Johnson. I suggest you sober up so you and your guests can vacate the premises. We'll send you an invoice including damages and a full cleaning bill, courtesy of your secretary after she vomited more than once," Hannah seethes.

"It's a party. You know what a party is, right? We're supposed to have fun."

"You've had a little too much fun, Mr. Johnson."

He leers at Hannah, then grabs his crotch. "You wanna see my johnson, Hazel?"

Hannah squints her nose in distaste. "No, I do not want to see anything of yours. My boyfriend would likely murder you."

"Bet you're just saying you have a boyfriend. Come on, when's the last time you got laid?"

"This morning," Hannah says dryly.

"Nuh-uh."

"Oh, I can confirm, considering she's dating my brother, and I stayed at their house last night. She got laid this morning. And around four. Around two in the morning, and definitely around midnight. Honestly, after the fifth or sixth time, I stopped counting," I tell him. Hannah blushes as she fights to hide the smile on her face.

Drunk Mr. Johnson stares at me. "Really?"

"Yep. You know who my brother is, right?"

He shakes his head. "Should I?"

"Considering this is my family's hotel, you should."

Mr. Johnson immediately pales. While I know he's not from Eternity Springs, it's clear he knows the area. This means he's narrowed it down to the Santo family and doesn't know which brother Hannah is with. Which one is the worst?

Probably Luca.

No, Alex and Leo would be the worst. They can get rid of a body and make it look like an accident. Or, better yet, it'll never be found.

Mr. Johnson shakes his head, a wry chuckle escaping his mouth. "Nah. You're lying. You ain't related to them."

I raise my eyebrows. "Oh? Care to test that theory?"

He gets a defiant expression as he nods. "Bring it on, bitch."

Oh, that's how he's going to play this? Let's fucking go. "Hmm. Who should we call, Han? Your man? Wait. He's on the ice in New York right now, so we can't do that. I could call Dom, but he had to go home. Alex just got home, so I don't want to call him. I know! Let's call my dad. I'm sure he'd love to hear about how you're belittling his daughter and future daughter-in-law."

Before I can get my finger on my phone, Mr. Johnson rips it out of my hands. "I think the fuck not, little girl."

"Give me back my phone!" I shout, but he shoves me hard. Hard enough that I stumble, the heel of my stiletto catching on a small tear in the carpet. As my heel stays put and gravity takes me down, my ankle buckles, and I swear I feel a pop as I hit the carpet hard.

"What the fuck is going on here?" A loud, booming voice shouts from the door. Guests scatter as I'm lifted off the ground. Mr. Johnson no longer stares distastefully at me, as my brother Alex has him by the throat. "You got a death wish, motherfucker?"

I'm too rattled to realize I'm in Stone's arms, and only when I smell his familiar cologne do I sharply inhale and stiffen in his embrace. "I've got you, Princess."

"Put me down," I whisper.

"I need to look at your ankle," he replies.

"I'm fine. Put me down."

"You're not. I saw you go down. It's at least sprained."

"How can you tell that by a fall?" I ask exasperatedly.

"It's not the fall. It's the angle. I've seen it before with my mom," he confesses. Holy shit. Stone never talks about his mom. I'm unsure of how to move forward. Ask him about his mom? The injury? Act like he didn't even speak?

"Your mom?" I end up saying.

Stone sets me on the bar and tenderly slides his hand down from my knee to my ankle before painstakingly removing my other heel. He grabs both ankles, carefully pushing my feet together, and studies them. I bite the inside of my cheek to keep from crying out. It's worse than I let on. "Yeah. She sprained her ankle a bunch of times. Mostly when she was drunk. She'd get all dressed up after convincing herself my dad was going to show up out of the blue, and she never could handle heels when she was drinking."

"Apparently, I can't handle heels when I'm sober," I joke, trying to diffuse the tension. Stone chuckles bitterly.

"Your fall had nothing to do with you, and everything to do with that asshole. What were you even doing in here, anyway?" he asks as he gently pushes against the side of my ankle.

"Two bartenders called in sick, and the crowd turned on Hannah. I was the only person left for her to call. Hannah already sent someone to concierge to call the police, but I was going to call my dad too."

"Your sixty-year-old dad shouldn't be trying to manage a crowd either, Princess."

"That was more of a scare tactic. We told the ringleader we were related to the owners. We were hoping he'd get everyone settled down out of fear."

Stone hits a tender spot on my ankle, and I cry out. He winces as if my pain somehow caused him to feel it, too, before bringing my foot to his mouth and kissing the spot gently. "I'm pretty sure sprained. We need to get you to a doctor or urgent care."

I groan as tears fill my eyes. "If I promise to go first thing in the morning, can I just go home? I'm so tired, Stone. I just want to eat dinner and go to bed."

He looks at me warily. "Promise?"

I nod. "Please. I want to go home."

"My house, or with Hannah?"

I stare at him before remembering I'm sort of homeless. "I listened to them have sex all night. I can only imagine they'll be having phone sex tonight. I really want to be somewhere quiet. Do you have any intention of having phone sex, or real sex, tonight?"

Stone must have swallowed wrong because he begins coughing. "Uh, no, Princess. I have no plans for sex of any kind tonight."

I sigh. "Fine. Your house. Since it's my left foot, can I drive?"

"I'd rather take you. I can bring you back to your car in the morning."

"Fine."

"Fine."

"What were you doing here, anyway?"

"Meeting Alex for a drink. He promised he would tell me all about his deployment."

I can't help but laugh. "He wasn't going to tell you shit."

Alex and Leo are so tight-lipped about their military deployments that it's become a running joke amongst the family. We have a bet on who will get either of them to confess something. Anything.

"I know, but I was going to try and get stuff out of him. But in all honesty, we brought his kids up here for dinner. Ran into your parents, so basically, I crashed a Santo dinner ... again. Your niece Abbie is going to be one hell of a teenager."

"Oh, yeah. She's already dealing with hormones and drama, and she's only ten!"

We both chuckle before an awkward silence wafts over us. I find myself staring expectantly at Stone, long enough to make him chuckle. "What, Princess?"

"I'm just waiting."

"Waiting for what?"

"You and I both know how this is gonna go, Stone. You're not going to let me hobble out of here. Get on with it already."

Stone tries to hide his smile but fails. "I thought maybe, just once, you'd ask nicely for some help."

I shrug. "I don't need help. I know you'll throw me over your shoulder like a caveman anyway."

He shakes his head as he carefully clutches me, but instead of putting me over his shoulder, he tenderly carries me against his chest. The adrenaline coursing through my veins only moments ago is beginning to wane, and I find myself on the cusp of tears immediately.

I hate how good this feels. How right. Like I've never given anyone else a chance because Stone was always the man I was supposed to end up with.

I hate how I recognize his scent. How I wake up smelling his cologne, even when I know he's nowhere around.

I hate that I can breathe easier in his arms than anywhere else.

But mostly, I hate that I don't hate him at all.

Before we can clear the ballroom, Bradley strides in.

"Asshole alert," Stone mutters.

"Princess, I heard you had a run-in with a paying guest," Bradley starts in, and I gasp in shock. I can tell by his tone of voice he's assuming I'm to blame.

"Back the fuck up, Bartlett," Stone booms. "That asshole assaulted her, and you act like it's her fault?"

"Well, Arianna is a flirt, and dressed like that, she's bound to bring attention to herself," Bradley sneers.

I feel Stone's body stiffen, and I struggle to think of a way to diffuse the situation. However, before either of us can react, my father arrives with my mother, and Alex's kids, on his heels.

"Mr. Wetherington, your tenure with this hotel is terminated. Remove yourself immediately before I call the police," Dad announces.

"What?" Bradley exclaims. "I didn't do anything!"

"In this instance, you are correct. You didn't do anything. The concierge staff alerted me to you watching the situation unfold on the security cameras, and you didn't bother to step in when my daughter was assaulted. Even worse, however, was how you plied the offending guest with free liquor and encouraged him to start trouble with staff, knowing we were short-staffed tonight. You purposely tried to get my daughter and soon-to-be daughter-in-law hurt, and for that, Mr. Wetherington, you are fired. Immediately."

Bradley stares at my father, his mouth open in shock, before he sputters a response. "You can't fire me! Who will replace me? I'm the head fucking chef!"

Mom gasps. "Watch your mouth, Mr. Wetherington! There are children present!"

"Well they shouldn't fucking be in here, now should they?" Bradley snaps.

"Enough," Dad says coolly. "Exit the premises now, or I'm calling the police. I will mail you your personal effects."

Bradley's face reddens as he turns to me. "You stupid bitch! This is all your fault."

Stone carefully puts me down on my right foot and turns so I'm behind him. "I'd think *very* carefully about how you want to act in the next five minutes, Bartlett. Touch her, and I will end you."

"My name is Bradley!" he screams.

"I don't give a flip what your name is. Arianna is the only name I care about, and if you so much as look cross-eyed at her, you'll regret it."

Bradley lets out a pained screech as he flies past me and into the hallway. We hear the main door open and slam into the stone entrance, then the undeniable sound of a trash receptacle being tipped over as Bradley flounces into the parking lot continuing his tantrum.

Everyone remains silent until we hear a car door slam, tires squealing, and finally, the sound of Bradley tearing out of the lot. I let out a relieved breath and rest my forehead against Stone's back.

"*Paperotta*," my mom whispers, her hand soothingly stroking my spine, "come home with us tonight. I'll take care of you."

I shake my head. If I go home with her, I'll break down. I know it. It's been one thing after another over the past week, and the last thing I need is to lose it. "I just want to eat and go to sleep, Mom. But thank you."

She sighs, giving me a sweet smile, before softly kissing my temple. She hugs Stone and whispers something in his ear before hugging Hannah. Alex approaches, handing me a bag of ice for my ankle, and asks if I want to press charges against Mr. Johnson. I almost forgot he was the reason I got hurt in the first place. "No. Just ban him from the property."

Alex nods before turning to Stone. "Raincheck on the drink?"

"Yeah, I'm gonna get her home and settled," Stone replies.

"Alright. I'll clear out this trash and make sure everything is kosher here. Get our girl home, and make sure she hits a doc tomorrow," Alex says, slapping Stone on the shoulder before giving me a kiss on the forehead.

"I'm not his girl," I whisper.

"If I can come to terms with it, so can you. You're his girl," Alex whispers back. I'm so rattled by Alex's words that I mistakenly put weight on my left foot. I cry out as my leg buckles, but Stone catches me immediately.

"You're trouble, baby girl," he mutters. Emotion clogs my throat, and I think about how only forty-eight hours ago, he called me baby girl, and it meant something different then. I lay my head on his shoulders as I can't stop the tears. "Don't cry, Princess."

I'm silent as he strides to his car. I've always thought his older 4Runner suited him perfectly. It's rugged but dependable. Older, yes, but still stylish and sleek. The shade of blue matches his eyes perfectly, and the soft interior always smells like the cologne he's worn for as long as I can remember. As I relax into the well-worn leather seat, Stone buckles me in and gently grabs my chin between his thumb and forefinger.

"Why the tears?" he asks quietly.

I shake my head before shrugging. Another tear slides down my cheek before he catches it with a finger. "Rough couple of days," I finally manage to squeak out.

He studies me, a deep line forming between his brows before he nods. Shutting the door, he quickly walks around the car before sliding in behind the wheel. Stone starts the car, but instead of driving, he turns to me. "I hate seeing you this upset, Princess."

I roll my eyes and laugh bitterly. "You're full of shit. You love getting me this riled up."

"Not even a little bit, Arianna. I can't stand making you cry."

I turn to look at him, assuming he will tease me about something, but his expression is solemn. "Then why did you do it so often?"

He sighs. "I never set out to make you cry. You always knew exactly what buttons to push to make me snap back at you, and our banter was so good that I'd forget you were just a kid. Then, when you weren't a kid, it was different. You were different."

"How so?"

His hand finds my cheek, his thumb stroking my bottom lip

slowly. "You only spoke to me when I baited you. And the more upset you got, the more real you got. Seeing your fire was like my kryptonite, Princess. Watching you take me on was the best fucking foreplay I've ever experienced. I craved it. Craved you."

"Then why are you fighting this?" I cry out, my lip quivering beneath his thumb.

"Because I'm not cut out for happily ever after. You are. I won't take anything else from you, Arianna. I've made you cry seventeen times. That's enough."

"You counted how many times you made me cry? That's kind of fucked up," I whisper.

He smiles, but it doesn't reach his eyes. "I remember everything about you, Princess. Each time you cried, I hated myself even more."

"Seventeen arguments?" I ask.

"Sixteen."

"What's the seventeenth then?"

He hesitates, struggling to formulate the words, before finally gritting out, "Sunday morning."

He didn't see me cry. I made sure of that.

But he knew, and somehow that hurts worse.

"I'm tired, Stone," I say wearily. Not only physically, but my soul is tired. I don't know how to move on from this ... and from him.

He may think I've only cried seventeen times because of him, but the number is much higher than that, and I know it will only go up.

Unrequited love is a bitch.

Stone

As soon as I said I knew how many times I made her cry, I regretted it. Not because she knew I kept count, or that it somehow emasculated me for doing so. No. I saw the look on her face and knew the number was much higher, and that fucking broke me. I hate knowing that.

After that first time she cried at Luca's hockey game, I walked on eggshells around Arianna. I was petrified of making her cry again. It was a couple years before I put my foot in my mouth and offended her again. After that, I avoided her as much as possible. It wasn't until after she turned eighteen that the arguing really ramped up, and I made her cry three times between then and her twenty-first birthday.

Once I realized I was attracted to her, the fury and disgust I felt for myself was unlike anything I'd ever experienced. I took it out on Arianna. Should I have? Absolutely not. She wasn't at fault for how I felt. But she was an easy scapegoat, and getting her riled up was the only way I could convince myself she wasn't who I wanted.

In hindsight, I realize I've wanted her since I saw her on her twenty-first birthday. I've never had such a visceral reaction to a woman before, and I should have known right then that she was different.

"I haven't even put sheets on the bed yet," Arianna blurts out, jolting me from my walk down memory lane.

"Hmm?" I murmur.

"My bed. It doesn't have sheets yet. Oh well. I can sleep on the couch my parents dropped off. They did bring a couch, right?"

"They did, but you can sleep in my bed." I'm not making her toss and turn on a couch with a bad ankle.

"You can't keep sending mixed signals, Stone. I can't — we can't —" she sputters.

"I meant you can sleep in my bed. I'll take the couch. It'll give you more room to maneuver if your ankle hurts. Or I can make up your bed if you really want to sleep in your room," I tell her before watching her yawn from the corner of my eye.

"I just want something to eat and to go to bed. I don't care where I sleep," Arianna mumbles, her eyes closing.

"I'll heat something up for you after I get you in the house," I say quietly as I pull into my driveway. When she doesn't reply, I turn off the engine, close the garage door, and quietly get out of my car. Once at her door, I unbuckle her seatbelt and slide my arms beneath her legs and back. Arianna raises her arms around me as I lift her, and her head lulls into my neck. I feel her inhale against my skin, and my traitorous dick twitches.

"You smell good," she murmurs, her lips vibrating against me, and I bite back a groan. "You know, after I turned sixteen, I spent all summer at the mall trying to figure out what cologne you wear?"

"That seems excessive," I choke out, my cock steadily thickening and forcing all blood from my brain.

"It bugged me."

"The smell bugged you?" Holding onto Arianna and opening the door into my kitchen is difficult, but I manage it.

"No, the not knowing what it was part. I loved the smell."

"Did you figure it out?" I ask as I stroll down the hall and into my bedroom.

"It's One by Dior," she whispers, and I feel her lips press against my neck in a barely there kiss. "I bought a bottle a few years ago. It came in ... handy."

"Handy?" I rasp.

"Handy. For times of ... need."

Arianna's hands tighten around my neck as I'm ready to deposit her on my bed, causing me to pause. "Times of need?"

"Uh-huh."

"What would you need with my cologne ..." I trail off as I bend down to place her on the bed, and her head dips back enough that our eyes meet. Clearly, all the blood is running straight to my cock, because I can't think. She stares at my lips for a moment before her tongue darts out to moisten hers.

"You know exactly what I mean, Stone."

Arianna drops her hands from my neck, allowing me to step back, and I don't stop until my body is flush against the wall. Clearing my throat, I say, "I, um, I'll go see what I can make for you to eat. Do you want me to get you some clothes from your room?"

"I don't know where anything is in my suitcases. I'll just sleep in my clothes," she says, but I can tell by her expression that she knows how uncomfortable it will be.

Walking to my dresser, I pull out an old tee shirt. "Here. This should be fine. I'll get you some food."

I exit my room as quickly as I can because I have a feeling Arianna would perform a strip tease for me if I had stayed a moment longer. I'm tempted to rub one out in the half bath by the kitchen to calm myself down, but the faster I get her some food, the quicker I can leave my bedroom and not go back in there. The thought of her in my sheets has me rock hard. I already washed the sheets from last night. Now I'll have to do it again. I won't survive feeling surrounded by her.

I wasn't kidding when I told Arianna I don't cook much, but our deal that she'd cook for us isn't happening now, so I guess I better figure something out for meals from now on. I combine food from two takeout meals, bag up some ice for her ankle, grab her a bottle of water and some painkillers, and say a quick prayer before heading back to my bedroom.

The prayer clearly didn't work, because I find Arianna wearing my shirt, perched on the edge of the bed, her legs dangling off the edge, and an expression far too innocent for what I know is going on in her head.

"Are you going to keep me company while I eat?" she asks sweetly. The minx has the sheer audacity to lift a hand to twirl a lock of her hair as she bites her bottom lip.

"I don't think that's a good idea," I say weakly.

Arianna smiles deviously. "Oh, I think it's the best idea I've had in a while."

I place the food on the nightstand before handing her the medicine and water. "Take this. It'll help with any potential swelling."

"If I'm being honest, not the swelling I'm concerned about," she mutters. After she swallows the meds, she makes a show of swiping her tongue across her lips luxuriously. She pats the bed next to her, but I shake my head.

"Here," I blurt out, thrusting the bag of ice at her. "Put this on your ankle. I'll check back in a little bit."

"Fine," she huffs. "Can you at least get my bag out of the car? I want to check my phone."

I quickly retrieve her belongings from my car and silently take them to her. Swiveling, I retreat from my bedroom before she can think of another way to keep me in there. I let out a long exhale of relief when I make it back to my kitchen. I don't know how long she will live here, but if this continues, I don't know how long I'll be able to hold her at arm's length.

Falling onto the couch, I scrub a hand over my face in exhaustion. I'm fucking tired. I hate admitting it, but I burn the candle at both ends most weeks. But this week, it's brutal. I'm not sleeping, eating like shit, and now I've got the equivalent of a wet dream down the hall. Short of knocking myself out with Melatonin, I don't see how I will sleep with Arianna here. When my phone buzzes in my pocket, I assume one of her brothers is texting to give me attitude.

Sam: (web link attached)

Shit. *The Eagle Has Landed* already has a picture of me carrying Ari to my car.

We aren't quite sure what to believe, as we're hearing reports that Arianna Santo was brutally attacked while at work, but also hearing that Stone Dixon threw the first punch when a paying guest at Everlasting Inn and Spa flirted with his paramour. Are these rumors true, or is the truth somewhere in the middle? In any case, Mr. Dixon does seem to enjoy carrying his decade-younger lover around. If, and when, they inevitably break up, who will be first in line to replace Ms. Santo? Yours truly, of course.

Fucking hell.

I really wish we knew who runs this site. On the one hand, I'd love to correct these ridiculous rumors. But on the other, they're half right. Arianna was assaulted. I didn't throw a punch, but I thought about it.

If I'm being honest, however, I'd like to get the originals of these pictures for myself. I may not get to have Arianna in real life, but these photos would show that I had a part of her, even if just for a moment.

Sam: Throwing punches?

Me: Hardly. Alex may have swung at the guy, but I wasn't paying attention.

Sam: And why is that?

Me: Arianna fell. The drunk dude shoved her, and she fell on her ankle. I got her out of the way of Alex and the drunk guy so I could look at her ankle.

Sam: Her brother probably could have done that.

Me: I didn't discuss it with him. We just acted. He went after the guy, and I went to her.

Sam: I find it hard to believe he'd go after some drunk guy instead of his sister.

Sam: It's almost as if he KNEW you'd go to Arianna.

Me: He didn't know that I'd go to her. For all he knew, I'd go after the dude and beat the hell out of him.

Sam: Now, why would you do that? Because you're in love with her?

Me: He assaulted a woman. It has nothing to do with feelings. It's about disrespect.

Sam: Maybe he went after the dude because he knew you wouldn't control your temper. Since he, you know, ASSAULTED THE WOMAN YOU'RE IN LOVE WITH.

Sam: You're not even telling me it's a lie, Stone.

Sam: You could at least acknowledge you're receiving these messages, though.

Me: It doesn't matter what I feel for her. Nothing more is going to happen.

Sam: MORE???

Me: There were moments over the weekend. But we stopped. I stopped. Lost my head for a little bit, but reminded myself she deserves better than some fucked-in-the-head loser who owns a barbershop and barely makes ends meet.

Sam: Damn. That's insanely negative self-talk, even for you.

Me: It is what it is. She's the Santo princess. She should marry some rich prick, live in a million-dollar house, and pop out little Ken and Barbie babies. She doesn't need any of my trailer trash history in her glass castle.

Sam: That's the thing about glass castles, though. They're all an illusion. Smoke and mirrors. Arianna doesn't strike me as the type who would choose a man based on real estate, or a bank account number. And frankly, I'm disappointed that you think so lowly of her. But it's even worse that you think all of that about yourself.

Placing my phone on the couch, my head falls into my hands as I let Sam's words marinate. Yeah, I've decided not to get married, or have kids because of my childhood. But other than Ari, I've never considered myself beneath women. What is different about her? Why do I think so poorly about myself when it comes to her?

I barely remember my dad. He left town twenty-five years ago, and I haven't heard from him since. I don't think he ever even told me he loved me. And my waste of space mother told me she hated me constantly. If genetics play a part in how people interact, their intelligence quotient, and even what jobs they're more likely to want to do, does it also play a role in whether someone can love?

What if I'm destined to be a cranky, miserable man for the rest of my life? What if I never know what it's like to be loved by someone like Arianna?

But what if she gives me a chance, and I fuck it up? Fuck her up?

What if I take that beautiful, headstrong, thriving, and amazing princess and I unintentionally break her?

"Stone?" Arianna calls out quietly. Raising my head, I find Ari braced against the wall, looking at me with a sad expression.

"What do you need, Princess?" I ask, standing to approach her. She studies me for a moment, wordlessly dissecting me with a look.

"What happened?" she whispers.

"What do you mean?"

"Just now. You're sad. You're never sad, Stone. You aren't exactly happy, but you never look like someone just killed your puppy. What's going on in that head of yours?"

I sigh as she cups my cheek softly, closing my eyes and letting her touch soothe me. "It's nothing."

"Don't lie to me," she whispers, her other hand grabbing my opposite cheek as she grips my face and shakes it lightly. "Would you agree that we've never lied to each other?"

I nod.

"We may not be the nicest to one another, but we've always been honest. So please don't lie to me now. What's going on?"

"What if I'm not capable of loving someone?" I blurt out.

Arianna's eyes widen almost imperceptibly as her hands tighten on my face. "You think you won't be able to love someone?"

"I don't know. Maybe," I mumble.

"Do you love Alex?" she asks.

I chuckle quietly. "Not what I was talking about, Princess."

"It's the same thing."

"It's not."

"It is! Stone, love is love. Alex is your best friend. Your ride-or-die. If something happened to you, or vice versa, you'd both be devastated. When you have a bad day, you turn to Alex, and he to you. That's love. Yeah, friendship and relationship love have different parameters, but the concept is the same."

"I didn't get to see how a woman loves a man," I confess.

"You saw my parents, Stone. They might not be your birth

parents, but they've loved you like one of their own from the first time you had dinner at our house."

"You weren't even born yet, Ari," I comment wryly.

"I've heard stories. My mom said she'd double or triple the lasagna whenever you came over because she knew it was your favorite. Another example of love right there."

"I still think falling in love will feel different than what I feel for your brother or your family, Princess."

Ari's eyes close as she nods. "It does feel different. But you asked if you were capable of loving someone. Not a woman. Someone. And when the right woman comes along, you'll know it."

I struggle to respond, as I want to shout that it's her. She's it, right? I've had five years of thinking about Arianna. Pushing her away because I was so painfully attracted to her, and I didn't know how to comprehend having a thing for my best friend's sister. Is it love? Am I in love with Arianna? Maybe. But those doubts creep back into the forefront of my mind, telling me she needs someone younger. Better. Smarter. Wealthier. Anyone but me, the kid from the wrong side of the tracks who just happened to find his ride-or-die in the back row of a second-grade classroom three years before Arianna Santo was even born.

Arianna came screaming into the world one fall day. When I went with Alex to the hospital to meet his new sister, their parents told me she'd barely stopped screaming since her birth. I didn't want to go to the hospital. Babies freaked me out. But my dad was in and out of the trailer a lot, my mom was drunk more often than not, and their epic fights were becoming gossip fodder for the town. Nonna Santo picked Alex up from school that day and demanded I come as well. The school already had the adult Santos down as emergency contacts for me, even though my mom definitely didn't sign off on it. Everyone, it seemed, knew my home life was a shitshow.

"You want to hold her?" Mrs. Santo asked after Alex had a quick turn. I remember staring at her in horror. Babies were tiny. Flimsy. I'd only seen a couple, but they all had that weird cone head shape and a smooshed face.

Mrs. Santo laughed and handed me this swaddled thing. I was two seconds away from handing it back to her when the thing let out a loud squawk before opening its eyes. As soon as our eyes met, the thing stopped screeching and stared at me. Her eyes were an odd bluish-gray.

"Thought it would have brown eyes," I commented.

"They'll probably change to brown, but maybe they won't," Mrs. Santo explained. "You have a way with her, Stone. She hasn't stopped crying all day."

"I've never held a baby before. What's its name?"

"It's a girl, so you say 'she' or 'her,' Stone. Her name is Arianna."

"Pretty," I whispered.

I don't remember anything else anyone said that day. But I remember her. And her eyes. And how much she captivated me, even as an eleven-year-old.

"I finished my food. I just wanted a glass of water," Arianna whispers. I'm thrust back into the present day, my hands holding her waist, her own hands having fallen from my face, and I'm aflame with embarrassment.

"I'm sorry. Lost in my head. How's your ankle? I'll get you some water." I let go of her waist and step around Arianna to get her another bottle of water. When I exit the kitchen, I find her hopping on her right foot down the hallway, and my gaze zeroes in on the delectable curve of her ass as my shirt sways up and down with each hop. Holy shit. One glance and I'm hard as steel, my only thought is how I want to drop to my knees and worship that crease with my tongue.

"Nonna. Mr. Santo. Old man balls. Alex. Alex will kill you. Mr. Santo will kill you. Old man balls. Balls. Balls. Balls." I whisper, trying to calm myself down. I cannot go in there with any kind of chub. Knowing Arianna, she'll pounce like a panther and devour me whole.

And until I get my emotions in check, I can't do anything with her. I won't be that guy to her again. I won't take something from Arianna without being able to give her all of myself.

*A*rianna

So much makes sense now. I've never fully understood how Stone's parents damaged him until now. I knew his home life was bad, but it didn't occur to me that he'd think he was incapable of loving someone else.

He's capable of so much more than he thinks.

Without a doubt, I know Stone would kill for Alex if needed. He'd adopt Alex's kids if it came to that, and spend every waking moment raising them to remember Alex. Stone will do, and has done, whatever my mom wants around the hotel. I hadn't known how much he helped out until he mentioned it, and when I asked my mom, she winked and told me I wasn't in a place to realize it yet. What the hell does that even mean? I've never told her about my adolescent crush on Stone, but did she know? Was she waiting for me to confide in her?

I'm so confused.

I hate knowing that Stone isn't ready for anything with me, but it's worse not knowing if he'll ever be prepared. Obviously, we have chemistry, but he's stuck in this rut, thinking he's not good enough for me. I wish I could convince him otherwise. Show him that I think he's perfect exactly as he is.

I'm twenty-six years old. I've slept with exactly five men and have seriously dated two. I've been on countless first, second, and third dates, and as soon as I put the "does he compare to Stone" card up, I'd realize that I was wasting my time. No one has come close to igniting me the way Stone does. Now that I've kissed him a few times, I realize that even my more serious boyfriends didn't compare. There's no one like Stone, and I wish I could get him to see that.

As I carefully climb back onto Stone's bed, I take in a deep inhale, trying to quell my emotions. The evening has been exhausting, both mentally and physically, and now it's taking on a new emotional turmoil I didn't think was possible. I feel like the only way I could make myself feel better is to either cry myself to sleep, or to have life-altering sex. Since one of those clearly isn't happening, I'm hoping I can get Stone to leave the bedroom and allow me to quietly cry alone.

"Do you need anything before bed?" Stone stammers from the doorway. I look at him and find his gaze zeroed in on my legs. When I look down, I realize it's because his tee shirt has ridden up, revealing my baby pink thong. My own gaze tracks to his crotch, and I detect a substantial bulge.

In some cases, I'd be excited to get this reaction from him. But at this moment, it pisses me off. I slam my knees together, prohibiting him from continuing his lascivious perusal.

"Hey!" I growl, snapping my fingers in front of my legs, then drag my hand upward. Stone's eyes follow my hand until our eyes meet. "You made yourself clear, Stone. There will be no 'us,' so you don't get to look at me there."

"I made myself clear?" he finally asks.

"More than once," I whisper. I shake my head as if to stop the conversation and rise to my right foot. Jumping to the en suite bathroom, I stop when I reach the sink. "Can you get me a toothbrush? I have one in my purse."

I hear him rifling through my purse momentarily before quietly shuffling into the bathroom beside me. I brace myself against the counter while I begin brushing, all too aware of Stone's presence next to me. When he finally speaks up, I'm not ready for his words.

"The first time I dreamed about fucking you was just after your nineteenth birthday," he states clearly, and I immediately choke on the toothpaste on my tongue. "I chalked it up to being a one-off, and it didn't happen again until right before your twenty-first birthday. That time, though, I saw you again right after, and I realized you weren't a kid anymore. But God, Princess, I felt so fucking guilty. Like I was some dirty old guy, skeeving on a little girl. It didn't matter that you were technically an adult. It mattered that Alex was your brother, and I was eleven years older than you. It still matters."

"Stone —"

"No. Let me finish. Five fucking years, Arianna. Five years I've dreamed of you. Lusted for you. I couldn't get off without imagining your face. Twice, I said your name during sex, and I can't even tell you how often I called a girl princess because I was imagining your body beneath mine. Do you know how fucked up that is? And whenever Alex asked, hinted, for me to check in on you, I felt like a liar to both of you. I couldn't tell you that I wanted you with every piece of my soul, and I couldn't tell him either."

I spit out the toothpaste as he continues.

"But that's not the only thing. You're meant for greatness, baby girl. You're meant for a husband, kids, the perfect house, and the perfect family. You deserve those things. I don't. I've always known that. I'm trash, and I came from trash. I'm not the guy you bring home to your parents. I'm the guy you fuck in an alley behind the bar because your friends dared you to. I'm the guy who you complain to about your boyfriend after I've finished going down on you, but not the guy who gets all of you. I've come to terms with that. No self-respecting woman should want to take me on, you know? Which is why I've never allowed myself to think about actually pursuing you. Dreaming about you is one thing, but chaining you to this life is another. You deserve the world. And I know I'll never be able to give that to you." His tone is soft, but resolute, as he stares down at the sink. He's not angry or sad. He's resigned himself to what he thinks is his lot in life.

Openly crying, I can barely see Stone's reflection in the mirror. When I think I understand him, he reveals another layer I didn't see coming. "I had no idea you thought this of yourself, Stone. I didn't know."

"No one knows."

"Not even Alex?"

"Not even Alex."

"Why not?"

Stone sighs, scrubbing a hand harshly on his face. "Because I'd have to explain that I've wanted you for years. I couldn't lose him over something I had no intention of acting on."

"You really think he wouldn't forgive you?"

"Couldn't take that chance, Princess."

"I don't think you're giving him enough credit, Stone. He wouldn't end your friendship over being attracted to me."

"It's not just an attraction," he murmurs.

"It's not?" I ask.

Stone's eyes meet mine in the mirror. "You know it's not. I've never wanted more with a woman before, Arianna. But it's always been different with you. I just don't know how much I can give you, and that's not fair to you. You deserve someone who is all in with you. And I don't see any reason to make you waste time with me when you could find someone you have a future with."

"And I don't have a future with you?" I ask, speaking slowly so my voice doesn't tremble.

"I don't know. I'm not saying no, but I can't say yes with certainty, either. I'll always think you deserve more than me."

"I disagree," I say clearly. Stone's confused gaze meets mine. "I'll always think you are more than you believe. Jesus, Stone. I've been comparing every guy I meet to you in my head for as long as I can remember. Surely that means something."

His mouth tips up in a hint of a smile. "You compare everyone to me?"

I nod.

Stone steps closer to me. "What do you compare?"

"How I feel when I'm with someone. Whether or not I can feel the chemistry. How they smell. How they dress. If they'd fit in with my family. How I imagine it would feel to be with you …" I trail off as his head ducks to my shoulder, then whimper when his lips softly touch the sensitive skin behind my left ear.

"Go on," he whispers against my neck, his hot breath causing goosebumps to scatter down my arms.

Clearing my throat, I whisper, "How it would feel to be taken by you. To have you inside me. To come because of you."

"Have you thought of me often?"

"All the time," I moan. His lips drag along my neck before tracking back to my ear, nibbling gently on the lobe. "I've gotten in trouble for saying your name too."

"Oh yeah?"

"Yeah." Stone's arms now bracket me against the counter, and I can feel his length nestled into my ass crack. I want to reach around and touch him, but I'm balanced on one foot, and I fear if my knee buckles, I'll collapse in a very unladylike heap.

As if he can read my thoughts, one arm slides around my waist and pulls me backward. His voice is deep and gritty against my ear. "I'm worried you'll regret anything with me."

"Not possible," I breathe, my eyes closing as I sigh in bliss. Stone's hand curls around my hip, his fingers digging into my skin.

"I don't know how to promise forever, baby girl. All I can promise is you'll get more of me than anyone else has before. I'll try my best because you're fucking worth it. But I can't promise you everything you deserve. If you aren't on board with that, then this stops right now, and we'll move on like it never happened."

I shiver against him as I consider his words. "What can you promise me, Stone? Honesty? Exclusivity? Time?"

"Open your eyes, Princess," he demands. Once my eyes are open, he nods. "I've never lied to you, Arianna. Never. And that won't change now."

"Okay."

"And if we do this? If we really do this, then fuck, yes, it's exclusive. You're mine, and I'm yours. Alright?"

I nod.

"As for time ..." he trails off, hesitating. "I'll give you what I can. But when I'm available, you'll have me."

"I know you're busy, Stone. So am I. I just want to know that I'm important to you," I say quietly. I feel him stiffen behind me momentarily before his arm tightens around my waist. He turns and lifts me so I'm sitting on the counter.

"Baby girl, look at me," he says. "Don't ever doubt that you're important to me. No one comes close. You and your mom. That's it. Your mom is wonderful, but it's you, okay? You're the most important woman in my life."

"Really?" I whisper.

"Really," he replies, his eyes widening as if it suddenly dawned on him how he feels about me. "Holy shit, Princess. I should have realized that. Should have noticed sooner how important you are to me. How important you've always been to me. Yeah, we argue. We fight. But I'd burn down the world if you needed me to, and I should have recognized that. Should have realized it years ago."

"Would it have changed anything?" I ask softly.

Stone stares at me, contemplating his answer, before he slowly nods. "If you had asked me that a week ago, I would have said no. But now? Right now, baby girl, fuck yes it would have changed things. Dammit, all this wasted time —"

"It's not wasted time, Stone," I blurt out, interrupting him. "Not if you needed it. It doesn't matter how long it took you to realize your feelings for me. But, what happens if ..."

"What?"

I take a deep breath, metaphorically putting on my big-girl panties, and trudge forward with my most feared question. "What if this doesn't work? You change your mind and decide you don't want me. That this is too hard to do."

Stone sighs as he rests his forehead against mine. The subtle movement is so poignant and heartfelt that I almost begin to cry again. "I can't answer that, baby girl. All I know is I don't want to fight this anymore. And I can't fight you anymore. So how about we just take it one day at a time? We don't need to worry ourselves about a future that is irrelevant to today. One step at a time."

"One step at a time," I repeat. "Stone?"

"Yeah?"

"Take me to bed."

He lets out a rushed breath against my mouth and chuckles in relief. "Gladly."

I gasp as Stone grabs my thighs, lifting me and walks back into the bedroom. "You'll tell me if your ankle hurts?"

I nod against him as I bury my face in his neck. If he stops now, I don't think I'll survive. I feel like we're finally on the same page.

"Princess," he says softly as he sets me on the edge of the bed, "are you absolutely sure about this? Say the word, and we can act like this entire conversation never happened."

"Don't you dare!" I yell. "You are not taking this back. We're finally on the same page, dammit. Now get on with it and fuck me!"

Stone throws back his head with a loud guffaw of laughter. "As you wish."

I expect him to push me back and lay on top of me, but he steps back a few feet from the bed.

"What are you doing?" I ask nervously.

"What?"

"Shouldn't you be on the bed instead of moving further away?"

"How about you let me 'get on with it' how I see fit, Princess?" he teases with air quotes.

"But ... seriously, what are you doing?" I ask as his eyes take a leisurely stroll down my body. My skin prickles with anticipation as I watch him. His gaze stops on my chest, sharpening imperceptibly, and my nipples tighten in anticipation. Stone licks his lips in response, and I whimper. His hands find the hem of his shirt, and he slowly raises it to remove it. Every inch he exposes makes me breathe harder. It's been six months since I saw him shirtless when he rescued me after the flat tire debacle, and the memory has starred in every single fantasy since then. I don't know if Stone understands how beautiful his physique is. He has a fantastic set of abs and has the best forearms I've ever seen. I'm sure it's due to years of using his hands, but a smattering of tattoos covering one arm also adds to the mystique of the man. When I catch Stone chuckling, I realize I'm unabashedly staring at him and blatantly salivating over the promise of pleasure with him.

"You about done?" he asks, one brow cocked, his hands on his hips.

Two can play at that game.

Figuring I can wipe that smirk right off his face, I grab his tee shirt at the hem and whip it off. As I suspected, the smile drops from his face as he stares at my chest. I'm not the most well-endowed woman out there, but I've got healthy handfuls, and I'd say from Stone's expression that he's a fan. His expression becomes hooded as he licks his lips sensuously. I decide to flirt with danger a bit, dragging my hand up to grab one breast, pinching the nipple between my thumb and forefinger. He tsks and shakes his head. "Uh-uh, Princess. Hands off my merchandise."

"Yours?" I choke out, surprised at how turned on I am by Stone referring to my breasts as his.

"Mine. You need to understand this about me, baby girl. I may fight with you. I might even enjoy going toe-to-toe with you and get off on it. But right here? In my fucking bedroom? I call the shots. I run this show. I'll make you feel so fucking good, Arianna. You won't regret giving me control. You with me?" His pupils blown out,

Stone's intensity is unnerving. Sensuality oozes off of him as he patiently waits for my response.

Woah. Having forgotten how to speak, I nod emphatically. Stone's smirk turns feral as he saunters toward me. His hand reaches out to gently grasp my neck, one finger resting against my pulse point. My pulse is wild, and Stone's eyes darken when he realizes how turned on I am.

"Hard limits, Princess?"

"Huh?" I ask.

"Limits. What are your deal breakers?"

"Oh," I respond, embarrassed. I've never thought about limits. I guess my experiences so far have been pretty vanilla. "I don't know."

Stone's hand finds my chin, pulling up until my downcast gaze meets his. "There's nothing to be concerned or embarrassed about, Arianna. Day by day, remember? Step by step. Just tell me if there's a certain area of your body you'd rather I not touch, okay?"

"Oh, no. There's nothing, I don't think," I stammer. Stone cocks his head to the side, studying me for a moment, before slipping his hand down my side. Dragging his fingers along the side of my breast, I inhale quickly as a burst of pleasurable sensation engulfs my skin. Stone's hand dips down to my hip, sliding along my ass, before tracing along the seam of my thong. He stops just above my asshole, and I forget how to breathe.

"What about here, Princess? Anyone ever touch you here? What about sex here?" he asks quietly. I vehemently shake my head no, but even I can tell by my increased breaths that I'm curious. Just having his finger so close to my forbidden hole has me drenched. "Would you let me? If I asked, would you let me take your ass?"

"Mm — maybe," I stutter. I feel like the temperature has risen twenty degrees in Stone's bedroom. My skin is on fire. If he doesn't actually touch me in the next few minutes, I'm liable to burst into flames.

"Let's have a safe word, Princess. I think that would be helpful, in case I push you further than you're ready to go," Stone says, his hand skirting away from my ass and instead sliding between my thighs. Just the tip of one finger drags along my seam, and he groans when he feels how wet I am. "Jesus, Arianna. Can't fucking wait to get your taste on my tongue."

"Yes, God, yes, please," I moan. I attempt to lay back on the bed, but Stone stops me.

"Stay upright. Watch as I eat you," Stone murmurs as he grabs both sides of my thong. "You partial to these?"

I shake my head. A very basic thong. Nothing special about it. I had no idea today would go the way it did. Stone gives me a grin before ripping the thong off my body. I gasp, more in shock than from actual pain, as he discards the broken fabric next to his feet and pushes my thighs further apart.

"Castle."

"What?" I ask.

"Your safe word. A princess is safe in a castle, so it's perfect," he says, and before I can respond, he leans down and drags his nose through my folds. I feel him take a deep inhale as he does, and it's remarkably raunchy and sexy at the same time. "Jesus fuck, baby girl. You smell spectacular."

Given Stone's earlier comment about him controlling the bedroom activities, I expect him to tease me mercilessly. If anyone I know would be into edging, it would be Stone. Which is why I'm completely unprepared for him to latch onto my clit and suck so hard that I immediately come. My eyes roll back as the most brutal orgasm I've ever experienced rolls across my body with aftershocks so intense I collapse on the bed. Expecting him to be like every other guy and immediately impale me so he can get his, I'm surprised when he doesn't let up. In fact, he doesn't even give me time to rest. His pace doesn't slow or falter. I'm on the edge of another orgasm quickly, and he catapults me over the cliff by sliding one finger into my pussy and finding my G-spot.

"Give me one more," he growls against me, the deep vibrations of his voice exciting me even more.

"Stone, I can't," I moan brokenly, thrashing on the bed.

"Yes, you can. Give it to me, baby girl. Give me what's mine," he says, adding a second finger against my G-spot and nipping at my clit with his teeth.

Stone's remaining hand slides up my abdomen to cup my breast, and he pinches my nipple harshly. With my clit still sucked into his mouth, and his tongue flicking against it, the zing of pain from my nipple shoots directly to my clit, and I come again.

"Castle," I whimper.

"Good girl."

I feel my pussy clench around his fingers, and I realize I'm totally screwed. In more ways than one. There's no way Stone won't completely own me after this, and if it ends, I don't think I'll come back from it. Stone has officially ruined me for any other man.

Chapter 17

Stone

*A*rianna has officially ruined me for any other woman.

There's no other way to explain it.

I figured she'd put up a fight about who has control. Honestly, I did. She fights with me about everything. I figured I'd be able to convince her, eventually, but she was on board from the get-go. We haven't talked numbers, but I'm fairly certain she hasn't been with that many guys, and her experiences are clearly on the vanilla side of the spectrum. But to see her pupils blow wide when I suggested taking her ass?

My Princess is a dirty girl, and I'm the lucky son of a bitch who gets to bring that side out of her. This is going to be so much fucking fun.

As I rise to my feet, I'm unprepared for her to grab me and yank me down on top of her, taking my lips in a deep kiss. I know she can taste herself, and it seems she gets off on it. The kiss is passionate and sensual. This kiss describes Arianna perfectly. Fire, sass, and sex appeal. It's a kiss I'll compare to every kiss I have for the rest of my life.

When her hand reaches down to cup me against my jeans, I jump back. I'm so aroused right now I could come from even the smallest amount of pressure.

"What's wrong?" Arianna asks.

"I need a moment," I grit out. Old man balls. Old man balls. Old fucking man balls.

"Are you second-guessing things?" she whispers.

Fuck. "No. No, absolutely not. I'm two seconds away from coming, and you haven't even touched me. I'm trying to get a handle on things before embarrassing myself," I confess. Her eyes brighten. "Let me get a condom."

"Oh, um, I'm on birth control," she stammers uncertainly. I groan, the thought of taking her raw like adding fuel to an out-of-control fire, and I struggle to keep my composure.

"While I'd like nothing better than to feel you like that, I need a layer between us, or I'm really going to embarrass myself. And Princess, I want this to last longer than five seconds."

"Okay," she whispers, but I see the hurt in her eyes. Shit.

"Arianna," I say. "Trust me when I say that I want you bare. God, I fucking want you so badly it hurts. But I can't go without this time. I need to feel you come on my cock right now. I need it. Do you understand? I've dreamed of this so many fucking times, and now that I have you, I'm not going to be a two-pump chump. I want to blow your mind."

She giggles lightly. "You've already done that, Stone. But we can talk about it another time."

There will be another time, I say silently to myself. There has to be. I already know Arianna will be the best I've ever had, and I'm not cool with this being a one-time thing.

"Unbutton my pants," I demand, my voice breaking slightly as I try to keep calm. Arianna's delicate hands slowly unbutton my jeans, and she pushes them off my hips. My swollen cock, finally freed from one layer of fabric, strains to explode out of my boxer briefs. Her eyes widen when she sees the outline. "Ever seen a pierced dick before?"

Arianna shakes her head as she drags one finger along the ridge outlining my Jacob's Ladder piercing. I've been blessed in the penis department. I'm rocking a girthy eight inches, and I've added four barbells of the Jacob's ladder along the underside of my cock. I've always enjoyed a little pain with my pleasure, and I haven't had any complaints from women. But as Arianna grabs my boxer briefs by the hem and slowly drags them down my length, I realize a second too late what she's about to do, and I can't stop it.

One luxurious lick from the base of my shaft to the tip before she sucks the head into her mouth, and I can't stop the tsunami of my release. "Shit, fuck, I can't — I'm coming —"

My hands find her hair as I unload, unable to even pull out of her mouth. One fucking lick. That was all it took. That's how turned on I was. How badly I wanted her. How I *needed* her. I can't focus on anything, the room spinning as my body shudders through the release.

And the little vixen doesn't miss one drop.

"Jesus Christ," I pant as my dick finally pops from her mouth. My knees buckle, and I barely have time to step to the side before I collapse next to her on the bed. "What the fuck was that?"

"I'm sorry. I couldn't help myself," Arianna says sweetly.

"I don't think you're even a little bit sorry."

"Yeah, I'm not sorry at all," she giggles. I chuckle as I struggle to regulate my breathing. I've never come that fast. "I shouldn't have done that, though. I really wanted you to fuck me. I didn't think it through."

"What do you mean?"

"Well, you came, so we're done for the night, right?" she asks.

"Damn. Give me about thirty minutes to recover, and I'll be good to go."

"Seriously?" Arianna's eyes bug out. "That can't be normal. Can it? I mean, even you? You're old ..."

"Nice."

"I didn't mean it as it sounded. At least not this time," she giggles. God, I love making her giggle.

"I can't speak for other men, but I'm typically not a one-and-done guy. So get some rest, baby girl. I can go all night."

"Oh, praise Jesus," she murmurs.

"How's your ankle?" I ask as I pull up my boxers. Arianna has the nerve to pout as my dick disappears below the fabric. "I'm just stepping out to get some water, Princess. Do you need any ice for your ankle?"

"I can't even feel it anymore, to be honest," Arianna responds. I take a quick look, nodding as I confirm no extra swelling or discoloration, before leaning down to place a soft kiss against her ankle. Jogging to the kitchen, I grab two water bottles before returning to my bedroom. Arianna is exactly where I left her, stretched out in all her naked glory. It's a pity she ever wears clothes. Honestly, if I had my way, she'd be naked all the time. Her body should be celebrated like the female version of Michelangelo's David statue. I'd worship at her feet every damn day. When her eyes open and she smiles, I almost drop to my feet right then.

"You okay?" she asks, and I realize I must be staring at her.

"Yeah, I'm good. Better than good, actually," I answer. Arianna's smile widens, her eyes sparkling.

"You shouldn't have fought this as long as you did, Stone. We could have been doing this all along," she teases.

"Doing what exactly?" I ask, dropping my boxers before I stretch on top of her. Her cheeks blush adorably as she bites her lip. I lean down and catch her lip between my own teeth, pulling it away from hers, then lave her lip with my tongue. My tongue slips into Arianna's mouth, where it tangles with hers, and she slides her hands around my back to dig her nails into my skin.

Our kiss turns salacious. Like a summer thunderstorm approaching the shore, it was nothing until it was everything. *Until she consumed me.* I find myself losing control as Arianna's taste and scent are all I can feel. When her legs wrap around me, forcing my cock to hit her warm and wet center, it's a natural reflex to slide inside. Arianna lets out a guttural moan as my piercings slowly push against her channel.

"Stone, I feel them," she whimpers. A Jacob's Ladder is designed to be felt best in non-missionary positions, but I can't move her. Not right now. Buried to the hilt, with every inch of her skin pressed against me, and our eyes locked, I can't break this connection. I push my arms under her upper back so we're as close as can be before I slowly begin to move.

I feel Arianna in every molecule.

Every cell.

My skin vibrates with pleasure as I make love to her. That's what this is. It's not sex. It sure as hell isn't fucking. This is making love. Our souls speaking to one another. And I see it the moment Arianna realizes it, too. Her eyes fill with tears as one hand cups my cheek. "Stone —"

"I know, Princess."

I should speed up. I can feel her orgasm gaining speed, and I could speed up to push her over the edge. But I can't. I won't. I've never felt this before and want it to last forever. If she changes her mind about me and decides to end this, I want to have this memory.

"Stone, I need to come," Arianna whispers. Her hands clutch at me, flying over my skin as she tries to find traction. I can feel my own orgasm creeping up on me, a tingling at the base of my spine. Each time Arianna digs her nails into my skin, that sharp pain sends a spike into my spine, sending me closer and closer. When she stiffens against me, her eyes rolling back in her head as she comes with a loud moan, I can't hold off any longer. The spasms around my cock force my own orgasm as I shoot my load deep into her. It's a much different sensation than I've experienced before.

I've never come inside a woman raw before.

The last thing I think before I collapse against Arianna's damp and sated skin is how I hope she ends up pregnant.

I've never thought about having kids. I assumed it wasn't in the cards for me. Assumed that it *shouldn't* be in the cards for me. But with Arianna, it's different. I'm different. The thought of her pregnant, watching her belly grow, and getting to experience that with her, makes me happier than I ever thought possible. For the first time in my life, I'm excited for the future. I can't help but smile against her hair, finally feeling like I'm where I'm supposed to be. Wrapped up in my Princess.

I'm ridiculously pleased when I find Arianna surrounding me the following morning. I have at least seven inches and seventy-five pounds on her, but Arianna is half on top of me and half using most of my king-size bed. I've been smushed into the farthest corner of the bed, one leg hanging precariously off the edge. But I'm not moving. Arianna's head is buried against my neck, one arm wrapped around my chest, and I'll be damned if I'm waking her up anytime soon. This reminds me of how we woke up in Vail, tangled together.

Laying here, holding her, allows me the extra time I need to wrap my head around everything that has happened over the past week. I know I've been all over the place with Arianna. Hell, I'm still not entirely sure of where we stand. I know she deserves better than what I can offer. She should want more than what I have. But I don't know if I'll be able to push her away now that I've been with her like this. Now that I know how she sounds when she comes with me inside her.

I don't know what I'll do if, or when, she realizes she's so fucking out of my league.

"You're thinking way too hard, old man," she purrs against my neck, her voice husky with sleep. "You're not supposed to wake a woman up with your dang thoughts. I need beauty sleep."

"You're perfect, Princess. You don't need beauty sleep," I murmur, pressing my lips against her hair while tightening my arms around her body. We're quiet for a few minutes, both lost in our thoughts until Arianna breaks the silence.

"No regrets?" she asks quietly.

"No. Absolutely not."

She sighs in relief, her body sinking further against mine. "Me neither."

"Did you think I'd have regrets?"

"I don't know. Maybe. You've been hot and cold, Stone. I'm freaked you're going to pull the rug out from under me again."

I let out a deep exhale as I realize how correct she is. "You're right. I don't know what the hell I'm doing here. This is all new to me. Not only a relationship, but it's *you*. I've had you pushed into that untouchable box in my brain for so long. It's hard to de-compartmentalize you."

"Are you going to tell Alex?" she whispers.

"I'd like to. I want to come clean to your family. But I'm scared of how they'll react. I don't have siblings, baby girl. I don't know what they're thinking. They're the only real family I've ever known, and I'm petrified of losing them."

"How would you lose them?"

I struggle to formulate my words. How do I explain what I'm thinking without hurting her feelings. "Sit up so I can see your face, Princess."

Arianna immediately sits up, turning to face me. The minimal light from my bedroom windows casts an ethereal glow around her shoulders. Her beautiful hair is in disarray, and there's a red mark on her face where she was positioned over my collarbone. Her eyes look tired, and her lips appear slightly swollen from all our kisses. Even with dried saliva on the corner of her mouth, she's the most breathtaking woman I've ever seen.

"I need you to look at this from my point of view, okay?" I ask, and she nods. "If anything goes south between us. I'm just talking about an argument, a full-on fight, or a breakup. They'll pick you. And frankly, of course, they would. You're blood. A daughter and sister. I'm just a friend who piggybacked through the majority of my life. I'm expendable. And that scares the shit out of me, Arianna. They're the only real family I've ever known."

A solitary tear slides down her cheek as she tries to smile. "You may not be blood, but they're your family too. I'd like to think they wouldn't choose between us, Stone. But it hurts my heart that you think so lowly of my family and automatically assume we won't work out."

"It's not that I'm assuming anything. I'm looking at it from all angles."

"I don't think I believe you," she says, her eyes narrowing. "Just when I think we've taken one step forward, you take a massive leap backward. It's exhausting."

"I have thought about what happens if we stay together," I reply.

"Prove it," she challenges. I almost roll my eyes. Damn woman and her desire to challenge me at every step.

"Fine. You want to know what I've thought about?" I ask, pushing up to slide back until my back hits the headboard. She immediately moves toward me, almost subconsciously, as if she can't be further from me than a foot away. And I fucking love it. "I've thought about how I'd ask your dad for your hand in marriage. How I'd propose. Keeping Alex from kicking my ass. Our wedding, and where I could afford to take you on a honeymoon. I've dreamed about all the places we could have sex, and wondering if you'd let me tie you up."

Arianna's breath catches, and my eyes dip toward her mouth, where her tongue darts out to wet her lips. I can't help the smirk that erupts on my face as I continue, knowing she'll definitely be on board with being tied up. "I've thought about what it might be like when you tell me you're pregnant, and finding out it's a boy. Telling your parents and Nonna about the baby. I've thought about family dinners, movie nights, and waking up every fucking morning like we did this morning. Even when I knew you deserved someone better, I've thought about you, baby girl. Dreamed about you. *Wished* for you. I've thought about it all, Arianna. I may not verbalize every damn thought I have like you invariably do, but I've thought things."

A hint of a smile graces her beautiful face as she replies, "And you think you can't love."

"That's what you got from that monologue?"

"That you're in love with me? Yeah, pretty much."

A moment of panic sets in as I run through what I said. "Wait, I didn't say that —"

"It's okay, honey. You haven't said it out loud yet. You'll get there eventually. I'm fine with waiting you out." Arianna leans forward and gives me a quick kiss before jumping out of the bed. "I have to get ready for work. You have a coffee maker, right? Can I use your shower? Can you bring my toiletries bag in? It's in the biggest suitcase, I think. Just root around until you find it."

I'm speechless as I watch her hobble to the bathroom. While she's not walking perfectly, she can put more weight on her foot.

"Stone?" she calls out from the doorway. When I look up, she smiles. "I'm cool with keeping this a secret for now. I know you need time to get your head sorted. The whole family thinks we're fake dating to save face with Bradley. Is that over? Just so I'm prepared."

"I guess we are still fake dating," I mumble, scratching my chin.

"Okay. Hurry up with my toiletries, old man," she teases. "I'll let you wash my back if I can wash yours."

As I absentmindedly go to Arianna's room and retrieve her things, I feel like I just jumped in and out of a hurricane.

Chuckling, I take her bag to the bathroom. Hurricane Arianna could be just what I needed in my life.

Chapter
18

Arianna

I assumed Stone would kiss me a few times, and maybe tease me about things, but I was unprepared for how he basically doted on me in the shower. It was exquisite. He held me against his chest as he carefully lathered my hair, his adept fingers massaging my scalp at the perfect pressure. When he tipped my head back to wash out the shampoo, his head dipped to give me the most tender kiss ever.

He could probably hear my heart screaming our love for him.

I've never felt so treasured before.

I may have been a little disappointed we didn't have sex again, but I wouldn't trade that experience for anything. No one has ever made me feel so special. So wanted. So loved.

Stone may think he is incapable of love, but he already gives so much. I just need him to see for himself what a catch he is. Then I need to lock him down before he realizes I'm a hot mess and leaves me for someone better.

"Do you need me to call someone for a ride so you can get to work?" I ask him as I carefully slide on a pair of unflattering boots. They aren't stylish at all, but they're comfortable, and I'm less likely to trip and screw up my other ankle while at work today. We agree that I must have just slightly twisted it because it feels much better this morning.

"Shop doesn't open for another hour. I'm taking you to work and making sure you make it to your desk okay," Stone says, raising an eyebrow as if to challenge me to argue with his statement. I just smile sweetly at him.

"Okay."

"Okay? You aren't going to argue?"

"Not this time."

"Just when I think I have you figured out, Santo, you throw me for a loop."

"Gotta keep you on your toes, Dixon."

As I gingerly walk past him into his garage, he swats me on the ass. I gasp, whipping around to face him. "Gotta keep you on your toes, too, Princess."

I don't respond as I hold a hand over the throbbing section of my ass. I'm weirded out by how hot that was. How hot it felt. I open the passenger door to Stone's car, and his hand reaches out to wind around my waist, drawing me back against him.

"You liked that, didn't you, baby girl?" he whispers against my ear. I whimper in reply, to which he chuckles. The sensation reverberates across my skin, causing goosebumps to dance down my shoulders and décolletage. "It really is a shame you're late for work. I'd like to find out how wet you are right now."

"Dammit, Stone, you're not supposed to send me to work like this," I hiss as he lets go of my waist and motions for me to slide into the seat.

"You have any idea how many times you gave me blue balls? I think you can handle one day of edging."

"That won't be necessary. I'll get myself off at work," I tell him haughtily. It wouldn't be the first time I'd needed a release at work, and most, if not all, of the times I've had to masturbate at work, were due to Stone. Seeing him in passing would get me so worked up that I couldn't focus.

"You better not, Princess."

"Or what?"

Stone throws the car in reverse, pulling out of his garage and onto the street before looking at me. "I'll make you edge so long you pass out without an orgasm. Hours, Princess. Hours."

"How on earth would you do that?" I tease. It can't be possible, can it?

"Well, first, I'd tie you to the bed so you couldn't move. Couldn't touch yourself when you got frustrated. Then I'd blindfold you so you couldn't see what I'd be up to. Maybe even fill your mouth with your own panties so you couldn't bitch me out. Then I'd play. I'd learn what gets you going, and how quickly you get riled up. Then, I'd avoid doing those things. Hours. I'd have you a sweaty and quivering mess all fucking night, baby girl. And the only one who'd come is me."

Stone's face remains composed as he glances at me, but I know his words turned him on as much as they did me when he reaches to adjust himself. My own thighs clench together of their own volition, trying to find the friction I need. My face feels hot, and my labored breathing gives away how turned on I am.

"Be a good girl and wait for me, okay?" he whispers as he opens my car door and helps me out.

He's got me all hot and bothered, and my bratty side comes out strong in the only way I know to affect him the same way. "Okay, Daddy."

Stone's eyes darken as he lets out a deep groan. He might claim he doesn't get off on being called Daddy, but as he pulls me against him, I feel the evidence of what that word does to him.

This day better go by fucking fast. I'm so hot and bothered that I think walking from the parking lot to my office could bring me to orgasm if I clench at the right moments.

Stone dutifully carries my belongings as he walks me into the hotel. My office is in the basement, in a mostly hidden area of the hotel. I have direct access to the spa and a quick exit out to the hot springs. When Stone follows me into my office and closes the door, I turn to question him. Then I see the lust swirling in his eyes.

"Sit at your desk, Princess," he says thickly.

"Are you — what are you going to do?" I stammer as I quickly sit behind my desk.

"I'm going to give my woman an orgasm so she doesn't take one for herself," he whispers as he crouches next to me. I'd be lying if I said my heart didn't jump when Stone referred to me as his woman.

"Did you lock the door?" I ask.

"No."

"Stone! What if someone comes in?" I hiss.

"Then you better come fast, or figure out how to come silently," he murmurs as he pushes up my dress and grabs the middle seam of my tights, ripping through them. I whimper at the vision in front of me. The man of my literal dreams, kneeling before me, ready to have his way with me. He yanks my legs, so I'm perched on the edge of the chair, then positions himself underneath my desk. Pulling my chair toward him, he gives me one lustful look before he buries his face between my thighs.

"Hey, Ari, do you have the final numbers for that Valentine's spa night ... are you okay? Your face is red," Hannah says as she unceremoniously opens the door without knocking. I attempt to shove Stone's face away from my pussy, but he bites one finger and resumes his voracious licking.

"Oh, um, I'm just hungry, I think. I didn't sleep well last night and woke up late," I lie.

"How's your ankle?" she asks as she sits in a chair across from me.

"Better. I can put weight on it this morning," I grit out.

"You really should eat something," she comments. "Your face is getting redder."

"I sh — should," I stutter. "I don't have the nn — numbers for the … thing … but I'll get those to you laterrrrrrrr," I drawl as Stone takes me right to the edge of an orgasm and then lets off. Asshole.

"Uh-huh," Hannah says, her eyes twinkling with mischief. "Bless your heart. You're all atwitter. I'll leave you alone, Princess. Get some breakfast after Stone finishes his."

She winks at me before standing up and walking out. The moment the door latches, Stone attacks. Two fingers slide in and push against my G-spot while he sucks hard on my clit. I fall back into my chair as one hell of an orgasm washes over me. Stone calmly strokes me through the aftershocks before peppering kisses along both thighs.

"You think she's going to tell Luca?" he asks quietly.

"At this moment, I don't care," I reply breathlessly. Stone chuckles against my leg, kissing my clit once more before repositioning my panties.

"Sorry about your tights. I was in the moment."

"Again, I reply the same. At this moment, I don't care. If you continue that tradition, I'll wear these every day."

"Duly noted," he says as he pushes my chair back. Stone winces as he climbs out from under my desk. "I'm too old for that cramped space, Princess. We'll have to get creative in the future."

"I'm cool with creativity." Honestly, he could tell me he wanted to lay me out on the hotel buffet, and I wouldn't have an issue with it. I'm the most relaxed I've been in ages. I foresee a nap on my lunch break.

"I need to get to work. What time are you off work tonight? Do you want me to pick you up, or do you think you'll be fine driving your car?" he asks. Goodness, he sure can be sweet when he wants to be.

"I think I'll be okay driving. I can always ask Hannah to drop me off on her way home if needed."

Stone leans down until our noses touch. "I didn't offer to be nice, Princess. I'd love to pick you up after work."

I can't help the beaming smile that spreads across my face. "You want to pick me up?"

"I do," he replies, a big smile gracing his face. "What time?"

"Five is fine. Can we hit the grocery? I want to make dinner."

"Only if you let me help. Too much standing could make your ankle get worse."

"You can help. I'm craving spaghetti, so it won't be anything too fancy," I tell him.

"Anything you want to make is fine with me, Arianna. I'm sure it'll be better than any takeout I could bring home." His nose nuzzles mine briefly before he presses a soft kiss against my lips. "I might hit the store for some things for my shop, so text me what you need. Kill two birds with one stone."

"I can do that," I tell him as he opens my office door and peeks out. "Hey, Stone?"

"Yeah?" he replies, turning to look at me.

"Thanks. For, um, that."

"Anytime, baby girl," he says, winking, before sauntering out. I unabashedly stare at his ass until he's out of sight. Sighing, I pick up the phone and dial Hannah's extension.

"I almost stayed in there out of spite," Hannah answers.

"Please. The amount of sex I had to listen to for just one night in your house? You owed me."

"You weren't in the same room, Arianna."

"And? You didn't have to barge in. You could have knocked."

"I've never knocked before! And why didn't y'all lock the damn door?"

"Ask him. I didn't know that was going to happen," I mumble.

"I at least lock my office door when Luca pays me a visit," she says snarkily.

"Ew! Hannah, that's my brother. Please tell me I haven't walked in on you guys!"

"Don't ask questions you don't want answers to then," she replies.

"Fantastic. Listen, don't tell my brother, okay? I don't know what exactly is going on with Stone, but this stays between us," I say quietly.

"Of course, girl. Your secret rendezvous is safe with me. Although you might want to tell him to lock the door. Or use a hotel 'do not disturb' sign. Or a sock? Something. I need a warning," she giggles. "Should I start shouting 'cacaw, cacaw' as I walk toward your office?"

"I'm sure that'll go over well with the other staff and guests, Han. How about we both just keep office shenanigans to a bare minimum?"

"Well, where is the fun in that?" she replies before hanging up.

Hannah, the southern belle who seemed straight-laced and regal when I first met her, has blossomed since meeting my brother. She always seemed genuine, but now she's charming, adventurous, and incredibly sassy. It's been a joy watching her come into her own.

I quickly fire off a text to Stone, letting him know the few ingredients I need from the store, before buckling down to get work done. He replies a few moments later.

> Stone: For some reason, I assumed you'd be making the sauce from scratch.

> Me: Sauce from scratch takes hours and POUNDS of tomatoes. I don't have the time or patience for that, and I'm pretty sure you don't have a big enough pot to cook the tomatoes.

> Stone: I'm teasing you, Princess. Good to know you can make it from scratch, though.

> Me: Nonna taught me well. Mine is nowhere near as good as hers or Mom's, but it does the job. But tonight, you're getting good ole jarred sauce, but I plan to doctor it with spices. Do you have dried spices?

> Stone: I will by tonight.

Me: Sigh. Add garlic and onion powders to the list and dried basil, thyme, oregano, and parsley. Oh, and if you want homemade garlic bread, I'll need bread, butter, and parmesan cheese. A fresh block, not that powder crap in the plastic jar.

Stone: No to the powder crap. Got it.

Stone: As if I'd EVER get the powder crap. You wound me, Arianna.

Me: I'd retaliate, but I just realized you probably don't have a cheese grater. Powder crap it is.

Stone: I actually DO have a cheese grater, Princess. I'm not quite the Neanderthal you think I am.

Me: I definitely viewed you as one step up from Neanderthal.

Stone: Obviously, I gnaw on the parmesan block to shred my cheese.

Me: Obviously.

God, I'm so in love with this man.

One lunch nap later, and I'm chomping at the bit to get home to Stone. Home. Is it home? Could it be home? Most girls imagine what their lives will be like as adults. Their perfect home. Perfect husband, those two point five perfect children. I've never looked at it that way. When I envisioned my future, all I ever saw was Stone. The background was blurry in my dreams, but Stone was always crystal clear. I could even see our kids. A boy and a girl. I never saw perfection. I just saw comfort. Happiness. Honesty.

But my dreams have morphed since Stone kissed me at the gala.

The blurred background has materialized into the fireplace Stone is restoring in his house. My toothbrush is next to his by the sink. Kids toys haphazardly strewn around the house, and watching Stone teach our son how to ice skate. Cooking as a family.

As I turn off my office lights and lock my door, I find my brother Dominic striding toward me.

"I wanted you to hear this first from me. Bradley is pressing charges against Stone."

"For what?" I shout. "Stone didn't even come close to him. He came right to me!"

"I know. Bradley is claiming Stone made threats against his life."

"Seriously? Wait. Oh." Shit. He may have actually done that. He joked that he told Bradley my family would make him disappear.

"Yeah. As far as I can tell, there's no evidence that Stone did anything wrong. I'm not even entirely sure what the rules are for this."

"This is bullshit," I whisper. "Stone was just trying to protect me."

"I know, sis. I'm getting the attorney involved, but since he typically handles mostly legal hotel business, he will probably refer us to someone who deals more with criminal matters."

"Is Stone going to be arrested?" I ask fearfully, my distress clearly evident in my shaking voice.

"I'm not sure. It depends on how far Bradley takes this. He had his father show up for his belongings today, and Mr. Wetherington is the one who let it slip that Bradley was pressing charges."

"Is Alex in trouble, too?" I ask. Dom looks confused, so I add, "I think the threat was that Stone, Alex, and Leo would be the ones to ensure Bradley didn't bother me anymore."

"Fuck, I didn't know that," Dom mutters. "I will talk to Alex. My gut says it's just Stone because it's a personal vendetta against you. Hurting Stone is the fastest way to do that."

"Hurting my brother would do that too," I respond.

"I know the way a man's mind thinks, Ari. You go for the jugular.

Hurt the guy who took your place, which hurts the girl the most. Bradley knows you were never in love with him, and the fact that Stone swooped in to steal you away pisses him off. He probably knew early on that he was never going to live up to your Stone expectations."

"You're really giving Bradley a lot more credit than he deserves. I don't think he knew how I felt about Stone."

"Ari, I love you, but you're living in a cloud if you think we all didn't know that you had a thing for Stone. Jesus, growing up, you used to write your initials with a 'D' instead of an' S'. We all knew."

"I thought I hid it better after high school," I whisper.

Dom smiles softly. "Maybe to some, but not to me. He'd bait you, and you'd hook him right back. It was fascinating to watch, really. I'm surprised it took this long for something to happen. Not that I was cool with it happening as it did, but it was evident for at least the last couple of years that the two of you were just circling around each other."

"He doesn't think he deserves love. He thinks I'm too good for him."

"You remember what Nonna used to tell us? Shit, you probably don't. She used to tell us about falling in love with Papa. Then he got sick, and those last ten years were just brutal for her."

"I remember that," I whisper. Our Papa finally passed away a handful of years ago after a ten-year battle with colon cancer. It was awful watching the life fade from his eyes, but even worse watching our Nonna lose her husband and partner. She struggled for a year to even smile. It's only been over the past year or so that she's shown signs of the Nonna we remember.

"Well, she used to say that falling in love with someone, and choosing to love that person, were two different things. Falling in love is easy. It's sunshine and rainbows. Once you learn about their habits, their likes and dislikes, and the things that irritate you? That's when you choose to love them."

"So what are you saying?" I ask.

"Show Stone that you choose him. You want a life with him exactly as he is. Choose your love story," Dominic says quietly, his eyes intense as he looks at me. He claims not to want love, but I can see how desperate he is for it. How badly he needs it in his life. But I can't say that to him yet. He's not ready.

As if he knew we were talking about him, Stone rounds the corner and hesitates briefly when he sees Dom.

"Everything okay, Princess?" he asks. I attempt to nod, but the motion pulls tears from my eyes. Stone immediately pulls me into his arms, his forehead against mine. "What happened?"

I fail to find the words, shaking my head against him. Stone's hand finds the nape of my neck, and he grasps it, the feeling helping to center me and calm my nerves. I realize our breathing has synced, my hands wrapped tightly around his waist. Just like my dreams, the background has faded away. It's just the two of us, Dom having disappeared at some point.

"I choose you," I blurt out.

"What?" he asks, a light chuckle bursting from his lips as he lifts his head to peer down at me.

"I choose you, Stone. You're enough. Do you understand that?" His smile fades as he comprehends my words. "I'm choosing my love story. I choose you."

"Princess, I — I worry you're going to regret that," he says quietly. "You deserve better."

"No. I deserve you. I deserve the happiness you bring, and the way you make me feel. I deserve everything we are together. Neither one of us is perfect, Stone. I don't deserve more because you think I'm on a fake pedestal. I deserve you because no one has ever made me want more before, and no one has ever made me want to be a better woman. A better woman for you."

Stone's eyes glisten with unshed tears as he clears his throat. "I'm the one who put you up on that pedestal, Princess."

"Then get up here with me. You deserve to be up here, too."

He chuckles as a tear cascades down his cheek, and I lean up to kiss the salty trail.

"You're wrong, you know. You are perfect."

"No, I'm not," I huff. "I'm argumentative, and I'm routinely late. I spend too much money on shoes, and have road rage."

"You're perfect for me, baby girl," Stone whispers as his lips find mine in a soft kiss.

"And you're perfect for me. No one will ever love you like I do," I say, watching Stone's face as he hears my words. His responding smile is blinding.

"I love you too, Arianna," he whispers hoarsely. "I think I always have."

Slipping my arms around his neck, I giggle. "Take me home, handsome."

"Home?"

"Yes. Our home."

"I guess it's a good thing I spent my lunch break unpacking your suitcases into our closet," he says, dipping down to pick me up in the bridal hold.

"I can walk, you know," I tease him, my hand finding his hair and scratching against his scalp. He sighs in bliss as he strides toward the stairs leading to the lobby.

"I kinda like taking care of you, Princess," he says, turning his head to kiss my palm. "That okay with you?"

"As long as you let me take care of you."

"For the rest of my life."

"Promise?"

"Promise."

Chapter 19

Stone

As soon as Arianna told me she chose me, it was as if my entire life had somehow sharpened before me. I don't know how I lucked out to get her, but I refuse to let my fears push me away from her again. I've always thought Ari deserved better than me. That she was destined for a relationship better suited to the lifestyle I thought she wanted. When she told me it was all about the happiness I brought and how I made her feel, I finally realized what Arianna had always needed.

Me.

I feel like I'm enough for the first time in my life.

All because of her. Yeah, I put her up on that pedestal. I'm the one who started calling her Princess. Instead of fighting me, or making things difficult, she slowly dragged me up on the pedestal with her. And there's nowhere I'd rather be.

If I had to repeat my entire life, knowing I'd still have the shitty home life, the absentee dad, and the lousy mom, but I'd still have Alex as a best friend, and Arianna as my partner? Yeah, I'd redo the whole damn thing again, without a doubt. I never would have considered myself to be lucky before, but hindsight tells me I'm one lucky motherfucker.

"Babe, can you start a coffee for me?" Arianna calls as she frantically dries her hair.

"On it." I didn't mean to make her so late this morning. But she shimmied against me, pushing perfectly so my cock hit her center, and I couldn't just ignore that. Then I might have delayed her even more when I went down on her in the shower, but she certainly didn't stop me. I just wanted her taste on my skin so I could think about it all day.

When the doorbell rings, I don't think about it before swinging the door open. Mark Baxter, one of the county deputy sheriffs, stands next to Dominic.

"What's going on?" I ask, clearly confused.

"Arianna didn't tell you?" Dom replies.

I shake my head.

Dom sighs. "I'm sorry, man. Bradley is pressing charges against you."

"For what?" I ask.

"Oh shit," Arianna gasps behind me. "Fuck! Stone, I completely forgot to tell you!"

"It's okay," I murmur as she comes to wrap her arms around me. "What is he pressing charges for?"

"Menacing," Mark explains.

"I'm not even sure what that means," I admit.

"Mr. Wetherington is claiming you threatened to hurt him. He reported you said you knew places to dispose of a body where no one could find it," Mark says. Shit. I did say that, didn't I?

"Stone, don't say a word. I've got our hotel attorney getting someone for you. Do not answer any questions without the attorney present, okay?" Dominic demands.

"Dom, I did this as a favor for you, but don't impede this process," Mark warns.

I feel Arianna shaking against me. When I look down, tears are coursing across her cheeks. "It's okay, Princess. It's going to be okay."

"No. None of this is okay," she cries. "Are you arresting him? Right now? Can this wait?"

Mark sighs. "I have to take him to the station for questioning. It's not the same as being arrested, but he needs to cooperate."

Arianna refuses to let go as her hands tighten around my waist. "Can I go with him?"

"No," Dom and I both respond simultaneously.

"Why not?"

"It's procedure, Arianna. Stone will be questioned alone, or with an attorney present. Whichever he prefers."

"Fuck," I whisper. I can't believe this is happening. I feel my jaw clench as I watch Arianna's tremble. Leaning down, I kiss her tenderly. I hate that this kiss is in front of a sheriff and Ari's brother, but I don't have a choice. It's not a deep, passionate kiss, but I pour every emotion I can into that short kiss. Breaking off the kiss, I wipe the tears from her cheeks. "I love you so much, sweetheart."

"I love you too, Stone," she whispers brokenly. I wrench her hands from my waist, pausing to kiss each wrist before letting go and turning to the men.

"Can I put on shoes and a coat?" I ask. Mark nods.

"Of course. Hopefully this will be quick."

Fucking hell.

Jail.

I quickly put on my coat and shoes, avoiding Arianna's gaze. I can hear her whimpers as she struggles to maintain her composure. I kiss her temple quickly before looking at Dom. "Stay with her, please."

"Of course. The attorney's name is Dillon King. He will meet you at the station. We'll get this figured out, man." Dom slaps me on the shoulder as I walk past him. Arianna's cries grow louder the further I get from her.

Mark opens the back door of his cruiser, grimacing when I stare at the car. "I'm sorry, Stone. I can't let you ride in the front."

"I understand."

"This is all such bullshit, anyway. Wetherington's dad pulled some strings with the county. Kid has no proof. But we're going as by-the-book as possible to ensure they can't keep you on a technicality. I'll read you your rights when we get to the station so there are witnesses."

"I thought I wasn't being arrested?" I ask in horror. Maybe he misspoke in front of Arianna to keep her calm.

"No, but as soon as we begin any questioning, it's in your best interest to have your rights read. That is when you should invoke your right to an attorney."

"Okay," I murmur as he pulls out of my driveway. Arianna stands in the doorway, visibly sobbing, and I'm suddenly horrified that I've brought this pain to her.

In my thirty-seven years of life, I've never even been inside a police station, let alone been questioned. Hell, I've only gotten one speeding ticket in the twenty years I've been a licensed driver. If I weren't so worried about Arianna, I'd find the entire situation weirdly fascinating. But right now, I only want to get home to her.

The lawyer Dom arranged for me, Dillon King, is not what I expected. He shows up in jeans and cowboy boots, an MC leather cut, and appears to be chewing on a toothpick. While he's probably somewhere around my age, I assumed he'd be a big-city attorney, wearing a bespoke suit, and looking down at all the small-town folk of Eternity Springs. Dillon immediately shakes hands with half the police force within this county substation. He appears to know each of them by name and asks more than one about their family at home.

When he finally reaches me, he shakes my hand and acts like we're not meeting for the first time.

"Stone. I'll have you home by dinner so your woman doesn't worry too much," he tells me with a smile. "I'm a little surprised Arianna hasn't shown up here yet."

"Dominic is with her," I reply uncertainly. I'm taken aback by Dillon's entire demeanor. When he sits next to me in the incredibly uncomfortable folding chair, he lounges back and pops one well-worn cowboy boot on the opposite knee. His jeans appear dusty, and he has a smudge of dirt on his forehead.

"You were expecting someone a little more clean-cut, huh," he comments.

"I was, yeah," I confess. This entire situation is surreal.

"If we go to court, I'll be every bit the shark you expect. But when I get called while working on my land, you get what you get," he shrugs. When his gaze narrows at something over my shoulder, I turn to see Bradley Wetherington staring triumphantly at me, and two older men bracket him. One is an older version of Bradley, and I assume it's his father. The second man looks familiar, but I can't place him. Bradley looks tired. Agitated. His skin is dull, with large dark circles under his red eyes and greasy hair that looks like it hasn't been washed in a while. "Game on, Stone. This is gonna be fun."

Fucking hell. Did Dillon really just say it was going to be fun? What the hell did Dom get me into?

"Mr. Wetherington, Congressman Peterson," Dillon says, shaking both men's hands. "To what do we owe the pleasure of your company today?"

"Just wanted to ensure everything was done by-the-book, Mr. King."

"And you thought something would happen if you weren't here?" Dillon asks, cocking his head thoughtfully to the side as he waits for a response.

Bradley's father clears his throat. "Mr. Dixon is known to have connections with the Santo family. We want assurances that he's being treated like every other criminal in Park County."

"He is detained for *questioning*. That's quite a bit different from actually committing a crime. Now tell me, Mr. Wetherington, why did you need to bring Congressman Peterson with you?" Dillon asks. The two men glance quickly at one other.

"We were having breakfast when we were alerted to Mr. Dixon's arrival. We stopped by to make sure it really happened," the Congressman responds.

"Oh? Are you sure it doesn't have to do with the fact that you and the county district attorney play golf together twice a week? Or maybe it's because your niece is engaged to Bradley, and you wanted to make sure nothing messed with that connection. Or, possibly, it could be the fact that all three of you were in on the charade where Ms. Santo was assaulted at her workplace. Then again, it might also be that you three and the DA are in an underground sex club, and you want to make a deal with me so none of that information gets out to the public." Dillon looks at me with a mischievous twinkle in his eye, clearly loving the limelight being placed on him.

"What? No, I don't know what you're talking about!" Bradley sputters.

Dillon chuckles before pulling a manila envelope out of his waistband. He taps the envelope against his opposite hand, and I watch, captivated, as the color drains from their faces. "Question is, what do you think I have in here, gentlemen? Because, honestly, there's a lot of amazing options."

Congressman Peterson shakes his head, chuckling bitterly. "You're bluffing. You've got nothing."

Dillon raises an eyebrow. "You willing to take that risk?"

I watch as the two Wetheringtons engage in hushed whispers. When Bradley's eyes meet mine, his gaze narrows to slits as his lips press into a fine line of contention. He's unwilling to budge in this weird competition I didn't even know we were in. But, then again, I got the girl. He's obviously still pissed he couldn't have his fiancée, and Arianna too.

When another deputy rounds to stand between us, I expect him to read me my rights and put me in the holding cell. I'm completely shocked when he turns to Bradley. "Bradley Wetherington, you're under arrest for conspiracy and menacing."

"What?" he shouts. "I did no such thing! Father!"

"Who is accusing him?" the elder Wetherington bellows, his attention turning to me. "You —"

"Actually, it was me," Arianna states from across the room. Her parents flank her as Arianna stands proudly, her head held high as she looks at Bradley. "You really didn't think you'd get away with talking that man into assaulting me at his work Christmas party, did you?"

"You stupid bitch," Bradley snarls as he attempts to lunge toward Arianna. Before I can intercept him, two deputies grab Bradley's arms and haul him away from Arianna. When I see the subtle tremble of her chin, I know she's barely holding on, and I desperately want to take her in my arms. Mark is still beside me, holding onto my arm, and Arianna gives me a pained smile as she nods. She's telling me she's okay. I get that. But until I can touch her, I'm the one who isn't okay.

"Deputy Baxter, has Mr. Dixon been officially arrested?" Mr. Santo asks.

"No. He's been detained, so we can ask him some questions. But, seeing as how the events have changed with Mr. Wetherington, I think we can safely let Stone return home for the time being," Mark answers. He turns to me, lowering his voice, and says, "Don't leave the county, Stone. I assume we'll work out a deal with Wetherington that gets you off the hook. No more threatening bodily harm with your special ops friends, okay?"

I let out a relieved chuckle. "Absolutely."

"Tell Alex I said the same thing," Mark says quietly. "Go get your girl before she collapses."

As soon as Mark lets go of my arm, Arianna flies across the room and into my arms. We sigh simultaneously. I bury my head in her hair as I feel her tremble against me.

"I was so scared," she confesses. "I know that sounds dumb. But I've never seen anyone get arrested, and certainly never someone I love. Dom had to hold me back."

"I know, Princess. I was scared, too," I say hoarsely. I'm not correcting her on the difference between getting arrested versus being detained. Hell, I didn't know the difference until thirty minutes ago.

"Stone," Mr. Santo says clearly. Raising my head, I meet his cold gaze. "A word."

"Dad, not right now —" Arianna begins, but I cut her off.

"It's okay. I'd rather get this over with."

"Get what over with?" she asks, her expression full of worry.

"Him reading me the riot act, and then me finally fighting for you. It's time he knows I'm not backing down," I tell her. Arianna gifts me a breathtaking smile as I kiss her quickly before following Mr. Santo outside. He turns to face me, his arms across his chest in a defiant stance.

"I don't like getting a call from my daughter telling me the man she loves has been arrested for menacing."

"Well, I didn't like being arrested for menacing," I reply. A deep groove forms between his eyes as he frowns. I've never talked back to Mr. Santo. I've always tried to respect him, first as Alex's dad, and now as my future father-in-law. He doesn't know that yet, but I'm marrying Arianna, one way or another.

"You want to explain to me what the charges were?"

"Alex and I threatened Arianna's ex-boyfriend that we'd make him disappear if he fucked around with her again," I state bluntly. Mr. Santo's eyes widen before he shutters his expression.

"You'd make him disappear."

"Yep."

"Did you detail how you'd do that?"

"Not in specifics."

"What did you say you'd do?" he asks exasperatedly.

"I reminded him that Arianna has more than one brother in the military, and we know many places in the mountains with deep lakes."

I don't miss the quick smirk that covers his face as he nods. "So he wanted to press charges?"

"Yes."

"And Arianna saved the day by also filing charges against him for his hand in her injury at the hotel."

"Yes, but the attorney Dom called for me had all kinds of dirt on Wetherington and his dad anyway, so I think I would have gotten off, or had a reduced charge."

"Dom didn't get the attorney. I did."

Now it's my turn to be surprised. "You did?"

"Yes."

"Why?" I blurt out. "You hate me. You've always made that clear."

He chuckles sardonically. "Hate is a powerful word, Stone. I could see the hearts in Arianna's eyes from when she was barely out of diapers. Her mother and I knew you weren't interested, and you didn't see her, *really* see her, until she was an adult. I saw the change in your eyes around her nineteenth birthday, and I knew it was a matter of time."

"For what?"

"I knew eventually she'd wear you down. Sofia and I talked often about you two circling one another. We'd laugh about a story we'd hear, about one of you antagonizing the other. My sweet daughter fights hard, but she loves harder. Arianna is brazen and opinionated. A fiery personality. But I've never met anyone who could put out the flames without extinguishing her fire. Until you, Stone. I know she's trouble. Infuriating, that one. But one day, if you're lucky enough, you'll have a strong-willed daughter who defies you at every turn. And then you'll understand." Mr. Santo looks over my shoulder with a look of unconditional love as he clearly watches his wife and daughter just inside the doors.

"I'll understand?"

Mr. Santo smiles wistfully. "You'll understand what a gift she is. She's worth the trouble."

"I already know that, sir. She's worth everything I have and more," I reply honestly.

"I'm glad you finally see that, Stone. I know that you and Arianna are finally on the same page. It's been a long time coming."

As Mr. Santo raises a hand to squeeze my shoulder, I take a chance and confess my deepest thoughts. "I'll never stop thinking she deserves better. But I promise I'll spend every day making sure she's the happiest she's ever been, Mr. Santo."

"I know you will, Stone. Because, like you already know, my family has ways to make you disappear," he whispers ominously. I'd laugh if he wasn't looking at me with the most intense look I've ever seen. A wicked smile pops on his face as he steps behind me.

"I'm not saying it's happening soon, but just know I'll be coming to you and Sofia to ask you for your blessing. As soon as I know Arianna is ready, I'm locking her down," I tell him.

"I'd expect as much. And Stone," Mr. Santo says, and I turn around to look at him, "you can call me Nick now."

As he walks back into the precinct, I let out one hell of a relieved exhale. It's about fucking time.

Chapter 20

*A*rianna

"*I*'m taking the day off," I tell my mom. She smiles softly at me and nods.

"I figured you would."

I try to inhale, but a sob threatens to surface. I look toward the exit, barely making out the silhouette of Stone and my dad talking outside. They need to be done. I'm two seconds away from a breakdown, and I just need a hand on Stone. I need a connection to him.

I know it's stupid. It's not like he was carted off to a maximum-security prison. He was escorted to a tiny sheriff's precinct in my tiny town. He wasn't handcuffed, and I never heard his rights being read. If anything, it would be a he-said versus he-said situation. If Alex and Stone actually did threaten Bradley, they wouldn't be dumb enough to do it with a paper trail.

It's the fact that Stone and I were finally on the same page, and that was threatened. I've wanted Stone for as long as I can remember. I have vague memories of putting on pretty dresses when I was six or seven and twirling in front of him. I didn't know what I was doing then. It certainly wasn't sexual in any way. All my life, I've felt a pull toward Stone. Now that he's finally admitting he's felt something for me, the thought of that being brutally ripped from my grasp has me petrified.

When my dad comes back and hugs me, I look over his shoulder to find Stone standing outside. "Is everything okay?"

"Of course, *paperotta*. Do you need a ride to work?" Dad replies.

"No, I'm taking the day off."

"Should we drop you off at Stone's?" he asks.

"No, I'll figure something out," I murmur absentmindedly. "I'm going to go talk to him."

I vaguely hear both of my parents chuckling as I push them out of the way in an effort to get to Stone faster. As soon as I open the door, he turns to me. "Hey. You alright?"

"Yeah, I'm fine, Princess. Are you okay?" he asks, his arms sliding around my waist as soon as I get close enough. I sigh as soon as we connect.

"I am now," I whisper, resting my head on his chest.

"I need to go to the shop and call my clients for the day. I need a day off," he murmurs. "What time do you need to be at work?"

"I took the day off."

"Would you like to walk with me to the shop? Then we can grab some food and go home. I'd like nothing better than to take a nap and watch a movie with you."

I giggle. "Shouldn't it be watching a movie and then taking a nap?"

"I don't care what order we do the things, Princess. I just want to relax with you." Stone's hands slide down my arms to grab mine, bringing both up to his mouth. "Come on. Let's get going."

As we begin to walk, Stone stops suddenly.

"What?" I ask.

"Is your ankle okay for this? Fuck, baby girl. I didn't think --"

"It's fine," I say, interrupting him. "As long as we walk slow, I'll be fine."

Eternity Springs is a relatively small town, and it should only take five minutes to walk from the precinct to Stone's shop. Still, with my ankle, we're trudging along slowly. Stone has one arm wrapped tightly around my back, holding me up so I don't put too much weight on it. We're both quiet, content to be as we are in the moment. By the time we arrive at his shop, I'm looking forward to sitting down. His other barber, Sam, is already inside, and he's gleefully reading something on his phone.

"Did you really try to murder some dude?" he bellows.

"Fucking hell," Stone mutters. "Whoever runs that site should be arrested for spreading rumors based on nothing."

"Look at this!" Sam screeches, thrusting his phone into our faces.

Trouble in Paradise?

Stone Dixon was arrested early this morning, with a tearful Arianna Santo watching from their shared home. Sources claim Stone was arrested on menacing charges after apparently threatening to harm an ex-boyfriend of Ms. Santo. While it appears Mr. Dixon was cleared of any wrongdoing soon after that, yours truly wonders if this is the beginning of the end for this age-gap romance or if it's just a tiny speed bump on the way to their happily ever after.

Editor's note: the ex-boyfriend in question, Bradley Wetherington, was also arrested on charges of menacing for his part in the assault on Ms. Santo at Everlasting Inn and Spa. Mr. Wetherington was a previous employee of the hotel and is also nursing his own broken heart after his fiancée broke their engagement. It turns out Ms. Tasha Steele was also harboring her own secret: she's a lesbian.

"Seriously?" I say incredulously. The fiancée's name was Tasha. Huh. I'd have expected something a little more stuck up and pompous. The lesbian thing I never saw coming.

"Well, that was unexpected," Stone murmurs.

"So you really did threaten to murder him?" Sam asks.

"Not exactly. I just reminded him that Arianna's brothers are in the military, and they know things," Stone says sheepishly.

"When did this happen?" Sam asks.

I gasp. "Holy shit! I just remembered all of this. It was at the gala!"

"You forgot?" Stone says, chuckling.

"You had just kissed me. I wasn't operating on all four cylinders."

"Rocked your world, huh," he muses. I half-heartedly slap his bicep.

"You kept me in front of you while you talked to Bradley, and I'm pretty sure it was to hide your hard-on," I tell him.

"Yup." Stone gives me a malicious grin. "Not even gonna lie."

"About damn time the two of you finally did the damn thing," Sam shouts. "God, I was getting so fucking sick of hearing him bitch about you, Ari. It was so obvious he had the hots for you."

"Oh yeah? What did he bitch about?" I ask.

"Nothing, baby girl. I never bitched about you. Sam, shut your fucking mouth," Stone warns.

"Your shoes, mostly."

"What?" I screech. "My shoes? Why that?"

Sam winks at me. "My opinion? He was focused on them because he wanted to feel them digging into his back."

"Jesus Christ," Stone mutters.

"What else?"

"Your obsession with Diet Pepsi."

"I'm not obsessed with it," I respond.

"Yeah, you really are," Stone murmurs. When his eyes raise to mine, I motion for him to explain. "You've gone off on people more than once, telling them how disgusting Diet Coke is. You wouldn't let your parents switch to Coke products at the hotel. And you made me start carrying it in the vending machine here."

"That's not entirely true," I defend. "Coke wanted a ton more money to make the switch. I didn't see the point in that. And Diet Coke is disgusting. But I didn't make you carry it here —"

"Nah, girl," Sam boasts, "that was all Stone. He just suddenly switched our stuff to Pepsi. I knew it was for you."

Stone's cheeks blush as he sheepishly scratches the back of his neck. "I guess I didn't realize I was doing that."

"When did you make the switch?" I ask. Stone shrugs.

"Probably four or five years ago," Sam answers. Stone silently sits in his chair, his eyes trained on the floor.

"Four or five years ago," I parrot. I carefully move to sit in Stone's lap, my arms sliding around his neck. "What else have you done for me over the last four or five years?"

His eyes raise to mine as he smiles softly. "Just love you."

"While arguing nonstop with me," I respond.

Stone chuckles. "Not my finest moment, but it worked out in the end, didn't it?"

"I guess it did," I reply, kissing him tenderly.

"Listen, I'm thrilled for you guys, but I'm gonna need you to keep that disgusting lovey-dovey shit to the bare minimum around me. I'm single as a Pringle, and I don't need you rubbing it in my face," Sam teases.

"Want me to set you up with one of my friends?" I ask. I gasp and then clap maniacally. "My friend Claire would be perfect for you! She really skirts the line between sane and batshit crazy that I bet you'd be gaga for."

Sam shrivels up in horror. "Uh, thanks, but no thanks, Arianna. I prefer to stay off the crazy train."

I shrug. "Your loss. I figured you'd enjoy her ... uh ... kinkier side."

"Say what now?" Sam says, sliding across the floor to stand in front of us. Stone muffles a laugh against my shoulder.

"No, you're right. You're way too vanilla for Claire. I mean, she has a wall of pain in her apartment. Whips, chains, strap-ons. She'd probably want to dominate you. I doubt you'd like her kind of pain and degradation, Sam. She'd eat you alive," I tell him. Sam's expression of abhorrent shock is evident. I wish I could hold in my laughter longer, but I break with a loud burst of cackling.

Claire is the furthest thing from a madame. I'm not even sure if she's had sex doggy style before. She wants to be wined and dined, and I know that Sam won't be a match for her. I remember Sam from hanging with one of my brothers, and he's as outdoorsy as Claire is bookish. He is to sports as she is to coffee shops. While opposites like Luca and Hannah often attract, I feel Claire and Sam would combust in the worst way.

"Come on, Princess. Let's get home," Stone murmurs against my hair.

"I thought you needed to make some calls?" I ask.

"Sam will, won't ya, buddy?" Stone asks, looking at his friend pointedly.

"I guess I'm making some calls," Sam mumbles. "Good to see you, Ari. I'm glad this dipshit finally wised up and locked you down."

"Me too," I gush as I slide my arms around Stone's waist.

"Hey, it started snowing again," Stone comments as we exit the front door. "Do you want me to call a rideshare?"

"No, let's walk. It's so peaceful walking in the snow."

"How's your ankle?" he asks.

"It's okay. I'll tell you if we need to call someone."

It's a little under a mile to Stone's from his shop, and we set off quietly, only the sound of the snow squishing beneath our shoes accompanying us. I couldn't be happier at this moment, but part of me fears we haven't heard the last of Bradley. I don't know what I'll do if Stone gets arrested again. Did he even get arrested? What did Mark Baxter call it? He said Stone was detained. What an interesting expression. It's like getting half-arrested.

"You okay?" Stone asks quietly.

I snuggle into his chest, my arms tightening around his waist. It's as if I can hold him closer to prohibit anything from happening to him. "I'm not sure how to process everything that happened this morning."

"Me either."

"Do you think it's done? That the charge will be dropped?"

"I don't know, baby girl. I sure as fuck hope so. The attorney has his shit together. He seems like he'll do what needs to be done. I just don't know how much this will cost, and I don't have much savings …" Stone trails off.

"I have savings," I blurt out.

Stone stops moving. "Absolutely not."

"Why not?"

"I'm not taking your money, Arianna."

"Why? That's dumb. It's just sitting in the bank," I tell him, throwing my hands in the air in frustration. I know what he's going to say before he says it, but I'm mentally pleading with him to change his mind. But he doesn't.

"I don't know how much money you've got in a trust, or an inheritance, or whatever, but I'm not fucking taking a dime of that. That's your money. Your family's money. Not mine."

I growl at him. I literally growl. I'm so sick of him pulling the money card on me. He's done it for as long as I can remember. "I don't have a trust or an inheritance. I don't know what you've been thinking all these years, but I've never been given money, Stone. None of us have. We've all worked our asses off. We all started working part-time at the hotel when we were fifteen. During summers in high school and college, I worked a ton of hours. Every last cent went into savings. Other than what I give to the Children's Hospital or when I treat the staff to lunch, I rarely treat myself. If I had so much money, don't you think I'd own a home? Instead of living in a shitty one-bedroom apartment?"

"Shit, Ari, I didn't think —"

I poke one finger hard into his chest. "No, you didn't think. You assumed. You've got this block in your head about money. Yeah, I know I was raised with more money than you. I get it. But it wasn't a cakewalk. Most weeks, I work fifty to sixty hours. Did you know that? That's not even including the times I help when we're short-staffed. I love my job. I love the hotel. I'm not complaining about anything. But I'm sick of you making comments about money. That night at the gala? You commented on my dress, and how much it must have cost. It was a rental, Stone. My one vice is shoes. You can yell at me for how much my shoes cost."

"Okay," he mumbles, one corner of his mouth turned up in a smile. "I'm sorry. You're absolutely right. I shouldn't have made assumptions about money."

"What happens when we get married?" I blurt out.

"Huh?" Stone's eyes widen as he stares at me. His hand covers mine on his chest, clutching it against his pounding heart.

"Marriage. We're gonna get married at some point, right? So, do you not believe in us having a joint bank account? Are we going to be married on paper only and just continue living separate lives in every other way?"

"Well, I don't know — I mean, I didn't think —"

"That's obviously the case. You didn't think. I want a *partner*, Stone. Someone I'm in the thick of things with. I don't want a room-mate, who has the same last name as me, that I occasionally fuck. I want us to be *together*. We take on every trial and tribulation as a team. That means it's not my money, or your money. It's ours. So I don't fucking care how much the attorney costs, Stone. It'll get paid because I love you, and that's what you fucking do when you fucking love someone."

"It's weird that I find it really hot when you say fuck so much," Stone finally says after a moment of shocked silence. We burst into laughter simultaneously as he yanks me into his arms. "God, I love you. I'm sorry. I've been doing the adult thing alone for so long. I'm just used to figuring it all out by myself."

"You have me now," I murmur as I snuggle into him. I feel him press a kiss against my hair.

"I know, Princess. And I'm so fucking lucky to have you. Thank you for not giving up on me. I know I'm not easy, but you've never let me rest on my laurels before, so don't start now."

"I have no intention of doing that. But you'll tell me if I'm too much, right? I want to build you up, not emasculate you."

He chuckles against my hair. "Yeah, I'll tell you. You're pretty good about just busting my balls for shit that needs to be addressed."

I tilt my head up to look at him. Snowflakes dot his hair and eyelashes, but the look of adoration on his face is something I'll never forget. "I don't want to bust your balls. I like them."

"That's good to know, baby girl. Let's get home. You're cold, and I need to warm you up," he says huskily, leaning down to press a kiss against my lips.

Twenty minutes later, we're stripping off our sopping wet clothes just inside the front door. "Should we warm up by the fireplace, or in the shower?"

"Bed, Princess. We warm up in bed," Stone says before crouching to shove his shoulder into my stomach. I shriek as he picks me up and swiftly walks down the hall to his — I mean our — bedroom. A moment later, we're under the covers, me snuggled against Stone, our arms wound around each other.

"Can I ask you a question?" I ask after a few minutes of silence.

"Of course."

"Does our age difference bother you?"

I feel Stone hesitate before he answers. "It used to. It took me a while to come to terms with it. I felt like a dirty old man lusting after you. It probably didn't help that you called me old man from the time you were about ten."

I wince, recalling the first time I called him that. "I only did that in retaliation for you calling me a princess."

"I know," he sighs, "but it still made me acutely aware of the decade between us. I already felt bad for wanting my best friend's sister, but it was worse in my head because you were so young."

"What made you finally decide to let it go?" I ask quietly.

"I couldn't fight it anymore. Couldn't act like I didn't recognize the pull toward you. I've never felt like this with anyone before, and I think I finally recognized that. And after that kiss at the gala, I knew I was a goner. It just took me a bit more time to come to terms with my feelings."

"You weren't as shocked as I thought you'd be when I brought up marriage on the way home," I murmur.

"You expected me to be?" he asks.

"I don't know. Maybe. I've never known you to have a serious relationship, so I figured you were anti-marriage."

"I'm not anti-marriage, or anti-relationship for that matter. I figured it wouldn't happen for me, and I would have to live with that. Honestly, I think I was waiting for you."

"Sure would have been nice if you could have figured this out a year or two ago," I tease him. He chuckles and presses a kiss against my forehead.

"I know. I'm bullheaded. I'd like to think we came together at just the right time, Princess. When we were both ready for it."

"So ... you aren't against marriage?" I whisper.

"No, baby girl. I'm not against marriage."

"And kids?"

Stone tenses beneath me. "You — you want to have kids with me?"

I turn my head up to look at him. His eyes are cinched shut, a look of torment on his face. "Stone, what's wrong? Why do you look like you're about to cry?"

He takes a labored breath, and a shudder wracks through his body. "I'd never thought about kids with anyone ... until you. Even when I didn't think I was worthy of you, I could *see* our kids. But I'm freaked out about how I might fuck it up. With how I was raised, I didn't want to put anyone through that. How could I be a good dad when I had shit parents?"

My eyes fill with tears. Poor Stone. He has so much trauma from his childhood. But before I can speak, he continues. "But you ... you were made to be a mom. I've watched you with your nieces and nephews, and you're spectacular. How you care for them and your patience with them is phenomenal, baby girl. If I was so lucky to have a baby with you, you'd teach me how to be a good dad."

I sigh as he cups my cheek and kisses my lips softly.

"I remember how you were when Alex's kids were babies," I murmur against his mouth. He pulls back slightly to look at me.

"How was I?"

"You'd watch them constantly. Laugh at their antics, but always keep a close eye on them, especially if Alex was deployed. I think you've had a little more practice with kids than you think you have. And hearing how concerned you are tells me you're going to be an excellent dad to our babies one day."

"You think so?" he whispers, and I nod. The breathtaking smile that widens on his face gives me butterflies. "Fortunately, I know I'm already well-versed in the practice part."

"Oh yeah?" I tease, and he nods as he leans down to kiss along my collarbone. "Better show me how good you are at it, Mr. Dixon."

He sure does show me.

Multiple times.

Stone

The following week, it's Christmas. We're heading over to Arianna's parents' house for Christmas dinner. It's been a very low-key Christmas morning, just the two of us. We discussed Christmas presents one night and decided to give each other one present that had to be under one hundred dollars.

Neither one of us sticks to the one-present deal.

Arianna gives me a set of tools, a box of coffee pods, and a pack of funny boxer briefs. She confesses she had gone over the dollar amount only slightly.

I didn't go over at all, but I know my gift has unparalleled sentimental meaning, and I'm nervous as fuck to give it to her.

First, I gave her a book I found at a used bookstore that contained Italian food recipes. The recipes had been passed down through generations, and each recipe accompanied a story about the family that shared the recipe. Arianna teared up when she opened it. She claims she doesn't have the domestic gene. Still, she's completely fascinated with Italian history, cooking things her mom and Nonna cook, and continuing to learn about her heritage. Besides one unfortunate incident where she burned some rice, I've scarfed it down every time she's cooked.

But my second gift, the sentimental one, made her sob.

Honestly, I debated on proposing. I did. But we've been dating for all of a second, and while I'm fairly confident she'd say yes, I don't want to rock the boat just yet. Instead, I give her the only thing I have that has meaning. Well, besides my heart.

My own parents were always a disaster. But I had a grandmother, and she was cool. She died when I was pretty young, but she gave me a necklace and made me promise to keep it safe. She knew her daughter would sell it for drug money if she got her hands on it, so Grandma gave it to me. I hid it in this tiny pocket inside my backpack, knowing my mom wouldn't look there. She never checked my backpack. Once I became close with Alex and his family, I asked his mom to keep it safe. I got it back from her a few days before Christmas.

The necklace was fairly simple — just a gold chain with a ruby pendant. Since it never had a proper box, I decided to give it to Arianna in my hand.

"Do you know what your birthstone is?" I ask her.

"A ruby," she responds.

"My grandmother's birthday was also in July. Did I ever tell you that?" I murmur.

"No, I don't think so. You've never talked about your grandmother with me before."

"She was the good one. Even when my mom was a mess, I could count on my grandma. I don't remember a ton of her from my childhood. Just odd bits and pieces. She's the one who introduced me to maple syrup on a toasted bagel," I tell her, chuckling as her face screws up in obvious distaste. She's poked fun of me each time she's seen me eat a bagel that way. "When she died ... I felt really lost, Princess. My dad skipped town, and my mom was drunk or high most of the time. She sold all of my grandma's things to feed her addiction. If it weren't for my grandma's foresight to give me something of hers, and make me promise not to tell my mom, I wouldn't be able to give you this today."

"You don't have to give me anything, Stone. Especially if it's the only thing you have of hers," Arianna says firmly, shaking her head.

"This was meant to be yours, Princess. I know it. My grandma told me I'd meet someone someday, someone who would turn my life upside down, a woman who would love me for me. I don't think she realized I'd be meeting you when you were born," I murmur.

Arianna giggles as she wipes an errant tear from her cheek. "I don't think I've ever known that. You met me when I was born?"

"Alex dragged me to the hospital. You were only a day old, I think." She's looking at me now with the same expression as she did then. Her eyes have always been burned in my mind as a core memory. "So my grandma left me this, and I hid it from my mom. Until I met Alex. Then I asked your mom to hold onto it for me. She gave it back to me a few days ago."

I lift my hand toward hers, and she copies me. When our palms touch, I drop the pendant from between my fingers. Arianna gasps when she sees the ruby. "Stone! This is gorgeous!"

She touches the gem reverently before looking up at me. "Will you put it on me?"

"Of course," I whisper. Arianna turns around, picking her hair up and holding it on her head. I lay the necklace against her décolletage. Once clasped, I bend to place a soft kiss against her skin. "She would have loved you. I think you would have been exactly who she'd pick for me."

"Why?" Arianna asks quietly.

"Because you aren't afraid to stand up to me. You'll tell me when I'm wrong, but you can admit defeat as well. You make me want to be a better man, and you've helped me realize that I *do* deserve love," I confess. Arianna swivels, climbs into my lap, and puts her nose against mine.

"My family taught you all of those things, Stone. I just reminded you that *I* have the privilege of being loved by *you*."

"And I do love you, Princess. Not enough words in the English language to explain how much I love you," I whisper.

"I love you too," she responds before giggling. "Can I confess something?"

"Yeah?"

"I was a little freaked out that you might be going to propose."

"I thought about it. But I kinda want to enjoy this stage for a little bit. I have every intention of wife-ing you up, baby girl, but I'm in no rush. As long as you're in our bed every night, and I get to fuck you awake every morning, I'm good."

Peals of laughter break from Arianna's lips as I lean down and blow a raspberry against her neck. She squeals and tries to slide away from me, but I tighten my arms around her and pull us both to the ground. Her lips find mine in a searing kiss, and within moments, I'm frantically ripping her clothes off.

I make love to my girlfriend, my future fiancée and wife, by our fireplace and Christmas tree, on a brand new rug that Arianna claimed we just had to have until we refinish the floors. I'm no longer spending my nights and weekends working quietly on projects. Now, there are at least two of us, and sometimes a rogue Santo brother, who work on the house. There's music. Laughter. Lots of sex. I can honestly say she is the best Christmas gift I could have ever gotten.

"*H*as anyone explained the Santo curse to you?" Arianna says suddenly as we pull into her parents driveway. I'm weirdly nervous. I've been to this house hundreds, if not thousands, of times. But this time is different. I'm here as Arianna's man, and I'm not sure how to act.

"I think Alex mentioned it once or twice. Why?"

"You're gonna need to participate."

"What?"

Arianna unbuckles and opens her door, quickly jumping out of my SUV and walking to the trunk. I follow her and await a response.

"Princess."

"Hmm?" she mumbles.

"Look at me."

Arianna sighs before her eyes turn to mine. "What?"

"I need more information. What do you mean I have to participate?"

"You just have to carry me over the threshold."

"Oh. And?" That seems absurdly easy, so I don't understand why she's freaking out.

"Well, it's just … no one really makes it. Usually, but Gia and Luca did, so …" she trails off.

"Wait. Are you saying Alex didn't even make it?" I ask incredulously.

Arianna shakes her head. "We blew it off because he was the first one. And he was the one who started the whole bet thing in high school. But then Dom failed. And we thought, what are the chances? Gia's high school boyfriend wouldn't even take the chance, and Isabella had an asshole guy who really lit into her about her weight and his fear of hurting his back."

I can see she's spiraling. "Baby girl, you have nothing to worry about."

She looks up at me, worry and pain evident in her eyes. "How do you know?"

I smile so widely that my cheeks hurt. "Because I already carried you over the threshold."

"What?"

"You don't remember?"

"Obviously not," she snaps. I fight the chuckle that threatens to burst from my mouth. My Princess looks mutinous right now.

"You remember I was at your nineteenth birthday in Denver, right?"

"Yeah, Alex made you keep an eye on me."

"Yep. And someone snuck past me and kept handing you drinks in the bathroom. You were completely hammered."

"Okay, and?"

"There was a guy you were hanging on. He was trying to drag you to his car, and I intercepted you. I had to forcibly put you in my car and buckle you in. You bitched at me the entire drive home and refused to get out of my car. I had to throw you over my shoulder and take you to your room."

Arianna looks at me widely. "Seriously?"

"Yeah. I didn't think anything of it at the time. I remember Alex talking to me about the curse, but I figured that wasn't about me because you and I weren't meant to be."

"We're not?" Arianna looks momentarily hurt before she shakes her head, as if to physically clear the intrusive thought that clearly worked a way into her brain.

"No, Princess. I meant then. That's what I thought then. You were nineteen, and it was the first time I really saw you. I was almost thirty. Even realizing that I found you ridiculously hot, I didn't think anything would come to be with us."

"So you've already passed the test," she murmurs. "Wow. Does anyone know?"

"I don't think so. Unless your parents watched the doorbell video."

Arianna snickers. "Doubtful. They only look at it if someone in their neighborhood asks for videos or complains about a crime. Or when there are reports of Mason roaming around."

That damn marmot gets into too much trouble.

I shrug. "So, do I need to carry you over it again?"

"I don't know. I bet they ask you to. They'll want to witness it."

I hear a high-pitched whistle, and we both look toward the

sound. Arianna's entire family stands by the driveway, looking at us expectantly. Arianna sighs. "Yeah. They're gonna expect it."

"Obviously," I mutter. I have no problem carrying her over the threshold, but I don't like being the center of attention. I'm worried I'll trip and drop her or something.

"Come on, lovebirds! It's time!" Luca yells out. I assume it's Luca. Dominic wouldn't yell like that, and Alex doesn't have the word "lovebirds" in his vocabulary anymore. He might tease me, but when his wife died, he lost all hope for love.

Arianna grabs my hand and pulls me toward her family. I find myself avoiding looking at Arianna's dad. He might claim to be on board with our relationship, but I fear he's waiting for me to fail.

"Guys, we don't have to do the thing," Arianna announces.

"The fuck we don't!" Luca shouts out. "Ow, Mom! Don't hit me."

"You get that from your mother," I mutter.

Arianna turns to me. "What?"

"The popping people on the cheek. You do that, too."

"Oh," she giggles. "I do."

"Why don't you need to do the thing, Arianna?"

"Well, Stone just told me he carried me over the threshold a few years ago. So we already passed the test."

"That's not how that works, baby sister," Gianna shouts gleefully. "*You* have to carry *him*. Remember?"

"Oh, shit!" Arianna exclaims. She turns to me, her expression stricken with worry. "I completely forgot. The Santo girls have to carry their men, not the other way around."

Well, this just got more interesting.

"Best way to do it is piggyback-style," Gianna says. Luca snickers and Hannah swats him.

"Dammit, the violence is really ridiculous in this family," he mutters.

Gianna's husband coughs to hide a smile. I don't know Travis well, but Gianna looks at him adoringly. "It worked for us, so it'll work for you, Ari."

"Do you have to carry me from the driveway or the front porch?" I ask. I'm nervous. I'm not saying she's going to drop me, but I can't assume this will be easy for her.

"From the front porch. At least that's where Gia and Luca have succeeded, so we're going with that. Because this has to work," Ari says, her brow furrowed. I'm not the only one nervous, it seems.

"Hey," I whisper, my hand finding her cheek and tilting her head to look at me, "We've got this. I won't tell you that this is dumb because I know you're worried. And I believe in you. I believe in us. What a turn of events, Princess, that I'm having to convince you to believe in this, huh."

Arianna sighs, leaning into my touch. "I love you."

"Love you too, baby girl. Your ankle is okay, yeah?"

She nods.

"Alright. Let's get this over with. Your mom's Christmas dinner is always phenomenal, and I'm starving."

"You should have eaten more today," Arianna says as I wrap my arms around her from behind.

"I ate quite a bit today," I murmur against her neck. "I ate for a good hour around lunchtime if I remember correctly."

I love the gasp that I feel against my lips. "That's not what I meant, Stone. But I'm not sorry that's how you spent lunch."

"Neither am I." I lift one leg, and Arianna grabs me around the knee.

"Jump up. It's gonna suck no matter how you do it, so just jump up there and get it done," Travis calls out. I look over to him, and he nods. "I know what you're thinking. You're worried about hurting her, so just get it over with."

"I agree. Sooner you do this, the sooner we can eat," Arianna murmurs.

"Fine," I mutter. "Gonna jump on the count of three. One, two ..."

Arianna braces, knowing I'll jump on three, and launches toward the door. I feel her stumble, and a collective gasp fills the air around us, forcing me to squeeze my eyes shut as I assume we're going to hit the ground. I'm already planning how I'll turn us both so she doesn't take the brunt of the hit, but no fall comes.

"You can get down now," Arianna whispers. I look through one eye to find us inside her parents' home. Jumping down, I spin her around. Her eyes meet mine, and they're filled with tears.

"Why the tears?" I ask.

Her chin trembles slightly as she looks up at me. "When I tripped, I thought it was over, and I — I can't go back to the way things were with us. I can't lose you. My life flashed before my eyes, and I saw how unhappy I was. How miserable you were. And now ... the thought of losing what we have is devastating."

"You're not losing me. You wouldn't have lost me if we had fallen, Princess. You're not going to lose me over a weird curse. You guys might believe in that, but I refuse to. You were meant to be mine, Arianna. And I was definitely meant to be yours."

Arianna gives me a beaming smile as she stands on her tiptoes to press her lips against mine. When I feel a sudden pinch on my backside, I break off the kiss to tease her. "Pinching? Really?"

Arianna's eyes narrow as she growls. "That wasn't me. Dammit, Nonna! You've got to stop pinching their butts!"

"Don't tell me how to live my life, young lady. I might die tomorrow, you know. Gotta enjoy all the tushies while I can," Nonna replies as she toddles past us.

"Their butts? Who else has she pinched?" I ask.

"Travis and Hannah. She leaves everyone alone until they've broken the curse. Then it's like her weird version of hazing or something."

"Is this the only time she'll pinch me? Or is it open season now, and I can expect to be pinched whenever I see her?" I ask, chuckling.

"Hannah only got pinched the one time, but —" Arianna breaks off when we hear a shout from the kitchen.

"Dammit, Nonna! Stop pinching my husband!" Gianna shouts, and Nonna cackles in response.

"Uh, I think it's safe to say you're on her radar for a while, old man," Arianna says with a grin. She grabs my hand and leads me into the kitchen, but I stop when I feel my phone vibrate in my pocket. Assuming it's Sam wishing me Merry Christmas, I'm incredibly surprised to find a text from my mother.

Mom: Merry Christmas. I got evicted.

Me: Why?

Me: I'm guessing you stopped paying the rent?

Mom: Well, when I have NO money, there's NO money to pay rent, now is there?

Mom: What am I supposed to do? Can you lend me a couple thousand?

Me: First of all, your rent isn't a couple thousand. Second of all, I don't have it to give you. And to answer your question: get a job.

Mom: I don't even know what that means.

I sigh, rubbing my fingers across my eyes in frustration. My mom has always enjoyed living off the government as much as she can.

Me: It means you literally go get a job. Apply places.

Mom: I haven't worked since before you were born.

Me: I'm aware of that.

Me: In most places that are minimum wage, you only need a high school education.

Mom: I don't know where my GED paperwork is.

Me: It's in your lockbox. Unless you sold it or burned it for fun.

Mom: I have a lockbox?

Me: It pains me how much you don't know about your own fucking house.

Me: It's in the bottom of your closet.

Mom: I don't even know what I'm good at, Stone. I bet no one even hires me. Who wants a recovering addict working at their joint?

Me: Recovering?

Mom: Got my gold chip yesterday.

Me: What does that mean?

Mom: Sixty days sober.

Me: Wow, Mom. That's awesome.

Mom: I haven't been sixty days sober since before I had my first hit.

Me: I'm happy for you, Mom. I don't have any money to give you, though.

Mom: I never should have asked you. I'm sorry. When I saw the eviction notice, I freaked out.

Me: They handed out gold chips on Christmas Eve? AND you got an eviction notice on Christmas Eve?

Mom: Addicts and landlords still work on holidays.

Me: Good to know.

Mom: Do you think maybe you'd want to try to have a relationship with me? I know I was a shitty mother. But I'd like to make amends if I can.

Me: We can try. I make no guarantees, Mom.

Mom: I understand.

Shoving my phone back into my pocket, I process that conversation. Did she really get evicted? Is she really sober? I'm not sure what to believe. It wouldn't be the first time she's lied to try and get into my good graces. She might not even be up for eviction.

"Stone?" Arianna says softly. I raise my eyes to hers, and find myself smiling. "You okay?"

Looking at my future, my everything, I realize that no matter what is thrown my way, I'll be able to handle it as long as she's by my side. "Yeah, baby girl. I'm okay."

As we walk into the kitchen, Sofia is waiting for us.

"Go get some food, *paperotta*," she says. Arianna raises a brow at me, and I nod. I don't know what Sofia wants to talk about, but it's clearly something she doesn't wish to discuss with Arianna present.

Once Ari is out of the room, Sofia turns to me with a victorious grin covering her face. "How good is your memory?"

"About what?" I ask warily.

"About a time when I asked you if I could rub it in your face when you fell in love and a girl knocked you on your ass," she brags, as she dances around the kitchen with her arms up triumphantly. "Told you so! Ridiculous that I had to wait this long for it, but I told you so!"

Nick peeks around the corner and smiles at his wife. "She doesn't get to do her victory dance very often. It could use some work."

I shake my head while laughing. "This family is nuts."

Sofia comes to stand in front of me, and grabs both of my cheeks. "But we're your family. Which makes us incredibly lucky, Stone."

A mischievous glint sneaks into her eyes as she slaps both cheeks soundly.

"Mom! Don't hit my boyfriend!" Arianna calls out from the other room.

"I'm not hitting your boyfriend," Sofia responds, before lowering her voice. "I'm hitting my future son-in-law."

I've never considered myself to be a lucky man, but maybe that needs to change. Because in this moment, I'm the luckiest man in the world.

Arianna

I wake up encased in Stone.

I never used to want to cuddle. I appreciated the quick cuddle before sleep and then needed the guy to move his sweaty ass over to the other side of the bed. I needed space, crisp sheets, and not feeling hot breath on my neck. But now I can't sleep unless Stone is suctioned up to me. The steady vibration of his breathing against me helps to calm me. When he spoons me, he buries his face in my hair, and his arms squeeze me at just the perfect tightness. And when he falls asleep on his back, I rest my head on his shoulder and breathe him in. It's utter perfection, just as I knew it would be when I realized over a decade ago that I wanted to be with him.

Stone was somewhat quiet after he received the texts from his mom yesterday. He told me all about it on the way home. I'd never met his mom, and he made it clear he didn't anticipate us meeting anytime soon. Both he and Alex have insinuated how volatile and toxic Stone's mom is, and I don't think I want to meet her. I'll probably give her a piece of my mind for almost destroying my happily ever after with her bullshit throughout his childhood.

When I realize Stone is still deeply asleep, I fret about what to do. Carefully slide out of bed to get a cup of coffee and watch the snow fall? Take a shower? Read a book on my Kindle? I've been meaning to read the new hockey romance from Bella Matthews. I snicker when I realize it's an age gap, which has always been my favorite trope. Clearly, I enjoy it because of my own age-gap romance.

Stone sighs in his sleep, moaning quietly, and I'm suddenly aware of the tent he's popped. Hmm. I wonder what he's dreaming about. Me, I hope. I subtly slide one hand down and softly grasp his length. His breath catches momentarily before he resumes his steady and deep breathing.

Well, that's not going to fly.

Forget the coffee and snowfall. The shower. The book. I've figured out what I want to do right now.

I want to wake Stone up with an orgasm.

Moving the covers carefully, I slither down, keeping Stone covered until the last second. I replace the blankets with my mouth, taking him deep into my throat. Hollowing my cheeks, I suck while flicking the underside of his cock with my tongue. As I move up his length, I take time to swirl my tongue around each of the four barbells. I'd never seen a pierced dick in person before, but I've seen pictures. Two-dimensional images do not do it justice. Or maybe it's just that Stone's cock is the most spectacular thing I've ever seen or felt, and it doesn't compare to anything else.

When Stone moans again, I double down my efforts and increase the speed at which I suck. When I feel his hand slide into my hair and grip it tightly, I smile around him.

"Baby girl," he grits hoarsely. "Jesus, your mouth."

I moan happily as he groans and grunts closer to release, ready to swallow every last drop of his essence. I'm unprepared for his grip to tighten on my hair as he yanks me off of him, twisting us both so I'm beneath him. "If I'm coming, I'm coming in your cunt, Princess."

"You could have had both," I reply breathlessly as he maneuvers me into the position he wants. Gripping his cock, Stone drags the tip through my core. I'm soaked. Taking him to the brink is the biggest turn-on.

"Fucking love how turned on you get from sucking me off, Arianna," he says huskily. "And while I love you wanting to do that for me, there's no better orgasm than when I'm wrapped up in you as you milk me dry as you come."

Stone thrusts forward, encasing himself in one smooth stroke, and I cry out. He begins a steady pace, burying his face in my neck as I thrash beneath him. I can feel the orgasm hurtling toward me, beginning at the base of my spine, and suddenly Stone stops. Pulling himself out completely, I don't have a moment to complain before he spins me. "All fours, baby girl. I need you hard and fast."

Oh yes.

Stone has mentioned to me that his Jacob's ladder piercing would feel better from behind, but I assumed he was exaggerating. Our sex so far has been face-to-face, which has always been my favorite. I want to see my partner. I want to watch him fall apart and know that I was partially responsible for that. While I know it will feel good in any position because it's Stone, I can't help but think it won't be any better.

I stand corrected.

Well, I'm definitely not standing.

As soon as Stone impaled me and those barbells rubbed against my front wall, my arms buckle as I scream. Every piece rubbed against my G-spot, flirting with that minuscule line between pleasure and pain. I attempt to push myself up, only to feel Stone's hand slide down my spine and grab ahold of my hair again, keeping me in place as he pummels into me.

I can't control the feral sounds coming out of my mouth. Moans, shrieks, grunts. Stone could be talking to me right now, and I wouldn't know. I'm on a level I've never experienced before. As the orgasm to destroy all orgasms charges toward me at breakneck speed, my arms flail as I try to find purchase on anything besides the sheet beneath me. I hear myself calling for Stone, begging for him, crying out for him to please ... do something. His chest hits my back, his hands grabbing mine, our fingers intertwined tightly as my body seizes up in torturous bliss. I'm squeezing him so tightly he can barely move, and when the orgasm wave breaks, I fall forward, taking him with me.

Stone groans his release as he collapses on top of me, our bodies shaking with aftershocks. I can barely breathe with my hair covering my face and Stone's weight fully covering me, but I've never felt better. More alive. Exhilarated. Invigorated.

"Told you so," he mutters against my neck. I can't help the giggle that bursts from my lips.

"You said it would feel *better*, not ... whatever the hell that was. What was that?"

"I'm not even sure. That was — that was something, Princess." Stone reaches up to move the hair that covers my face with a chuckle. "Are you okay? Give me a sec to get feeling back in my legs, and I'll get off you."

"It's okay," I murmur. "I kinda like you on top of me like this. You always brace yourself so you don't put your full weight on me. It's nice to know you were as affected as me."

Stone slides off to the side, leaving one leg on top of mine. I wince as his cock slides out of me. I feel the evidence of both our orgasms leaking onto the bed, but I couldn't care less. My entire body is humming.

"It's never ..." I trail off, hesitating to ask him what I really want to know. "Is that normal? Is it always like that with you behind a woman?"

Stone's eyes had been closed, but they pop open and sharpen on me. "No, that's not normal, Arianna. It's never been like this. Ever."

"Really?" I whisper. "You're not just saying that to shut me up, are you?"

"What's going on in that head of yours?" he asks.

I shrug, trying to seem nonchalant. "It's just … well, you have a lot more experience than I do."

"That's what happens when I'm eleven years older, Princess," he says wryly.

"Yeah, but even if we were the same age. If we met this year, and you were your twenty-six-year-old self, you'd still have a ton more experience than I do. I can't help but compare myself to those girls."

Stone studies me for a moment before reaching to cup my cheek. "Yeah, I've had more sex, Arianna."

I wince slightly at the brutal honesty of his words. "Stone, that's what I mean —"

"No," he interrupts me. "Let me finish. It doesn't matter. What I've experienced with you? It's unlike anything else, baby girl. Our connection, our history. What I feel with you … Jesus, Arianna. It doesn't matter if it's fast or slow. Doesn't matter if you're riding me or I'm hitting it from behind. Because with you, it's love. We're making love, baby. My soul is connecting to yours. I've never had that with anyone. Looking back, I think I fought any possible feelings or relationships because I wanted this. With you. This exact moment? It beats everything else. It doesn't matter that I've fucked more. I'd take what we have over all of that combined. With you, it's *more*."

Tears fill my eyes at the sincerity in his voice. "I just worry that I won't be enough."

"Hey, that's supposed to be my line," he teases softly. "Have I ever lied to you?"

"No."

"Not gonna start now. I'll repeat every aspect of my life as long as it gets me to this point with you, Princess. It's all been worth it."

"I love you, Stone."

"Nowhere near as much as I love you, Arianna."

"Are you seriously going to argue with me about which one of us loves the other more?" I ask.

"No. You know I'm right," he tells me with a cheeky grin. He leans over to kiss me quickly before popping out of bed. "Come on. I think this calls for celebratory pancakes."

"What are we celebrating?" I ask as I turn over and stretch against the sheets. When Stone doesn't immediately answer, I turn toward the bathroom door to find him staring wolfishly at me. "Stone?"

His eyes meet mine as his gaze turns predatory. "I'll explain in the shower."

"I highly doubt you're going to explain anything in there, which is why I'll shower after you — Stone!" I shriek when he stalks toward me, shoves his shoulder into my stomach, and throws me over his shoulder.

"I'm an expert nonverbal explainer," he says as he swats my ass. I retaliate by swatting his, and he spanks me again. "If I recall, I told you I'm in control in the bedroom, baby girl. Spank me again, and you'll be punished."

"Promise?" I snap sassily.

"Don't test me," he warns. Bending down, he carefully slides me off his shoulder. Once my feet are on the ground, I gaze up at him innocently.

The loud crack of my hand against his ass is well worth whatever Stone will do.

"Good choice, baby girl," he whispers. "On your knees."

Oh yes.

"Where are we going again?" Stone asks absentmindedly, his hand stroking my knee as he navigates the expressway entrance. It's New Year's Eve, and we're supposed to have a winter storm this afternoon. Dark grey clouds hover against the mountains, making me wonder if the storm may hit earlier than forecasted.

"I have to return some items to the Children's Hospital that were mixed up in our things from the gala."

"Yours personally, or the hotel?"

"The hotel."

"How do things get mixed up like that?" he asks.

"I don't know. I was a little preoccupied that night."

"Bartlett."

"No, you were the one who preoccupied my thoughts," I tell him.

"How?"

I sigh. "Mostly the kiss. I wasn't expecting that, and I didn't know how to process it."

"Me neither," he admits. "I was just going to act like your boyfriend, throw Bartlett off his game. But when I heard how they talked to you, it was like my body just reacted. Then I couldn't have stopped the kiss if I tried."

"You do know his real name, right?" I tease.

Stone glances at me with a smirk. "Does it matter?"

"No."

"Still can't believe his fiancée left him."

"Bet his whole family is up in arms about that."

Looking out of the corner of my eye, I can see a myriad of emotions across Stone's face. "Do you think about him ever?"

"No. Absolutely not. Hindsight is twenty-twenty, and I can honestly say I got caught up in watching Luca fall in love, and I wanted that for myself. I allowed Bradley to get closer to me than I should have, but I knew he wasn't my end game. I was more embarrassed than truly heartbroken when he announced his engagement."

"And you do want that, right? Marriage? Kids? The whole nine yards?" he asks quietly.

"I do. Well, I definitely want to have kids. I think having the wedding ceremony and marriage isn't a deal breaker for me. As long as you and I are on the same page and we're committed to each other, then I'm happy. Kids are non-negotiable, though."

"I still think you're gonna have to teach me how to be a dad," Stone whispers.

I cover his hand with both of mine, grasping it tightly. "You really think so?"

He nods. "My only role model skipped out on me. I guess I had your dad as a secondary father figure. And your grandfather. Alex, too, and Dom, I guess."

"Sounds like you have quite a few guys who taught you how to be a dad," I say quietly.

"I'll still need your help," he says, his eyes catching mine briefly before returning to the road.

"That's why I said I'm cool with whatever, as long as we're on the same page, Stone. You're my partner. We have to support one another through everything."

Stone brings my hand to his mouth as he kisses it softly. "I'll do my best. How long do you think you'll need at the hospital? It's already starting to snow."

"No more than an hour. I just need to find my contact within the foundation department to ensure she gets all of the items she needs."

"Okay, good. I don't want to be on the road any longer than we need to be."

"You'd think we'd both be comfortable driving in snow as Colorado natives," I joke.

"It's everyone else I'm worried about. Good ole Jimmy, driving his massive quad cab truck, thinks he can fly past everyone on the shoulder. Then the family from Florida, on their Christmas ski trip, assuming the minivan they rented has all-wheel drive. Those are the people I'm concerned about, baby girl. You're precious cargo."

The snow steadily falls as we get to the Children's Hospital. After quickly finding where I needed to drop off the hospital materials, we're back on the road faster than I expected. I'm silent as I watch Stone navigate the snowy roads. I breathe a sigh of relief when we make it back to the interstate, where the roads appear clear.

I don't even see it coming.

I hear the car as it attempts to whip around us and then the sound of wheels failing to gain traction. The crinkle of plastic and metal as our cars collide. Glass shattering as Stone's SUV flips.

The last thing I remember hearing is Stone begging me to stay with him.

Then, the darkness. And the cold.

S tone

⚜

I've always heard your life flashes before your eyes in near-death experiences, but that didn't happen to me.

Her life flashed before my eyes.

Arianna's.

The love of my life. *The other half of my soul.*

Every pivotal moment of her life runs through my brain like a slideshow.

Holding her after she was born.

Luca's hockey game.

Threatening to beat up some piece of shit douche who bragged about taking her virginity in high school.

Actually beating up the piece of shit douche.

Watching her graduate from high school.

All her birthdays.

Our first kiss. My last first kiss. My last first everything.

If Arianna Santo dies today, I die with her.

There's no living without her.

I refused to leave Arianna's side, forcing EMT's to put me in the same ambulance as we carefully navigated the snow-packed roads. I remember nothing except how pale Arianna was and the sound of her heartbeat on the monitor.

Stay with me, baby girl.

We were separated in triage, and I only allowed it so more people could focus on her. It's quickly determined that I've broken my arm. They put a temporary cast on it, planning more detailed scans once things calm down. Once doctors were confident I had escaped significant injury, they move me into the waiting room. I pace like a caged lion. I just need to know what's going on. Maybe they'll tell me, and I'll have time to formulate how I want to tell her parents —

"Stone!" Sofia shouts as she runs into the emergency room waiting area, the rest of the Santos on her heels. Seeing their terrified faces makes my knees buckle, and I fall into the closest chair.

"I'm so sorry," I weep when she reaches me. "I don't know what happened. I was being so careful, and I don't know what happened ..."

"Oh, Stone," Sofia whispers, sitting beside me and wrapping her arms around me. I actively sob, vaguely aware that I must be embarrassing myself, but I can't find one iota of strength to pull it together.

"If she dies, I don't — I can't —" I whisper brokenly.

"This wasn't your fault, Stone. You hear me? This wasn't your fault," Sofia states. I feel a hand on my back from the other side and turn to find Alex.

"I'm sor —" I start, but he holds up a hand.

"This wasn't your fault. Drivers here suck on a good day, man. This wasn't your fault."

"I can't lose her," I finally choke out.

"And you won't, son," Nick says, crouching before me. His hand reaches out to grasp my neck, and I realize he called me son. Arianna was right. I've had one hell of a father figure in my life for quite some time. "My *paperotta* is one of the strongest women I know. I raised her to be strong. Her mother raised her to be steadfast and honest.

She has always been meant to do great things in this world, and that doesn't end today."

I hear a throat clearing and look up to find a nurse staring at us. "Are you the family of Arianna Santo?"

"Yes, we're her parents, and this is her fiancé," Sofia states clearly. I almost correct her, but Alex pinches my hand.

"If she's in the ICU, they'll only let family back there. They won't let you back as her boyfriend," he whispers. "Besides, we all know that's where this is going anyway. You bought a ring yet?"

I nod. I didn't tell anyone. I was in Denver a few days ago, grabbing some supplies for the shop at a bulk store, which happened to be next to a jeweler. I don't know what caused me to walk in there that day or what made me walk directly to one section off to the side. But I knew it as soon as I saw it. The ring screamed Arianna, and I immediately opened up an account with the jewelers to pay for it. I wasn't kidding when I told Ari that I lived paycheck to paycheck. Dropping seven grand on a ring wasn't in my budget by any means. But as soon as I saw the one-carat peach sapphire stone wrapped in pavé diamonds and set on a rose gold band, I knew Arianna had to have it. I intended to sit on it for a bit. See how she felt about marriage. That's partially why I asked her about kids and marriage today.

And now she might never know that I was already waiting for her. Already planning to ask her dad for her hand and thinking ahead to when she'd have my last name.

"Come with me. A surgeon will speak to you shortly," the nurse says briskly, beckoning us with a quick flip of her wrist as she spins and begins walking toward large double doors. Alex shoves me forward, so I follow Nick and Sofia. My feet are sluggish as I follow them, and I turn to see Alex, Luca, and Hannah huddled together with varying expressions of fear on their faces.

"Stone, have you been checked out?" Nick asks, forcing me to turn and notice he's slowed his gait to walk beside me. I shrug, showing him my wrapped arm. How I walked away with only minor injuries is unknown.

I nod. "Arianna took the brunt. I've got cuts from the windshield shattering and where the seatbelt and airbag hit, and they're pretty sure my arm is broken, but Arianna ... it hit on her side. The other car, I mean. And then, when we flipped, we landed weirdly. She was smushed in her seat ..." I can't continue as emotion clogs my throat. I'll never forget that image as long as I live. My beautiful girl, unconscious and at an odd angle, as I hung above her, screaming for her to stay awake. Stay alive.

Stay with me.

Please.

"Dr. Adamson will be with you momentarily," the nurse says, jarring me back to the present. We've been taken to an interior waiting area. I hear Sofia struggle to breathe, and Nick comforts her.

We all know we were brought to this room for bad news.

I've seen enough medical dramas on television to realize doctors give good news in public and bad news in private. They wanted us to have a space to lose it when they tell us she's gone.

I know it has to be coming. That's why we're here. But I don't feel it. If she were really gone, I'd feel it, right? I'd feel empty and lost.

There's no way this is where our story ends.

As adrenaline crashes, I struggle to walk to a chair in the corner. I'm suddenly aware of my entire body hurting. Maybe I'm worse off than I thought.

A physician wearing a surgical gown steps into the room and closes the door. Sofia gasps, and Nick grabs her, anchoring her. Arianna was right, again, that I had a phenomenal set of role models for what a marriage and partnership should look like. I inwardly chuckle to myself, wondering when is Arianna not right. I'm sure she'd get a kick out of my internal thoughts, and I pray I get to tell her.

"Arianna is still in surgery. She suffered damage to her spleen and bladder. She has a broken tibia, which may have to be surgically repaired down the line, but it isn't a priority today. We've also repaired multiple lacerations to her arms and face, but they should heal with minimal scarring."

"They should heal?" I hear myself shout. "Wait, she's alive?"

The doctor looks at me with a crooked smile. "Yes, Mr. Dixon. Your fiancée is alive. She'll have a long road to recovery, but she should be fine."

"Are her kidneys okay?" I blurt out. "She's had two transplants. I don't think I told anyone on the way here."

The doctor chuckles softly. "You actually did. You yelled it at everyone. We immediately checked her kidneys, and they show no signs of damage or injury. All in all, your fiancée is one lucky woman."

Sofia and Nick begin to cry and thank the surgeon profusely. As he's about to leave, he turns to us. "Oh, and the fetus is fine. We'll keep her admitted for a few days for monitoring, and have OB check on her, but both should be fine."

Dr. Adamson knocks on the door as he leaves with a flourish, his surgical gown flowing behind him as he strides out of the room. If he had looked, he would have seen the faces of three shocked individuals who clearly did not know about any fetus.

"She's pregnant?" Sofia cries. "How far along is she?"

I find Arianna's parents staring at me, expecting answers. "I don't — I — we didn't know she was pregnant! I never would have had her on the road if I had known. I never would have been out in the snow ..."

"You really didn't know?" Nick asks quietly.

"I swear, I didn't know. I don't think she did, either. She would have told me. I would have noticed, I think," I murmur. Holy shit. She's having a baby. My baby. I don't think I've ever been this happy before. I feel complete. I thought I had it all once I realized my feelings for Arianna were equaled, but now ... I have a family of my own.

I know if Arianna were awake right now, she'd yell at me and tell me her family has always been my family. But this is different. I'll have a baby that will look up to me and depend on me. And that is the most poignant and humbling thing I will ever experience.

Another surgeon comes in to tell us Arianna is being transferred to a recovery room, but they'll try to get us in to see her as soon as possible. Somehow, Luca and Hannah snuck back to join us in the smaller waiting room, and Alex headed back to Eternity Springs to get his kids. Evidently, Dominic texted that there was some kind of disagreement between Alex's daughter and Dominic's son that resulted in a food fight.

I find myself yawning as the constant hustle and bustle of the hospital lulls me closer to sleep. Leaning back, I close my eyes for what feels like a second before someone shakes me awake. I open my eyes to find Luca peering down at me. "They said you can go back with my parents, man. She's not awake, but you can sit with her."

Jumping up, I run after Nick and Sofia. As we walk into a curtained area in the ICU, Arianna's parents gasp as they get their first look at her. Even being in the ambulance with Arianna, I'm unprepared for how broken she looks.

Jagged cuts crisscross her face, and large bruises cover one arm. A black eye is evident, and a deep gash is stitched above one eyebrow. Her right leg is perched on pillows to elevate it, a temporary cast keeping it in place.

"Oh, *paperotta*," Sofia whispers. "Can I clean her hair? She'll want — it will bother her if her hair feels matted."

"Of course, ma'am," the nurse says quietly. "I'll give you some time with her."

"When can we expect her to wake up?" Nick asks.

"It really depends. There's no set time for how the body responds to trauma and anesthesia. We're not forcing her to wake up just yet, instead letting her body recover."

Sofia asks more questions, but the room drains away as I stare at my girl. I find myself at her side, leaning down to press my lips to the only spot on her face, by her temple, that isn't bruised or cut. "Please forgive me, Princess. Come back to me."

Sofia stands opposite me and meticulously cleans the dried blood from Arianna's hair and skin. Nick pushes a chair toward me, motioning for me to sit near Arianna's head. He sits on the bed at her feet, his gaze unwavering as he looks at his wife and youngest daughter.

"A baby," he comments with a wry chuckle. "Our baby is having a baby."

"She's going to be shocked when we tell her. Do you think it's a boy or a girl?" Sofia asks.

"It's a girl," I blurt out. Both her parents stare at me, questions obvious on their faces, as I continue. "Gut feeling. I just know it. A boy would be easier, and Arianna doesn't do things the easy way. It'll be a girl, and with her personality. Hopefully her looks too."

Sofia sniffles as she smiles at me. "You're probably right. Another Santo baby!"

"Dixon. The first Dixon baby," Nick corrects. I inhale in shock at his admission. Looking at him, he gives me a slight head nod as if to say it's okay.

Carefully linking my fingers with Arianna's, I bring them to my lips and apply the softest kiss against her skin. My Princess is the best thing that's ever happened to me, and I'll spend the rest of my life loving her exactly as she deserves.

***

Hours later, Nick and Sofia have left. They grabbed a hotel room nearby and asked me to go with them, but I declined. I can't leave Arianna. Stepping foot outside the hospital without her would seem final, and I'm unwilling to do that. Instead, I leaned forward to rest my head against the side of her hospital bed.

It's uncomfortable, but nothing compared to what she's gone through. My arm throbs in the temporary cast, and a nurse brought me some pain medication. I finally fall asleep as dawn breaks across the sky.

Scratching wakes me up.

I can feel the most blissful scratching against my scalp. I smile against the bed, thinking how I love it when Arianna does this at home.

"Hi, old man."

My eyes pop open to find Arianna staring down at me.

"Princess," I murmur, grabbing her hand and bringing it to my mouth. I reverently kiss the palm of her hand, tears filling my eyes in relief and thankfulness.

"This wasn't your fault," she whispers. "I know you blame yourself. You can't control the other drivers, remember?"

"If it had been worse, if you had ..." I trail off, unable to complete the sentence. If she had died, what would I have done?

"It doesn't matter because it wasn't worse."

"It wasn't good either."

Arianna shrugs, then winces as the movement causes her pain. "It doesn't matter, Stone. I survived, and I'm choosing to focus on that. So did you. Are we a little worse for wear? Yeah. But I'll never *not* be thankful for being here with you."

Rising slightly, I lean over to kiss her lips quickly. "I'll never not be thankful for you as well."

She gives me a slight smile. "I feel like I was sort of awake, but not really. Did I hear my parents?"

"Yeah. Luca and Hannah are here too. Alex was here briefly, but he had to go back and rescue Dominic from some kid stuff."

Arianna looks at me, her brow furrowed in concentration. "Why did I hear the word baby over and over again?"

My eyes widen. I'd honestly forgotten about that. "You heard that?"

"Yeah. I knew it wasn't you calling me baby girl. It felt like it was something else. Like you referring to an actual baby."

"I was, Princess," I tell her tenderly, carefully sitting on the edge of the bed and bracing my hands on the sides of her head. "We're gonna have a baby."

"Haha, very funny, Stone. I literally just got you on board with a relationship. I'm not pushing for marriage and babies just yet."

"I'm not joking, baby girl. You're pregnant."

Arianna's eyes widen as she gasps. "What? How? When? Is it okay? How did they know?"

"While you were in surgery, they did blood work, I guess. Once they realized you were pregnant, they made sure your uterus wasn't damaged. They had to take out your spleen, and they're keeping an eye on your kidneys for now."

"I'm really pregnant? We're having a baby?" she asks tearfully. I nod, overcome with emotion. This girl, this extraordinary woman, has given me everything I didn't know I wanted. Needed. Craved. Arianna is the perfect ending to my chaotic storm.

"How do you feel about that, mama?" I ask her uncertainly. I've had a few more hours to process this information, but Arianna is already cradling her stomach protectively.

"I'm gonna be a mama!" she gushes. Her eyes swivel to mine as she gasps. "How are you feeling about this, Stone? This is a lot for you, and we've barely even started dating --"

I interrupt her with a kiss. "I'm so fucking happy, Princess. As long as you and the baby are healthy, I'm on top of the world. I'm perfect."

"Is your car totaled?" she blurts out, and I bark back a laugh.

"Completely."

"I'm sorry, Stone. You loved that car."

"Nowhere near as much as I love you and this baby. I can replace a car. I can't replace my girls."

"Girls?"

"Gut feeling, Princess. A gut feeling that you're incubating your mini-me, and I wouldn't have it any other way."

Arianna stayed in the hospital for three days. Surgeons feared they'd have to install a steel rod into her leg, but the leg wasn't as severely broken as they thought. We got matching blue casts and joked that together we made one whole person. My broken left arm with her broken right leg.

Arianna's family stepped up big time with our recovery, constantly bringing us easy meals to reheat, and taking shifts for doctor appointments and other necessities. Sofia enjoyed doing our laundry a little too much, I think. Nonna stopped pinching my butt, at least for the time being. She attempted to teach us the Italian card game Scopa, but both Arianna and I had difficulty understanding the deck of cards used and all of the different rules. Instead, we taught Nonna how to play Texas Hold'Em, and only after she fleeced us of quite a bit of money did we realize Nonna was a fucking card shark and completely played us.

Nonna isn't allowed to come over and play cards anymore.

With Arianna's broken leg making it unsafe for her to drive, I've been driving her car. Now that her surgical scars have healed and she's much more alert, Arianna has wanted to get back to work. I take great enjoyment in dropping her off at work each day, picking her up, and taking her to our home. She's been teaching me simple Italian recipes, and I never thought I'd enjoy cooking so much.

It probably helps that I lay her out on the table and eat her as an appetizer fairly often.

Around the time I purchased a new-to-me SUV, we found out I was correct.

Arianna is having a girl, and I already know my daughter is going to rob me of my ability to breathe easy for the rest of my life. But I wouldn't have it any other way.

I didn't think I was worthy of love. I certainly didn't think a Princess like Arianna would settle for me. But she's taught me that I'm so much more than what I've believed all my life. I've been broken, sure. But she painstakingly put me back together with her optimism, snark, sass, and laughter. There won't be a day that goes by that I don't worship at her feet, because Arianna deserves it. She's trouble, but she's worth it.

Arianna

"Patience, baby girl."

I growl at Stone. I legit growl at him. I'm one hundred months pregnant, I need to come right fucking now, and he's edging me to the point that I think I literally might die.

It's possible I'm exaggerating.

It's also possible I see why my mom is so thrilled I'm having a girl, because she claims it'll be karma for the drama I brought as a kid.

I'm seven months pregnant, not a hundred. It sort of feels like it though. I can't see my feet, and I've long ago lost the ability to see the area Stone is currently nuzzling against. It could be a vast forest down there, and I'd have no idea. Not that Stone is complaining. He told me it was like being on a pornographic adventure.

I threw a pillow at him.

I tried to throw my shoe at him, but that would have involved bending down to get it, and that wasn't going to happen. Frankly, Mother Nature better figure out what season she's on and stick with it, because it's flip flops or nothing.

"Stone, please," I pant. He's doing this weird figure eight thing where he dances his tongue around my pussy, skirting past my clit with just the briefest of touches. I feel like my skin is on fire. It's been a good thirty minutes of him just playing. As soon as he feels me start to crest toward an orgasm, he lets off the gas.

I am honestly pondering the difference between a felony and murder at this point.

Hannah is a few weeks ahead in her pregnancy, and she told me that she's been insatiable. I was still in the throes of all-day sickness — because whoever said it was just in the morning is full of shit — and I remember rolling my eyes and disregarding what she said.

She was right. Once that second trimester hit, I became unglued.

I need sex. I need to come. All. The. Time.

I've straight up begged Stone, more than once, to visit me at work and put me out of my misery. He, of course, obliged. I swear, the fear of possibly getting caught by my parents makes us come so much harder during those work afternoon delights.

"Stone, I swear to God, if you don't make me come in the next sixty seconds, I'm giving this girl my last name!" I threaten. Stone chuckles against me, his hot breath huffing against my core and making me clench tightly.

"What good would it do if you have my last name but our daughter doesn't?" he asks, resting his chin against the inside of my thigh and looking up at me with sparkling blue eyes.

"Stop with the teasing!" I whine.

"Are you not enjoying this at all, Princess?" he asks. "Because I can completely stop."

I growl again, making Stone snort. "You've been sending me provocative texts all day. I've been turned on since lunch, and now you're teasing me."

"I just want to make you feel good, Arianna. And if you remember, I told you I was in control in the bedroom. My rules. You need to let go."

I huff in annoyance before grabbing his hair and shoving his head into my pussy. Probably not what he expected, because he laughs, then bites my clit. The nibble is all it takes for me to explode. I'm oddly surprised when the orgasm is lackluster at best. "Huh."

"Yeah, huh. Bet that wasn't as good as you wanted," Stone comments as he slides two fingers into my soaked channel. "Here's where you apologize for doubting me, baby girl."

His fingers slowly, oh so slowly, slide in and out, as he rests his head against my thigh, his blue eyes sparkling as he looks around my bump. As he picks up speed, I can't even blink. His eyes darken as I reflexively shimmy, searching for friction and pleasure. I'm moaning as he adds a third finger, watching as his eyes grow hooded, and his pupils dilate with lust. When he takes his thumb and pushes against my clit, while his fingers find my G-spot and tap from within, my back arches and I come on a silent scream. White spots dance across my eyes as I shudder with pleasure. I barely have a moment to catch my breath before Stone impales himself inside me, beginning a punishing pace, and I wrap my arms around him blissfully. His lips take mine in a searing kiss, our tongues dancing together as I drag my nails up his back. I quickly have another orgasm, igniting his own immediately after.

"God, I love you, Arianna," Stone rasps as he stills above me, and I feel his release inside me. I hope I never get over how wonderful it feels to know that I can make Stone lose control like this.

He rests against me as he catches his breath, then carefully slides off. Stone is overly cautious with my bump. Just now, as he came, he made sure to keep all pressure off my stomach, and as his feet hit the ground, he maneuvers me so I'm on my side.

"I'm perfectly capable of rolling over, Daddy," I snap, mostly in jest, but I see the quick clenching of his jaw that tells me that using the word Daddy right now definitely hit its mark. Honestly, I should have used it ten minutes ago. Stone becomes feral when I call him that in bed, and I probably would have felt his dick in my ribs.

"Watch that tone, baby girl. I have no problem filling that sassy mouth of yours," he warns as he trots into the adjoining bathroom. I know he's getting a towel. Stone has always been extremely attentive to me after our bouts of lovemaking, whether it be soft and sweet or full-on rutting. It boggles my mind that he thought he didn't know how to love someone. Stone was made for this: being a partner, taking care of someone, and experiencing life together.

I'm one lucky bitch for snagging him, and I have no problem admitting it.

"You promise to fill my mouth?" I call out as he walks back into the bedroom. He chuckles while shaking his head.

"Christ, woman. Give me thirty minutes and I'll be ready," he says as he climbs into bed next to me, immediately placing his palm on my stomach, lovingly stroking it. The baby immediately kicks his hand. "Should we be worried that she felt any of that? I don't want to scar my poor kid before she's even born."

"My mom said I walked in on her and my dad more than once as a kid. I have no memory of that. She said I had questions that day, but never brought it up again, so she figured I forgot," I shrug. Stone looks at me in horror.

"Multiple times?"

"I guess you have a common problem with my parents, hand-some," I say, my eyes narrowing in mischief.

"Oh yeah? What's that?"

"Your inability to lock the damn door."

Stone bursts out laughing. Unfortunately, Hannah hasn't been the only family member to catch us in a compromising position in my office. Luca got an eyeful of Stone's ass when he didn't knock. Needless to say, we're much more careful about locking the door now ... and after hearing about our escapades, my parents asked Stone to stop visiting me in my office.

Thankfully, he hasn't.

"I still can't get over the fact that we're going to be parents in a couple months," Stone muses, a peaceful smile gracing his hand-some face.

"It is surreal," I say in agreement, covering his hand with mine.

"I hope she has your eyes," Stone says quietly.

"Really? Mine are boring. Yours are prettier."

Stone frowns. "You're not supposed to call a man pretty."

"Technically I called your eyes pretty, not you. Besides, I love how yours change colors depending on your mood. Mine are just brown all the time. Nothing special."

"Agree to disagree, Princess. Yours change color too."

"Really?" I ask.

Stone turns on his side more, popping up to rest his face against his bent arm. "They're lighter when you're sassy. When you're turned on, they're this phenomenal shade, like molten chocolate. And when you're sad, or sick, they're dark and dull. Breaks my heart when I see that last shade. I basically make it my goal to ensure you never have your eyes that shade. But if our daughter had matching eyes with you ... God. I'd feel like I won the fucking lottery with having you and your mini-me."

Tears fill my eyes at how sentimental he's being. "Stone ..."

Stone chuckles quietly. "Wasn't trying to make you cry, baby girl."

"I'm hormonal! I cried at an ad for one of those jewelry stores in Denver this week," I blabber. Stone reaches out to wipe the tears from my cheek.

"I hope she gets your sass too. She'll be unstoppable if she gets your tenacity and drive."

"I want her to have your patience, and hopefully she gets your handiness," I joke. We had an unfortunate situation where Stone trusted me with an electric drill, and needless to say, we had to replace a large section of drywall immediately after.

"And your cooking skills," Stone replies, before he chuckles. "Well, maybe your mom's cooking skills."

I laugh along with him. My ability to cook has come a long way, but I am nowhere near the absolute goddess level of my mom in the kitchen. She's already been freezing casseroles for when I give birth, and she's been teaching me how to make my own baby food. Baby Dixon is a lucky girl with Sofia Santo as a grandmother.

"Should we veto a few more names?" Stone asks, his hand slowly stroking my bump.

"Oh, yes! I came up with some good ones this week," I say giddily. Once we knew for certain the baby was a girl, we started a game for names. We each come up with five names, and we can veto a name on each other's list two times. Stone has taken to this with gleeful exuberance, and I swear he's been trying to come up with the worst names so I can't veto the ones he really wants.

"I gotta go get my list," he says, scrambling off the bed and running into the closet. I reach into my nightstand to grab the list I added names to just this afternoon.

"You keep it in the closet?" I yell.

"I move it all the time, Princess. I know you're snooping around here," he shouts back. I giggle because he's right.

"Alright, let's go. Ladies first," he says as he bounds back into the room and launches onto the bed. He whips a pen out of his notepad, pen at the ready to write down the names I suggest, as well as what we both veto.

"Luna."

Stone grimaces. "Ugh. Sounds too spacey."

"That's lunar, goofball."

"And that's why I said it *sounded* spacey. Veto."

I sigh. "Fine. Go."

"Hazel."

My mouth drops open. "Seriously? Is this the early nineteen hundreds? Veto."

"Damn. I thought it was cute and quirky," he says with a shrug, dramatically crossing it off on his list.

"My turn. Aurora."

"What is it with you and outer space names?" Stone says with a laugh. "I'll let that one stay on the list, just because I figure you have a ridiculous one coming."

He's right. I do.

"You're turn," I say, motioning for him to go.

"Simone."

"Huh." That's actually not a bad one. "I'll let that stay on the list."

Stone cocks his head at me, his brow furrowed. "That's surprising. I thought you'd hate that one."

"It's nice to surprise you on occasion, old man."

"Ha-ha. Since you're currently pregnant with my offspring, I think it's time you relinquish the nickname, baby girl."

"You call me baby girl, how is it different?" I ask.

Stone crawls toward me, until our noses are touching. His voice dips as he huskily replies, "You know it's different."

"So it's my turn," I say with a crack in my voice, as I fan my face with my paper. "Ready for my next name?"

"Hit me," he says.

"Alessia." I try to keep my face composed, but I burst into giggles with a very unladylike snort. "Isn't it perfect? We only met because of my brother, Alessio!"

"Over my dead fucking body are we naming our daughter after your brother," Stone says deadpan. His expression makes me dissolve into another fit of laughter.

"Come on! It's perfect. We could call her Ali or Sia for short."

"It pains me how much you've thought about this," Stone says, rubbing his forehead in frustration. "You are joking, right? Just to see if you can get a rise out of me?"

"Yeah," I admit. I'd never name my daughter something so close to one of my siblings. Alex already has one hell of an ego. He'd be unbearable if he thought we named our daughter after him.

"I'm not losing a veto on that, then. Moving on," Stone says with a swirling hand gesture. "Bianca."

I gasp.

"What?" He asks. "Is it the baby? Did something happen? Are you hurt?"

"Oh, God, no. Stone, seriously? Bianca? That was the next name I was going to suggest."

"Really?"

"Yes!" I shove my list in his face, showing him how I've circled the name. Turning the page, I point to how I've already written Bianca Dixon. A grin widens on his face as he stares at the name.

"I think we found our daughter's name, Princess," he says quietly.

I can't help the massive grin that covers my face. "I think we did."

Arianna

"Momma, sissy kick!" Emilia shouts, and I wince. Shouting is fine, but when her head is next to mine, I'd prefer her to table her outside voice. Emilia is three, and her two volumes are loud and louder. Her big sister, Bianca, looks on in amusement. At five, she's definitely my mini-me in looks, but her personality is all Stone. She's quiet, reflective, and introspective. She studies all outcomes of a situation before making a decision, even for simple things like playing with Lego sets, or messing with my sister's Easy Bake Oven. If Bianca had her way, she'd forgo elementary school and shadow her Aunt Isabella all day instead. She's been interested in cooking and baking since right after she could walk.

Emilia, on the other hand, looks more like Stone but acts like me. She's loud, optimistic, and incredibly extroverted. She's never met a stranger, and she can pull even the most steadfast wallflower into her web at preschool. Her blonde locks, which Stone assures me he also had as a child, and blue eyes are so striking that I fear she's going to be way too beautiful for Stone and me to rein in. Something tells me Emilia will either run the world or demolish everything in her way, and there won't be a middle ground.

This third baby was a pleasant surprise. My pregnancies weren't super easy, and Emilia's labor almost resulted in an emergency c-section because she was breech. Weeks later, Stone admitted he wanted more kids, but he was happy with two. He didn't need any more kids to validate his life as a man and a father. Never once did Stone insinuate he wished for a boy. He proudly rocks the girl dad life. He has no problems wearing a tiara in public, letting his daughters paint his nails, or embracing their interests in some stereotypical female activities like cooking and makeup. Honestly, he's taught *me* how to do their hair. I knew he'd be a great dad.

He's an even better husband.

I may have told him I didn't care if we ever got married, but I secretly wanted my last name to be the same as his and the girls. We had a very small wedding in our backyard a few months before Bianca was born. Stone said he wanted us married before she was born. I thought about doing a big wedding, but couldn't find the joy in planning it. Life was stressful enough without worrying about place cards, seating charts, and bridesmaid dresses. I just wanted the man. I didn't care about the day. A marriage is a lifetime. A wedding is one day.

Plus, have you seen how expensive weddings are? Insanity.

So we had an adorable backyard wedding that Luca officiated. We bought a cake from the town grocery store, I carried a bouquet of flowers my mom picked from her garden, and neither Stone, nor I, had any attendants.

It was just us, exactly as I wanted it.

The only thing I did splurge on was a dress. Looking back, I can say that I never dreamed about my wedding growing up. That should have been a big sign that I wasn't destined to have a huge wedding. I did, however, dream about my wedding dress. I knew I wanted something with lace and sleeves but also a princess-style dress that matched my personality and style.

Of course, that meant I ended up picking a very simple satin dress that showcased my baby bump. My veil, an heirloom every woman in my family has worn for three generations, blew behind me in a light breeze as I walked toward Stone. He couldn't even wait until I made it down our makeshift aisle, meeting me at the halfway point. He thrust his hand at my dad, thanked him for escorting me, and then said, "I'm taking my girl now."

Two hours after the ceremony, after we'd pigged out on an amazing barbecue spread by a local restaurant, Stone unceremoniously kicked everyone out of the house.

"Could you have made it more obvious?" I hissed, suddenly embarrassed at how my family would have known it was because Stone wanted to consummate our marriage.

"Baby girl, you're six months pregnant. I'm pretty sure they know we've had sex," he remarked dryly.

True.

Bianca Marie was born in late-August, on a Friday, fully cementing our family. Ironically, she was born on the day my ex-boyfriend was supposed to marry his fiancée. Bradley's ex-fiancée realized she couldn't marry Bradley for a multitude of reasons. She actually messaged me on social media about a month before I gave birth to apologize for her part in the mess with Bradley at the Children's Hospital gala. She explained that she figured he wouldn't remain monogamous with her, but thought she could handle that. She thought it would allow her to continue dating and sleeping with her own selected partners. We'd already known she was secretly a lesbian, but I think it was part of her coming out story to explain her reasoning behind the engagement farce. Her parents were less than thrilled. She may have been a virgin with men, but she certainly wasn't with her longtime girlfriend.

I deleted the message and never looked back.

Bradley disappeared into obscurity not too long after that. Last I heard, he was working at a chain restaurant in Wyoming. He is still unmarried, but I'm not surprised about that.

After the text exchange on Christmas with Stone's mom, we were surprised to find out she had skipped town. Cleared out her trailer and left with no forwarding address. Stone struggles with feeling like maybe he gave up on his mom years ago, and that he might have been able to help her. He also hasn't fully come to terms with his biological father's death. I convinced Stone to speak to a local counselor, and I was surprised when he agreed. The counselor is helping him work through the trauma of his childhood, his feelings of never being enough, and how he can break the generational curse by treating his own children differently.

He has nothing to worry about. As soon as we knew I was pregnant, I could see a shift in his world. Our kids are the center of his universe, and nothing makes me happier than watching him interact with them.

"Princess?" I hear him call out. Frowning, I look at my watch to see it's at least an hour before he's supposed to be home.

"In here!" I shout from Bianca's room. The barren bachelor pad that used to be Stone's home has turned into our perfect family home, a pink paradise. Bianca is obsessed with Barbie, and she picked out the most grotesque color of Pepto Bismol pink for her bedroom walls once she was potty trained. Emilia also loves pink but has already picked a much more subdued baby pink for her room once she is potty trained. Emilia is having more difficulty than I thought she would. As long as she's done by the time this third kid rolls around, I'm fine with however long it takes. I just demand that there only be one kid in diapers at a time.

Speaking of ... I need to tell Stone about this third kid of his.

"Hey, baby," Stone says as he strides into the room.

"Hi, Daddy!" Bianca says gleefully from her bed as she brushes a Barbie's hair.

"Daddy! Sissy kick me hard!" Emilia bellows. Seriously, what is it with these little girls and volume control? Dominic's daughter, Aspen, *still* has difficulty controlling her voice. I thought it was comical until I had my own banshee.

"How did your appointment go? I hate that I had to miss it," Stone says regretfully as he leans down to give me a quick kiss. He places a hand on my bump and is immediately kicked in greeting. "Damn. Active today."

"No kidding," I mutter.

"Everything went okay? Was this the diagnostic ultrasound appointment?" he asks. "God. I hate missing the ultrasounds."

Stone's other main barber, Sam, has been out with the flu this week, so Stone was covering a lot of Sam's clients. Normally, he would just close the shop for these types of occasions, but a plumber was servicing his stations and couldn't reschedule. So Stone dutifully went to do his owner thing, and I tackled the ultrasound with Hannah tagging along. Hannah's daughter Melanie is only a handful of weeks older than Bianca, and the cousins were instant besties from the moment we put them together for tummy time. Emilia is a little bit older than Hannah and Luca's son Caleb, and those cousins are much more like oil and water. Emilia loves Caleb, but the love isn't returned with the same ardor.

"Uh, yeah, I think everything went fine," I murmur.

His eyes sharpen on me. "What does that mean? You think? Did something come up? What are they concerned about? Did a radiologist view the report, or was this just the technician spouting nonsense, and you reading nonverbal cues?"

"They'll notify me in a few days if anything comes up on the ultrasound, but the technician said there wasn't anything to worry about. I grabbed some pics. Do you want to see?" I ask, grabbing the stack of pictures.

"Shit, yeah. Still hard to believe she's in you, you know? You'd think I'd be a pro by now, but this just boggles my mind." He studies the pictures, a beautiful look on his face as he looks at his offspring.

"I am being referred to a high-risk obstetrician, though," I say nonchalantly.

"What?" he barks.

"Look at the images, honey," I say softly.

Stone continues to study the photos, cocking his head to the side. "Wait. What the hell does Baby A mean?"

"It means that is Baby A."

"That doesn't actually answer my question, Princess ... wait a sec. Baby B? Are you having twins?" he shouts.

"Daddy loud," Emilia mutters.

"I'm allowed to get loud, Em. You do it all the time," he says. Crouching down, he covers my hands with his. "It's twins?"

I nod, my eyes filling with tears. They're not sure how I didn't find out before now, but Baby B was hiding behind Baby A.

"Four girls. Wow," Stone murmurs.

"Oh. That's not exactly correct," I tell him, a huge smile on my face.

"What?" he breathes.

"Baby B is a boy, Stone."

"A son?" he asks, his voice breaking with emotion.

"Book your neuter appointment, old man. The shop is closed after this buy-one-get-one-free deal," I tell him. My first two pregnancies were monitored due to my kidney transplants, but my OB already told me I'm definitely high risk for this unexpected twin pregnancy. I'm very content with this being my last pregnancy.

Stone bursts into laughter as he drags me into his lap.

"Knew you were trouble from the get-go, Princess, but damn if I'm not the happiest man in the world right now," he says as he nuzzles my neck.

"Was I worth the trouble?" I ask.

"Absolutely."

he End

Sneak Peek

**The following sneak peek is unedited and subject to change.

Dominic

"I'm done being nice, Katherine. Explain yourself right fucking now," I state, my voice deep and snarling. I can feel my blood pressure rising as I stare at Kate's defiant expression, her hands on her hips in annoyance.

"There's nothing to explain. Mind your own business, Dominic," she huffs.

"I found you in a ball on the bathroom floor. That deserves an explanation." I'm not sure I'll forget the visual for as long as I live. Sobbing and clearly in pain, Kate barely recognized being moved when I picked her up and took her to the closest bedroom, which just so happened to be mine. I try to ignore the feeling deep in my gut that screams at me.

I haven't had a woman in my bedroom since my ex-wife left. Hell, I've barely even had sex in five years. My job and my family take up all of my time, and frankly, any woman I meet never seems to get me excited. My hand does the job just as well as any of my past conquests.

"It's not a big deal," Kate says. The color is returning to her cheeks, probably more due to her frustration with me than anything.

Kate gets along with every single member of my family except for me.

"You were crying, Katherine. It is a big deal."

"Normal people cry, Dominic," she says pointedly, but movement casts my eyes downward. I notice she's gingerly holding her stomach.

"Are you pregnant?" I blurt out, then immediately wince when I realize how inappropriate that is. "Shit, I'm sorry. That is none of my business."

"No, I'm not pregnant, you moron," she snaps. "I've got so many damn female problems I'll probably never get pregnant."

Kate sits on the edge of my bed, misery etched on her face.

"Female problems?" I ask quietly.

Kate sighs. "I have PCOS and endometriosis."

I wrack my brain, trying to remember what PCOS stands for. "What is that first one?"

"Polycystic ovarian syndrome."

"And that means ..."

"My ovaries are full of cysts, basically. And then the endometriosis means I've got abnormal cells growing all over the place. So my entire reproductive system is fucked," she says, her voice clear. Still, a tremble in her words betrays her defiant demeanor.

"What do your doctors say?" I ask.

Kate laughs bitterly. "What doctors?"

"What do you mean? I assume you're under medical care, aren't you? What twenty-something woman doesn't have a doctor?" I chastise.

"The kind without medical insurance, Dominic. And even if any doctor near here would take cash, I don't have the funds for the office visits. Don't even get me started on the cost of prescription medication or the procedures they may suggest."

"How do you not have medical insurance?" I ask. She glares at me. "Katherine, you have so many different jobs. Surely one of them has insurance."

Kate has worked odd jobs for the entire time I've known her. Bartending, babysitting, and even temp jobs. Recently, she's taken on the majority of the nannying I need for my kids, but it's still only about twenty to twenty-five hours a week. I know that Kate pulls in around fifty hours per week cumulatively.

My kids are ten, seven, and almost six. Their mom, Savannah, walked out right after my youngest was born. After Savannah briefly tried to gain full custody, mainly in an attempt to anger me, I was awarded sole parental responsibility. At best, Savannah only comes around once a year, and I like it that way. My oldest, Sienna, remembers her the best. She misses Savannah and has trouble rebounding after visits. Carter, my son, doesn't like Savannah. He has fleeting memories but doesn't put much stock into his mother. Even at seven, he recognizes a waste of space. And my youngest, Aspen, has no memories of Savannah. She hates it when she's forced to spend time with her own mother.

I have to bite my tongue when my kids ask about Savannah, and I'll be damned if I give my ex one iota of ammunition to be used against me. I learned quickly that children have loose lips, and they'll innocently tell anybody anything if it gets their attention.

That's partially why I ended up hiring Kate as a nanny. More than once, I took her from the hotel to watch my kids when I had evening meetings. My kids adore Kate, and probably listen to her more than me. So, when she was evicted from her apartment, my mom suggested Kate move in with me. "It will be easier for her to handle the children, *birichino*. And we need to help her. She's family."

Technically, she's not family. Trust me, I've thought about it. It's a murky area, for sure. Kate's half-brothers are our cousins, but there isn't a blood relation. But my sweet Italian mother, who still calls me *birichino*, which means cuddly boy, wouldn't hear any arguments. When someone dear to her struggles, she will find a way to help, come hell or high water.

"Nope. None of my jobs are full-time." I take a breath, ready to tell her what to do next, but she holds up a hand to stop me. "Don't even go there, Dom. I know you're going to tell me to search for a job. I have been. There's nothing I'm qualified for. Because really, who wants to hire someone with zero college and a gazillion part-time jobs for experience?"

"Weren't you offered healthcare through the hotel?" I ask. I'm the CEO of Everlasting Inn and Spa, the hotel my family has run for generations. While I deal more with hotel issues, sales, and marketing, my mom still dabbles in human resources and concierge staffing. I vaguely remember her telling me she offered Kate insurance, but Kate turned it down.

"She wanted to just *give* it to me, Dominic," Kate says, her eyes blazing with fire.

"So?"

"I — I'm not a taker. I'm not a mooch. I don't like feeling like I'm taking advantage of someone."

"That argument is moot. You'd have been taking advantage of my family if you had suggested we give you free insurance. If my mom offered it to you, that was out of the goodness of her heart."

Kate vehemently shakes her head. "I'm barely working there these days. I'd think about it if most of my time was spent there. But I'm not taking insurance from your family when I maybe work ten hours a month."

"What would make you take insurance?" I ask, but as she's about to respond, she gasps and presses into her abdomen.

"Dammit," she breathes.

"What happened?" I sit next to her, ready to swoop in for whatever she needs ... but I don't have a fucking clue what that may be. I'm working blind here.

"It's probably a ruptured cyst," she murmurs.

"Ruptured?"

"Yeah. The pain will go away."

"You know that for a fact?" I ask in disbelief.

"Yeah."

"How many of these ruptured cysts have you experienced, Katherine?" I ask. I hear a sound that can only be described as a growl. She hates it when I call her Katherine, which is only partially why I do it. She just looks like a Katherine to me.

"Too many to count."

"What will make it better right now?"

"A bath sometimes works. And Tylenol."

"Seriously? Only Tylenol?" I ask.

"That's all I have, so it'll have to do," she retorts.

"If you had a doctor, what would they prescribe?"

"Something not over-the-counter, obviously."

"Is there a chance this isn't a ruptured cyst?" I ask.

Kate shrugs. "Maybe. But this isn't my first rodeo. I'm about eighty percent sure it is."

"Jesus, Kate. That's really giving a lot of room for variability."

"Not much either of us can do about it."

I pull out my phone and do a quick Google search, then stare at Kate in horror. "It says you might need surgery."

Kate rolls her eyes. "I thought I was the dramatic one here, Dom. I'd know if it was surgical."

"How so?"

"Well, the pain is different. It's way more intense."

"You've had this happen before?" I shout.

"Uh, yeah. Twice that involved a short hospital stay. Once that required a laparoscopic procedure to make sure the cyst had fully passed. The fucking ultrasound was inconclusive, so they did an exploratory procedure to find it. Damn thing had already passed, and I went under the knife for no reason."

"How much did that cost?" I ask.

"Oh, I was still on my mom's insurance, so I don't know."

Fucking hell. That meant she was a minor. "How long have you been dealing with this?"

"Basically since puberty," she says quietly.

I'm floored. I can't imagine having an exploratory surgery as a minor. She must have been petrified.

Clearing my throat, I ask, "How long will you have to deal with these issues? And how often can they happen?"

"I guess they could happen every month. Well, as long as I actually get my period. It's really weird talking to you about this, by the way. Can I go back to my room now?" she whispers.

"No." I hear her mutter "jackass" under her breath but choose to ignore her. "What's going to happen this time, or the next time, that you need another exploratory surgery? Will surgeons even do it if you don't have insurance?"

"They'll do anything," she says with a dry laugh, "but I'll owe them for the rest of my life."

Our fucking medical system at work.

Before knowing what I'm doing, I say, "I have excellent insurance. All the full-time employees at the hotel do."

"Jesus, Dominic. Way to rub it in." I see the hurt in her eyes, but I soldier on.

"It goes for families as well. Spouses and children."

"Okay?" she asks warily.

"So it's settled," I say, rising from the bed. "We'll go to the courthouse."

"What?" she screeches.

"You need insurance. We're getting married. End of discussion."

I walk out of my bedroom with my head held high, leaving a sputtering Kate sitting on my bed. Only later will I realize how right she looks in my space and how much that scares the shit out of me.

I said I'd never get married again or let a woman into my heart. But this is just helping a person in need, right? I'm not setting myself up for heartbreak. I'm just doing what my mom says I should do: giving to others.

I'll ignore the voice in my head that tells me I'm so completely fucked.

Coming Summer 2024

Acknowledgments

It's hard to believe this is my eighth published book! In some ways, it's flown by, and in others, it has dragged. The days are long and the years are short, my friends.

I'd like to thank my Q&C BFFs Tamara and Mandy for letting me vent, enjoying our off-the-rails conversations, and allowing me to name our group chat something completely inappropriate … and then never changing it.

To my PA Morgan, for putting up with my shenanigans and never giving me attitude, you're an absolute doll. Now go find make some graphics, because you're so much better than me.

Becca, Shauna, the team at The Author Agency, and all the influencers at TAA, you've made the last two releases so much fun. It's been a joy working with you.

My beta readers, Valerie, Anna, Amarilys and Daisy, thanks for always doing the pregnancy math so that I don't have to.

To my arc team, I love each one of you and how you allow me to reign over our chaotic group chats, most of which I'm responsible for starting.

And finally, to my family. Thank you for supporting me, telling me you're proud of me, and never reading any of my books. Hopefully you never see this message, or else I'm expecting a very awkward phone call soon.

Forever Series

Forever Sunshine

Forever Yours

Forever Ours

Forever Mine

Forever Us

Forever Together

Eternity Series

Worth the Risk

Worth the Trouble

Worth the Vow

Worth the Test

Worth the Heat

Mile High Sports Series

Blue Lines and Lullabies (prequel novella)

Forecasting the Forward

Paws on the Playbook (coming winter 25/26)

About the Author

Jennifer J. Williams writes steamy romance full of sassy characters, epic banter, and delivers amazing HEAs in her sports and small town books. She was born and raised in Ohio, but currently calls Colorado home. A lifelong lover of romance books, Jen enjoys writing older characters because love stories don't end at twenty-five. Jen prides herself on delivering realistic characters that struggle with normal problems. She spends most of her free time within her zoo: two kids, two dogs, and two cats! When not containing the chaos, Jen can be found lounging on her covered porch, devouring books on her Kindle.

www.ingramcontent.com/pod-product-compliance
Lightning Source LLC
Chambersburg PA
CBHW071246300726
48975CB00002B/563

* 9 7 8 1 9 6 7 8 2 9 0 2 6 *